OF OIL & SORCERY

A VOICE FROM THE VOID

BOOK ONE

REY ATHENS

Dedication

This book is firstly dedicated to my father who was taken a few years too soon to see me accomplish one my life's greatest ambitions. You supported me fully wherever my heart took me. You're my hero.
Secondly, this book is dedicated in part to my papaw, to whom the main character owes his namesake. You were taken only a year before you could finally hold the book in your hands. I took my time and did it right, as you always instructed me to do.

Lastly, this book is dedicated to my grandpa, who was also taken one year before he had another book to put on his shelf. You were a paragon of stoicism and responsibility, and I'll carry your lessons in my heart.
I love you all, and we'll meet again someday.

ONE

On a gloomy Tuesday afternoon, I laid eyes on Atlas Grimbrooke for the first time. I couldn't help but feel that his genetics betrayed the sweeping gravitas of his name. He was thin, on the smaller side, and he daintily held his books against his chest as he waited for the train. He wore a white button-up and had medium-length auburn hair with bangs that stopped just short of his bright green eyes.

I knew it was him because he stood next to his sister—a beautifully freckled young woman with blazing red locks. Her name was Fena, and every guy at school was talking about her. If they weren't scheming a way into her dorm room, they were talking about the weirdo brother who rarely left her side.

You see, Atlas came highly recommended from a prestigious primary school. He'd skipped a few grades and landed himself with us at Eye of Newt University, or ENU. Our school was for only the most promising of young mages, and Atlas was the first student with a magical handicap ever to be admitted.

But Atlas Grimbrooke was *blind to magic*.

That begged the question: how could he control his magic

or dodge incoming spells if he was unable to see them? I hunted for any reason to speak to Fena, but I was interested in Atlas as well.

Humming with magic, the train rolled into the station and glided to a stop. As everyone filed on, I wondered how Atlas would fare in an environment as competitive as ENU. As it turned out, I wouldn't have to wait long to see for myself why he had been admitted.

The first week had not even passed before Tovin Black-meyer smelled fresh blood. Tovin was the school's most noto-rious bully. He would tweak his spells to be needlessly cruel, he shoved newcomers around, and he had an entourage of ankle biters who clung to his backside, encouraging his behavior, and ridiculing his victims. Nobody liked Tovin, but everyone pretended they did. And nobody, it seemed, was willing to stand up to him.

He excelled in everything he was taught, and he was the pride of ENU. Thus, his antics went largely ignored by the staff. I had been killed by him once already for suggesting he ease up one of the first-year students. I shuddered as I remem-bered water endlessly rushing out of my lungs. It was pretty much the worst day of my life. I couldn't shake the sinking feeling that Atlas was about to have a similarly terrible day.

"I can't believe they even let you in here," I heard Tovin say from where I stood by my locker.

"Look at him; he's made of broomsticks." Tovin's followers joined in on the ridicule. "What's the matter Atwis?" asked one of them as they encircled him. "Gonna cwy? Gonna wun home and cwy?"

"I challenge you to a duel."

Never had a single sentence silenced an entire ENU causeway like that. It was as though a portal to a new dimen-sion opened up and swallowed all the air in the room. Everyone had the same horrified expression. I moved to get a better look. Atlas stood against his locker, his books pressed against his chest and his lips in a straight line.

"What the hell did you just say?" Tovin asked with an excited chuckle. "You're...*You*," he reiterated. "You're challenging *me* to a duel?" he asked as he exchanged glances with his posse.

"That's right," replied the boy, his tone cool as ice.

"Hey," a young woman came to Atlas's side. "You don't have to do this. Just take the joke. Let him ha—"

"Shut *up!*" shouted Tovin. "Wruthe!" he shouted, starting off with the vocal component of the spell and then thrusting one arm in her direction. A gale threw her backward, and she bounced off a locker, hitting the floor with a thud that made everyone in the hallway wince.

Now you might be wondering what kind of man lets a woman be handled like that. On this campus, women are every bit as powerful as men. Magic favors no gender; they are capable of fighting back on equal terms. Tovin, however, had no equal, man, woman, or otherwise.

The angry mage marched up to Atlas and got right in his face. "Let me tell you something, Atlas. I've been concocting a new spell, and you've given me the perfect test subject. Meet me in the hymnasium after school. You're going to wish you had never come here."

He turned and walked away, leaving the rest of us in stunned silence. The day seemed long. Nobody was talking about anything else. Everyone watched the clock through each class period.

I couldn't lie; I was just curious. I wasn't better than anyone else. I knew Atlas was probably going to die for the first time today. I still wanted to *see* it. Not his death, but whatever he was so capable of that he came to us so recommended. I wanted to know what he had up his sleeve that he could so calmly call out the most impressive student Galgia had ever seen with a straight face and still manage to keep his lunch down midday.

His sister tried to reason with Tovin in the hallway between the sixth and seventh periods, but he wasn't having any of it. He'd been disrespected in front of everyone, and he just couldn't ignore the blow to his ego.

The unstoppable force was about to meet the very movable object. Students had exited their classrooms while the echo of the final bell still hung in the air.

They migrated en masse to the hymnasium. One of the headmasters was among the crowd. He was cloaked from everyone else, but *I* could see him.

I was sick to my stomach that they were allowing this to happen. They weren't about to miss a chance to see their golden boy in actual combat. They probably saw him as their future champion to fight the Diesel Empire—a greedy, grimy, fossil-fuel based society that blanketed every territory they claimed in machinery.

ENU had been seeking a prodigy for years; someone who could rally all those in Galgia to take up arms and reclaim all that the Diesel had stolen. Someone powerful, and more importantly, young. The old guard were getting on in years, and many had serious concerns about the incoming generation having enough promising mages to replace them. They saw that in Tovin; I was certain of it.

I pushed through the crowd until I had a good vantage point. The hymnasium was similar in all aspects to the gymnasiums that you'd find at non-magic schools. But it had been built for the sole purpose of training melodic casters—mages who possessed the ability to sing creatures from other realms into battle and fight at their command.

It also served as the perfect arena for duels. I had never seen the hymnasium so packed. The whole building was buzzing as each of them appeared from opposite sides and made their way toward one another.

I was sick to my stomach as I thought about what would happen to Atlas. Plenty of mages had dueled within these walls, but none was like this. I don't think a single student wanted to see Tovin win, but we knew the odds. I was sure that we were all holding within our hearts the faintest hope that the mysterious new kid would put up a fight, but our hopes were tempered by the cold, hard reality that Tovin Blackmeyer really, truly was that good. He was the first to speak, and the room fell silent when he did.

"I give you credit for showing up at all," he said, smirking.

"I don't need your credit," Atlas responded, his tone sharp. "I need you to understand that I won't tolerate your bullying. Not toward me; not toward anyone else. It ends today."

The stands couldn't contain their excitement any longer. The collective swell of their voices lifted the mood from tense to electric. I couldn't take my eyes off the two of them. Whatever was about to happen next would be extraordinary.

Two

Tovin's face simmered dark red. I'd never seen him so angry before. He wasn't used to being talked to as an equal.

He was the product of two wealthy politicians, and he'd never known a hard day's work in his life. He seemed to effortlessly excel at anything he put his mind to. He mastered difficult spells within hours, spells that took others months of rigorous practice to learn to cast. He was gaining national attention before the age of ten. By the time he strode through the front doors of ENU, he was already one of the most powerful students to ever attend, senior or otherwise.

As renowned as Tovin was, Atlas was just as much a mystery. All we knew about him was that, despite his handicap, he surpassed his classmates in primary school and then skipped most of magi school to join his older sister at university. I couldn't help but feel uneasy about how calm he looked. He couldn't have any idea what he'd gotten himself into, could he?

Tovin turned and meandered left, with Atlas doing the same in the opposite direction.

"I'm going to teach you respect," growled Tovin.

"Oh, really?" Atlas shot back. "How do you expect to teach what you don't understand?"

Laughter filled the hymnasium. I smiled and leaned forward on the railing. Kid had guts. I almost believed he could pull it off. Tovin had lost the dialogue battle, and his mood was darkening.

Seething with rage, he leaped forward and threw his hands toward Atlas. A magical stream of energy erupted from his palms and connected with the boy's chest, carrying him through the air toward the other end of the hymnasium. Everyone gasped as his limp body bounced off the far wall, and he fell to the floor face-first with a sickening sound that echoed throughout the building.

I let out all the air in my lungs as Tovin lifted his arms and began his gloating. The poor kid was too young. He'd overestimated his abilities. The crowd's mood turned sour as Tovin cheered for himself. This wasn't a place for fairy tales, it seemed. We had all let our imaginations run away with what could have been, and we had nobody else to blame but ourselves for the blanket of depression that settled over the stands.

"Oh, was that it?" Tovin shouted with glee. "What are you even *doing* at this school? Where's Headmaster Rowan? I need an explanation for why this little worm was even allowed in these prestigious halls."

I made my way out. I couldn't watch anymore. I detested very few people more than I did Tovin. I hadn't come here to watch him jerk off his own ego. I had at least hoped it would be close.

Then, suddenly, the crowd was stirring.

"He's up!"

"Kid's not done!"

"Did he die?"

"No, look, there's blood coming out of his nose. He survived!"

I whipped around and pushed back toward my spot as everyone around me buzzed with excitement. I leaned over the railing to confirm it with my own eyes. He'd not only lived through the blast, but he was walking back toward his stunned opponent—and Tovin was right to be stunned.

My eyes were better than most. I *saw* how much energy Tovin packed into that blast. A criminal amount, the likes of which I didn't know he was capable. For most it was bright, but for me it was blinding. That's the kind of energy one uses to finish off their enemy.

Yet somehow, some way, Atlas was on his feet, and save for a bloody nose, no worse for wear.

"You seem surprised, Tovin," he said before coughing into his closed fist. "It's almost as though you intended to *kill* me."

"What—how did you...?" Tovin stammered in disbelief.

"It's okay," Atlas reassured him. "I'm not very good at holding back, either."

I couldn't make any sense of what I was seeing. You see, within the ENU campus, death isn't a rare occurrence. People didn't die every month, but it did happen from time to time. The school exists within a stasis field that revives and repairs one's body should their heart stop—a complex network of protective and restorative magic. And the fact that it hadn't restored Atlas's bloody nose meant that somehow, he had survived Tovin's monstrous assault.

Even the senior staff, who had watched the bout were leaning over the railing, struggling as I was to understand what they'd just witnessed.

"How are you not dead from that?" Tovin asked through his teeth.

"You're not the only one who's gifted, Blackmeyer," Atlas replied. "I must admit, I wasn't expecting that kind of power from you. I lost consciousness there for a second. I think I must have broken my nose in the fall."

"So, you're resilient. Is that it?" Tovin asked. "Well, I'm not done!"

Magic coalesced in his palms as he prepared the attack a second time, and it stirred a panic in the hearts of the crowd. Nobody wanted to see Atlas sail across the hymnasium again.

As the magical stream of energy left Tovin's palms, Atlas simply sidestepped the blast as though he'd done it a thousand times.

I couldn't tell you how he did it. The attack was too fast to track, even for me.

The magical blast fizzled against the warded walls of the hymnasium, and Tovin, for the second time in five minutes, stared at the boy with a perplexed look. It seemed like he was struggling, just as we were, to fully comprehend what he was seeing.

Atlas stared down his opponent with eyes that carried resolve and determination.

"Hey," Tovin yelled. "You're not handicapped at all are you? How did you dodge that if you couldn't see it?"

"I wouldn't have been able to dodge it if I were seeing it and reacting to visual cues," Atlas responded. "And I think," he narrowed his eyes, "you knew that already."

Tovin hadn't been the only one studying his opponent. It seemed that in the few interactions the two of them had shared, Atlas had sensed insecurity from his opponent. This battle wasn't born from vengeance alone; Tovin meant to set an example. As soon as he no longer felt like he was in control of the situation, he resorted to verbally attacking Atlas's character. But Atlas had seen right through it, and subtly called him out in front of everyone.

Tovin had expended a lot of his mana already. He

wouldn't likely be able to manage another blast of a similar caliber.

But Atlas...Atlas was beginning to glow. Brighter, brighter, and brighter still. I squinted and shielded my eyes as his energy climbed.

I glanced at Headmaster Alrune, who was a sensory type of mage, same as I was. He was holding his stomach and gripping the railing so tightly his knuckles were turning pale.

"You've...You've got to be using some kind of trick!" Tovin shouted. "You're cheating somehow!" He became unhinged. "There's no way you didn't die earlier! I won already!"

"I'll tell you the trick, if it makes you feel better," Atlas said. "I can feel the presence of magic. Like how one feels a tremor beneath one's feet. Once I understood the way your spell felt as you cast it, I could assess how to dodge it, should you use it a second time."

Tovin was lost for words. I could tell he wanted to interrupt, to dominate the conversation. But he was as taken aback as the rest of us.

"I've had to take a lot of painful spells right to the face to understand how to counter them," Atlas continued. "It toughened me up over the years. I guess you could say I've grown a decent resistance to magic overall." He folded his arms. "Whatever that spell was would have blown anyone else to pieces, if I had to guess."

"Magic...resistance?" Tovin muttered, intrigued at the possibility.

I had never heard of such a thing, but it wasn't outside the realm of possibility. Being born blind to magic and persisting down the path toward being a mage would create conditions where you're hit *a lot*. It wasn't just his endurance that made him special though. In fact, that appeared to be the least terrifying thing about him considering how brightly he was glowing.

His magic reserves ran *deep*.

"All of my elders told me to quit," Atlas spoke. "A magic-blind boy has no business being a mage, they said. They figured I'd only get myself killed."

Atlas lifted his hand, and a shimmering sphere of light appeared in his palm.

"But when they measured my mana reserves..."

The ball ignited and grew. Atlas lifted his arm over his head as the sphere of radiant energy grew until it blazed like the sun. Everyone stared in awe at his display of power, unable to turn away; unable to speak.

"Turns out I was made for this," he said as Tovin fell to his knees. Nobody else in the school, senior staff or otherwise, would be capable of such a feat. The heat was almost unbearable.

"Have you ever...feared for your life, Tovin?" asked Atlas, staring him down.

That's when the stadium filled with panicked shouts as everyone scrambled for exits. If Atlas launched that spell, he would likely obliterate the building and everyone in it.

Atlas looked up and around as the hysteria unfolded in the stands.

Headmaster Anther suddenly appeared behind him, uncloaking himself. He reached down quickly and snapped the boy's neck. The blazing inferno died, dissipating into dancing embers, as Atlas fell to the floor.

"It's all right!" Anther called out to the screaming students in his oaky old voice. "Everyone, settle down!"

Slowly but surely, decorum returned as the headmaster lifted his hands and waved everyone back. "Calm down, calm down. We won't have anyone burning to death, now."

I breathed a sigh of relief and leaned on the railing. As far as I knew, the stasis field had never been tested by mass death. I wasn't certain it could handle bringing that many people back at once. This sobering thought hadn't crossed my mind before—before I knew a mage like Atlas existed.

"Let this be a lesson," the headmaster continued, "not to hold unsanctioned duels."

Bastards. They *let* this happen. All the headmasters had made their way down to the hymnasium floor and were staring at the dead child in front of them. Blind to magic, but resistant to it, with deeper pools of magic than anyone could perceive.

Anyone but *me*. I saw it with my own eyes, and I knew what a special kid Atlas was. He'd put most of what he had into creating that massive deadly ball of magic. His core was dim, indicating that he'd meant to put on a show, to send a message, and to humble someone who needed to be humbled.

It was a secret I would keep.

Tovin got to his feet and looked around at the situation unfolding around him. He huffed and folded his arms, a scowl on his face.

A small smile found my lips. Maybe he'd been humbled after all.

Within a few moments, Atlas's body was surrounded by the healing glow of the stasis field. He opened his eyes and once conscious, was helped to his feet by the very headmaster who'd slain him.

"I apologize, Atlas," he said, resting his hand on the boy's shoulder. "I couldn't have you burning the building down, and killing you was the fastest way to heal that broken nose." He smiled, patting Atlas twice on the shoulder.

Atlas lifted his hands to his newly repaired nose.

I remained as the other students filed out of the building and the headmasters gushed over their new prodigy.

Tovin watched from a distance.

He might not have tasted death today.

But this was *better*.

THREE

The following morning, I awoke to find an envelope with a purple wax seal sitting in the basket beneath the message slot in my door. A purple seal could mean only one thing—a message from one or more of the *headmasters*.

They totaled seven in all: Rowan, Huede, Alrune, Norah, Edwin, Vega, and Anther. Each of them possessed incredible magical skill as well as a unique attribute that cemented their position within the college. Being born special in Galgia determined one's status as a mage. Intelligence, work ethic, physical fitness, the things that mattered in other societies were nothing when compared to being born lucky.

Several of our students were overweight, childish, or unintelligent. That didn't matter. If they could make the magic happen, then they'd go far. And if a headmaster noticed them, they were set for life as long as they did what was asked of them.

And it looked like I'd been noticed. As to whether that was a good thing, I could only wonder as I picked up my mail basket and placed it on my table. I used my letter opener to open the envelope, then pulled the message from within and unfolded it. It was written on some seriously expensive paper and the penmanship was oddly satisfying. The letter read simply:

Student: Gill Dragstenn
You've been summoned by Headmaster Alrune. You will report to him in room 52A located in the south wing at 12:00 P.M. This is not a disciplinary action. Please wear your school uniform to the meeting and be prepared to take notes.
—Vice Principal Wharl

I set the note on the table and glanced at the clock on the wall. It was just past nine–late for me. I was usually up and around by seven-thirty, but I'd had difficulty sleeping through the night. My mind bounced all over the place, but there was one specific question for Atlas burning a hole in the back of my head. I wasn't sure how to approach him. It wasn't like we were friends or anything. Really, all I had done was study him from afar.

I felt kinda creepy in that instant, and I shook everything away. I needed food to think straight.

I prowled the kitchen for something tasty, but I came up empty. Nothing in my cupboards, and the pantry was worse. The bread was molding, and the fruits were mushy and bruised. I let out a deep sigh as I realized I'd have to head down to the cafeteria for breakfast.

ENU was unusual in that was like its own little city. Students didn't have to leave for any reason other than to see family and friends. Real cafes and restaurants were in the west wing, but it was expensive and a real hike across campus. The cafeteria was in the east wing, same as the dormitories, and the school paid for the food. People liked to complain about the quality, but I never needed much more than a cup of coffee and piece of sweet bread for breakfast.

I made myself halfway presentable and left my dorm, locking the door behind me. I was dressed casually in a pair of black, slim-fit trousers and a long-sleeved polo. I would have plenty of time to come back and dress in appropriate attire for my meeting with Headmaster Alrune. As I made my way down the hallway, I noticed everyone had put out their trash by their doors. I remembered that today was trash day and headed back to my dorm. I had missed trash day once, and that was all it took. I nearly ralphed when I remembered the maggots.

Tovin was among the few students in the hallway, and he was heading in my direction. His eyes were to the floor as though he were in deep contemplation, and he was without his entourage. My body froze. I'd have to pass him. It wasn't so much that I was *afraid* of him, but my body had a natural reaction to him. Being killed by someone and living to remember it wasn't natural. All of my alarm bells were ringing, begging me to move, change course, anything but stand in his path. Then he did something I wasn't expecting; he turned, walked up to my dorm room door, and stood in front of it for several seconds.

I stared in confused anticipation.

He lifted his hand to knock on my door and stopped short. What could Tovin want from *me?* I thought about it only a moment longer before disappearing into the small crowd of students who'd just come up the stairs.

I glanced over my shoulder. I saw his face through the crowd.

I was sure we had made eye contact.

I hurried down the winding staircase and into the main causeway where there was a full crowd to hide in. It wasn't *hiding*, I convinced myself. I just didn't want to interact with him in any capacity for any reason at any time whatsoever.

I took the short walk to the cafeteria as I pondered the reason for Tovin's visit. I sat and stared out the window as I sipped on my coffee. It seemed obvious to me now. He was going to ask me about Atlas. I had deduced that Alrune's letter likely concerned the same subject. I took another swig. I was sure *everyone* was curious as to what I saw last night. My eyes had a knack for always being where they needed to be, and the senior staff knew it. For a new student to walk through our doors and cause the pride of ENU to fall to his knees. It was unfathomable.

"Hey." A voice came from above. I'll admit I jumped a bit.

Atlas was standing in front of me in full uniform, breakfast on his tray. "Would you uhh...mind if I sat here?" he asked.

"No," I said. "Not at all! Please."

He was just the person I wanted to see. I took a bite of my sweet bread as he sat down across from me.

"Thank you," he replied. "You don't have to talk to me or anything. I just needed a place to sit."

"No, it's all right," I assured him. "Why would you assume I wouldn't want to talk to you?"

He cut off a piece of his scrambled egg with the side of his fork and lifted it to his mouth. "Well, y'know...People tend to think I'm odd. They don't usually want to associate with me. I've made peace with that. You won't hurt my feelings or anything if you just ignore me."

"Gods," I said as I sat back in my chair. "You've got some real self-esteem issues."

"Not at all," he responded. "I'm very happy with who I am. I'm just stating facts. Other people tend to avoid me," he said, taking a drink of his tea. "It is what it is, and I'm not bothered by it."

I was surprised by his maturity. I assumed that because he was by far the youngest student in the school, he'd have a lot of growing up to do. Instead, he seemed well adjusted.

I decided that now was the moment. "Atlas, was it?"

"How rude of me," he said as he set his fork down and wiped his palms on his knees. He held out his hand and I shook it.

"Atlas Grimbrooke," he introduced himself.

"Gill," I responded with a smile. "Gill Dragstenn. I was hoping I could ask you something."

"Me?" he blinked twice. "Um. Sure, what is it?"

"There you are!"

I turned. Fena was walking toward the two of us. My heart fluttered. I hadn't expected to see her today. Gods, my hair had to be a mess. She was carrying a tray, also dressed to the letter.

"Thought you could hide from your sister, didja?" she asked as she pulled out the chair next to him and took a seat. "And," she said, looking at me, "You went and made a friend."

My blood froze. "Hello," I said in a singsong voice as I lifted my hand. I didn't know why I did that; it was unlike me. I hadn't had a crush for a long time. It was like I didn't know how to act all of a sudden.

"I'm Fena," she said, extending her hand. "Pretty sure you rode the train in with us the other day, right?"

She'd noticed me. Not bad news at all.

"Gill Dragstenn," I responded. "And yeah, I was visiting family for the holiday. Speaking of days off, you do know today is Saturday, right?" I said, looking back and forth between them. "You don't have to wear your uniforms."

Fena scanned the cafeteria and then buried her face in her hands. "Ohh, gosh," came her muffled groan. "That's embarrassing,"

"Speak for yourself," her brother replied, before taking another drink. "I was asked to dress in uniform today. I've a meeting with one of the headmasters."

"They want to talk to me, too," I said, tossing the last of my sweet bread in my mouth. "Probably hash shomething to do with the duel between you and Tovin yeshterday."

"What makes you say that?" asked Fena.

I leaned back in my chair, taking the opportunity to brag about myself. "Well. Since you asked," I said with a smile, "I was born with a gift. I can see things others can't. Always been that way."

"Like ghosts?" she asked with a flick of her fork.

"More like magic, I'm sure," Atlas said dryly.

"Y-yes," I answered with a nervous chuckle. "I can, for some reason, see magic better than anyone. I can see it inside of you right now, for instance."

"Incredible," Atlas said, wiping his mouth with his napkin. "You can see our mana?"

"That's so cool," Fena said, resting her head on her hands. "What does it look like?"

"Well," I said. "When someone isn't preparing to cast a spell, their energy is shallow throughout their midsection. It's a dim glow that I've got to focus to find. Whenever you rile your energy up though—even if you're just *thinking* about casting —your energy brightens and becomes noticeable."

"That could come in handy," Atlas said. "Nobody would ever get the jump on you."

"I read about that, actually," added Fena. "About how our bodies prepare magic at something as small as an aggressive thought."

"That's right," I nodded. "Headmaster Alrune produced that study fifty or so years ago. He can't see it the way I can, but he can *feel* it."

"I didn't know he was that amazing," she said, with a small smile. "Everyone here is incredible, aren't they?"

"Including you, I'm sure," I shot back.

"Oh, go on," she said with a smile as she swatted the air, turning and tossing her hair with one hand. The three of us shared a laugh before Atlas pressed me again.

"So, you can see the magic in peoples' bodies. Can you tell when...they're low on mana?" He had a poker face, but I knew why he was asking.

"I can," I answered. "But that doesn't mean I have to go talking about how deep anybody's reserves are." I winked at him, and he averted his eyes as though he'd been mentally violated.

"May I ask another question?" Fena interjected. "The degree to which one can control magic is tied directly to how well they can perceive it. If that's the case, then you must have *really* good control, right?"

Atlas sighed as he swirled the tea around in his cup. I eyed him for a moment before looking back at Fena.

She rushed to change the subject. "Oh! Um..." She glanced around. "Have you seen Tovin today? Walking around all butthurt?"

"Don't insult me," Atlas growled. "It's not a secret that I can't see magic, or that I have difficulty controlling it. I'm young, but I'm not a child."

I hadn't put two and two together yet. His reserves were mighty, but his magic-blindness would skew his control. If he couldn't see magic, then it would stand to reason that he had next to zero control. If Headmaster Anther hadn't stepped in when he did...we very well *may* have had an incident.

"Oh, come on, don't get all sullen," his sister said, rolling her eyes.

"Of course," I assured him. "My apologies, Atlas. Your

sister's deduction is accurate. I have, apart from Headmaster Alrune, the finest control of magic of anyone on campus."

"That's incredible!" Atlas smiled at me. "You must be a very talented mage, Gill."

I glanced down into my empty coffee cup.

"Not exactly. My mana reserves are...on the smaller side. The number of spells I'm able to cast before I run dry is, to be frank, kinda pitiful."

"Pitiful?" asked Fena. "Come on, your mana pool isn't *that* small, is it?"

"Thanks," I responded, lifting my eyes briefly. "But no. It *is* that bad. I have to make up for that flaw by controlling precisely how much magic I expend and targeting my opponents' openings for maximum effect. It's also the reason why I'm the school's only *tome user*."

"A tome user?" Fena blurted out. "At *this* school?"

"Sis."

"I'm sorry," she apologized. "That was rude of me!"

"No, it's all right." I waved my hands.

"I had heard there was a tome user at ENU," Atlas said, watching me. "I must admit, I'm curious about you too. How was it that a tome user came to be accepted here?"

It was a question I'd been asked often enough.

Magic can be cast in four main ways: kinetically, verbally, melodically, and via tome. Using a tome is considered elementary, like a grown man using training wheels to ride a bicycle.

Kinetic casting looks almost like dancing or practicing a martial art. Leaps, circular arm movements, wide steps, and rhythmic body motions channel a variety of spells. The mage can cast more powerful spells for their expended energy, but it requires a degree of physical fitness that not all maintain. High level mages favor it.

Verbal casters mold magic with ancient words of power believed to have been holy. The mage must not only remember the words associated with their desired spell, but they must also recite the words perfectly. The ancient tongue is difficult to pronounce. Not all mages contain the mental acuity or the calm during combat situations to wield verbal magic. Verbal is considered the safest method of casting, for unlike kinetic casters, the loss of movement is not a hindrance.

Melodic casting is perhaps the most powerful form of casting; however, it cannot be wielded by everyone. Only those born with the ability to sing well can become melodic casters. Those with the talent can sing monsters that will fight for them into our world from adjacent planes. Melodic casters can also sing into the world gouts of great flame, plumes of toxic smoke, or bitter cold winds. Those training to be melodic casters practice in hymnasiums under close supervision to test their pitch and find new realms from which to cast.

Tome casting is performed via ink and quill. Each page of a tome is inscribed with a seal of power, each unique to the spell with which they correspond. One can buy a pre-written tome at a store or purchase a blank tome to fill with one's own spell list. Tome casting is the easiest form of casting and provides the greatest selection of spells but comes at two major costs. The caster is required to envision the corresponding seal with almost 100 percent accuracy to cast it. They achieve this by opening the page of the tome to the selected spell and using it to cast the magic. The second major flaw is that spells cast via tome cannot be scaled up or down in power. The spell is ripped right out of the caster and achieves the same result every time. Because of these major drawbacks, tomes are discarded when a mage becomes serious and are rarely seen after primary school.

I stared across the table at the both of them and smiled.

"You really want to know how a tome caster was accepted into the most prestigious magic academy in Galgia?"

Four

The three of us made our way to the north wing of the university. Luckily for us, it was a ghost town on weekends. Practically all classes were held there, and it also housed the library and the hymnasium.

We were there for the latter.

I pushed the doors open, and the three of us walked in, cold air and the smell of old wood washing over us. The hymnasium was empty, save for a couple of students on the bleachers sharing a snack. The room was large and rectangular with high windows and seating on both sides. The lower bleachers were positioned behind warded glass where staff would be seated to watch the students. From the stairs to the upper deck, which wrapped around the entirety of the interior, people could exit into hallway D, the second floor of the north wing.

"I almost feel like I shouldn't be back here," Atlas grumbled. "I'm probably in trouble already."

"Ya think?" Fena asked sarcastically. "You started a fight on your *first day*."

"For what it's worth," I said, cutting in, "Tovin instigated it. And I'm glad you let him have it, Atlas."

"Oh, by all means, I'm glad you did it, too," his sister quickly agreed. "It was the right thing to do. He won't be messing with you again, that's for sure."

Atlas smiled bashfully and let his eyes fall to the wooden planks below. No doubt the praise meant a lot to him.

"I'm not sure about that," I responded as we made our way to the center of the floor. "If he hears about your secret, he'll want a rematch for sure." I stopped and turned to look at him. "And next time? He'll win."

"What?" Fena said in annoyed tone, "What makes you thin—"

"Because he's better than me," Atlas interrupted her.

Fena's features softened. "Aww, Atlas, don't say that!" she said.

"It's true," he insisted, staring up at her. "That first blast he hit me with? My body tingled all night long, pins and needles. It's unsettling that he's capable of a spell like that."

Fena and I exchanged glances.

"The second blast I sidestepped was just as powerful, maybe more," he continued. "My arm hair stood on end from just being close to it." He turned to me. "He underestimated me, didn't he Gill? He wore himself out early."

"For someone who can't see magic," I said, folding my arms, "you've got a pretty good grasp on what happened. But he didn't underestimate you. Tovin may be brash, but he's proud, too. He came at you with all that he had. He figured you wouldn't be able to dodge his attack, and it would finish the fight when it struck you. He was aiming for a spectacle. He wanted to make a clear example of you in front of everyone."

"Had I been any other opponent," Atlas said. "He would have come out on top."

"You really think so?" Fena asked.

"It's a blindingly fast attack." I came to Atlas's defense. "Few could have escaped it. The amount of magic Tovin had to pour into it, though." I closed my eyes, allowing the scene to play out before me again. "That's the spell's weakness. Tovin has good magic reserves, but the two shots wiped him. After you stood up, Tovin might have figured he didn't cast it right and tried again. As soon as he missed, it was over. His body dimmed. He was spent."

"I get what you're saying now," Fena said, putting the pieces together. "Atlas has such poor control that he spends himself out early. So, if Tovin, understanding that, were to come at him with a plan..."

"He'd annihilate me," Atlas said, finishing for her.

"But for now, he thinks Atlas is some sort of god." I grinned. "I'd like it to stay that way, at the very least until he cools off. He's a brutal, vengeful, dumpster-fire of a human being."

"I'm tired of talking about Tovin." Fena folded her arms. "You talked a big game back at the cafeteria. You gonna show us what you got or what?"

I didn't feel pressure before, but I did now. I smiled nervously and took a few steps away from them, "All right, all right. But I'm not showing you *all* my tricks."

"Oh, he's got *tricks* now," Fena said, playfully elbowing her brother.

"Tricks are my whole game," I said as I lifted my right hand and spoke the word of power, "Ha-*tôn!*" A crimson leather-bound book fell from out of thin air and landed in my hand.

"You cast verbally as well?" Atlas asked.

"It's one of the few power word spells I've memorized," I said as I clipped the book onto my belt. "It's so that if ever my tome is out of reach or taken from me in any way, I can retrieve it."

"Smart," he smiled. "But what good is your tome going to do you fixed to your belt like that?"

"I told you I had good eyes, remember?" I responded. "It just so happens that I was born with the ability to remember images, patterns, and symbols far more precisely than most. And that means..."

"You've memorized the seals in your tome?" Fena asked, her eyes widening.

"Is that...truly possible?" asked Atlas. "Such complex symbols committed to memory?"

"I've never heard anything like it," Fena responded in an almost combative tone. "In fact, I won't believe it until I see it."

"So then," Atlas turned to me, "you can cast spells from your tome without having the book open?"

"That's right," I smiled confidently. "As a child, I was told I had no future as a mage. Same as you, Atlas. But I had a fire in my belly. So my father researched the most mana-intensive spells I could cast with my weak reserves and wrote them down. We then catalogued all the known spells that were easier to cast than the written ones and ranked them by both usefulness and cost."

"I'm beginning to understand," Atlas said, nodding along. "Spells that are easy to cast and useful on the battlefield when deployed with care. Your tome is chocked full of those, isn't it?"

"That's right," I answered. "I've memorized every seal in this tome. I still study it from time to time to stay sharp, but I can use it without opening it. With verbal and kinetic casting, you build the power within yourself as you prepare to cast the spell. With tomes, it feels more as though the power is ripped out of you as the spell is cast. But because of my fine control and the fact that I've memorized my spells, I can measure *exactly* what each spell will cost me and what spells I can cast at any given time depending on how my reserves are looking."

"You turned both downsides into upsides," Fena said, her eyes sparkling.

"That's right," I replied. "And I'm not done, either. You see, without needing to have my tome open, I have my hands free." I lifted my right. "Ha-*ten!*"

A sword materialized above me, and I caught it by the grip.

"A freaking *sword?*" Atlas cried out, grinning from ear to ear. It was the first time I had seen him break his composure or act his age. "So cool!"

Fena took a few steps closer and inspected it. "Do you really use that thing? It's covered in nicks and dents."

"I have to," I said as I lowered the weapon. "I have to defend myself when my reserves run dry—and they always do. I work swordsmanship into my attacks to conserve my energy."

"Well, wait, hold on," Atlas said. "How is it that you even get close enough for a crude weapon like that to work? Wouldn't you just get blasted apart?"

"I thought you'd never ask," I said as I took a few steps back. "It's the reason I brought you here to the hymnasium. The floors are warded. They'll absorb the magic, so I don't make a mess."

"A mess?" Fena asked, taking a few cautious steps back. "What are you about to do, Gill?"

"I start by casting Fortify on myself," I said. "It's an outdated defensive spell; old magic that uses the body's entire mass to defend itself. If you punch me in the face, my entire body absorbs the shock rather than just my nose or my cheek. Kind of like how a mouthguard protects individual teeth by using the strength of all of the teeth together."

"There's a reason that's old magic," Atlas folded his arms.

"Mages don't punch people. You might as well not even be defending yourself at all. Why *Fortify* of all spells?"

"Well, for one," I said. "It's really easy to cast; insanely easy, actually. I don't even feel the expenditure. Second, it allows me to do this!"

I visualized the seal for Jetstream and concentrated it under my feet. The magic bubbled beneath my heels, and within seconds I was off. I skated around the floor at high speed on a stream of water localized under each foot. I couldn't keep the smile off of my face as the two students in the bleachers jumped to their feet and howled in excitement. I took a few sharp turns, changing direction at random intervals.

Fena was jumping up and down, making a ruckus as I blew past her. The wind whipped through my hair as I turned on a dime and rushed back toward the center of the floor. I slowed down and slipped to a stop. The floor absorbed the water as I made my way back to them.

"That was *amazing!*" she screamed. "I've never seen *anything* like that!"

"Very impressive, Gill," Atlas clapped quietly. "I've never seen finer control. I understand the use of Fortify now, from a physics perspective. I imagine without it, your feet would just slip out from under you from the force of the water."

"I've made *that* mistake," I laughed. "And I've got the scar to prove it."

"Can you teach me how to do that?" Fena asked, her eyes aglow. "That looked like so much fun!"

"I'm not sure," I said. "I don't know if I'd be a good teacher. I guess step one would be to come here often and practice focusing the Jetstream spell beneath your feet. And don't forget to Fortify yourself, or you'll do a backflip."

"Control like yours," Atlas asked, shaking his head as though in disbelief. "Can it be learned?"

"That's why you're here, Atlas," I rested my hand on his shoulder. "It's why we're *both* here. Because the headmasters see something special in us, and they believe that we can improve. I believe that, too."

We shared a genuine moment before I suddenly remembered something I had completely forgotten.

"The headmasters!" I shouted, snapping my attention to the clock.

11:43 a.m.

"Is your meeting soon?" asked Atlas.

"It's like, right *now!*" I shrieked. "And I'm not even dressed right!"

"It's too bad you can't summon your clothes," Fena joked.

"Gotta run!" I called over my shoulder as I sprinted for the hallway.

Idiot, idiot, idiot!

I'd spent so much time showing off in front of Fena that I'd forgotten about Headmaster Alrune. I'd also forgotten to ask Atlas that question I'd been meaning to ask. I turned the corner, but the bottoms of my shoes were still wet, and I slid into one of the columns in the causeway intersection. A group of students nearby got their laughs in as I scrambled to my feet and raced across the thoroughfare between the north and east wing. I glanced at the clock tower as I ran.

11:47 a.m.

I leaped two stairs at a time to the second floor and booked it down the hallway. I slid to my door, shoved my key in the lock, and twisted it. I did a panicked dance out of my clothes, grabbed my uniform, and got dressed in record time. I pumped my arms as I sprinted down the hallway toward the south wing.

My mind raced for shortcuts as I hurried down and around the steps, leaping entire sets of stairs. I ran down the hall and turned the corner too fast to stop. I slammed into someone and we fell to the floor. I scrambled to my feet, and as a slew of apologies flooded from my mouth, I reached down to help them up.

It was Tovin.

He glared back at me through glassy black eyes.

There was a non-zero chance that I was about to die again.

FIVE

When I was growing up, I never considered myself a coward. In fact, most would say I was among the more courageous people they'd met. My mother raised me that way: to always do the right thing even if it was hard—*especially* if it was hard. Thus, I found myself involved in other peoples' affairs and thinking of their problems as though they were my own. My mother called it virtuous, but my father called it dangerous. I brushed his warnings away. I guess I saw myself as the main character in my own story.

Everything changed when I started at ENU.

I was an eighteen-year-old, bright-eyed mage who'd graduated into his college of choice. My future had never seemed brighter. After years of being told I'd never make it, I strode under the golden archways and through the onyx gates. A longtime dream had come true, and I had a euphoric feeling that not everyone gets to experience. Despite my handicap, I'd been recognized, accepted, and chosen. I was the character I had looked up to in children's stories. The underdog who, despite his shortcomings, rose to the top and was admired by everyone.

I was feeling bulletproof when I shoved Tovin that day.

He was a year older than me. Long hair shaved on the sides, a pale complexion, and dark shadows beneath his eyes. He had been tormenting a new student, and I'd seen enough. I did what I always did in that situation. I played the hero.

In reality, that's *all* I'd been doing.

Playing.

When Tovin fixed his steely gaze on me...When the crowd dispersed and the victim ran away, I was in a new situation. His eyes were inkwells, devoid of light and filled with the fury of a slighted god. His magic rose within his body. He was angry.

But I didn't understand the extent.

I was surprised when he moved his arms. I never would have fathomed he would attack me in the halls—those pristine and prestigious halls that so many sought to walk. That he would even gamble on his enrollment for petty revenge was a thought so distant that by the time it had made itself at home in my mind, it was too late.

He thrust his palms at me, and in an instant my chest was icy. My nose ran, and it wasn't viscous enough to be mucus. It was water. I felt as though I were throwing up as I dropped to my knees and fell forward on my hands. Water forced its way out of my throat, my nose, and any orifice it could escape from. I was a leaking water balloon. I struggled to breathe.

Students were still in the hallway. They merely watched.

I wasn't their problem.

If I remained unable to breathe for much longer, I'd die. My throat instinctually continued to contract to swallow the water, but it was impossible. I reached my hand out toward Tovin as I struggled. Asking—*begging* him to stop, to show me mercy. It was a horrible feeling being utterly crushed by another human being. Even worse than that feeling was the hope. The hope that *someone* would step in, that *someone* would save me.

Nobody came.

Only Tovin remained, standing over me. My vision doubled as he knelt down by me and spoke a sentence that etched itself into my soul.

"Should have minded your damn business."

My muscles stopped responding. My reality turned dream-like as my synapses failed. My brain began to shut down. The lights grew dim, and sounds came from far away, as though behind panes of glass. Ocean waves from within a seashell. My light was being snuffed out, and nobody was there to save me.

Death was lonely. *Real* lonely. What good was a dream when you died early? Your ambitions, your hopes and aspirations—they all died with you.

Playing hero.

That's what I had done all my life. But heroes didn't always win, like in the fairy tales. They didn't always come out okay. I'd tossed the coin many times in my life, and it had always fallen my way. Only in my darkest moment, when I stood face to face with oblivion, did I understand that I wasn't the main character. I was nameless, in the background of someone else's tale.

Because mine was over.

Or so I thought. Nobody had told me that the school existed within a stasis field that prevented student death. Everyone seemed really surprised that I didn't know that. It made the behavior of the other students in the hallway easier to understand. They knew I would be okay. It didn't matter, though; I was never the same after that. I became a bit of an introvert, a shut-in, as some put it. I'd gotten better in the year since then, but I hadn't fully recovered mentally. Having to see the man who murdered you on almost a daily basis was a struggle, and I made a constant conscious effort to stay out of his way.

I had nightmares a couple times a week. Lying on the floor staring up at Tovin. The dream always ended with him staring at me as everything slipped away.

Those cold black eyes.

The very eyes I was staring into again after all that time I spent staying off his radar. All of those memories and night-mares flooded back into me as I stood over him.

He stared back at me from the floor with a combination of surprise and rage. My hand was still extended toward him. I didn't know whether or not to leave it hanging there. I realized my mouth was wide open and closed it, swallowing hard. I took a few awkward steps back.

Tovin rose to his feet, his jaw clenched. He dusted himself off and looked up at me, his energy flaring up in his midsec-tion. It was my worst nightmare, but I wasn't sleeping. I tried to speak, but my words got lost in my throat. The hallway was dead silent. Nobody dared move a muscle.

"Watch where you're going," he said through his teeth.

I lifted my hands and nodded. He started toward me, never taking his eyes away from mine. It was as if I were watching a slow-motion train crash. I thought to run but couldn't. My mind was screaming *move*, but it was no use. I knew how this story ended. Nobody would come to my rescue. I would die again.

Alone.

"Hey," a voice came from the crowd.

Everyone turned as Atlas approached the two of us.

"Gill. My meeting with the headmaster is scheduled close to yours. I'm still unfamiliar with the campus. I was hoping we could walk together."

He turned his eyes toward Tovin. "Good afternoon. I hope I'm not interrupting anything."

Tovin let out a deep breath, cast me one more glance, then turned and walked away. The students slowly returned to their usual business, the murmur of many conversations filling the silence as Atlas walked up to me.

"Are you all right?"

My heart rate was through the roof and adrenaline was rushing through my entire body, but I managed a pained nod and a thumbs up.

"You look like you've seen a ghost." He paused. "Wait, *can* you see ghosts?"

"Hey, Atlas, way to put Tovin in his place!" said someone in the hallway.

The boy turned and scanned the small crowd.

"Man, we've got a new hero on campus!"

"Way to go, little guy."

The students applauded.

Atlas turned to me, one eyebrow lifted. "Um...What just happened?"

I couldn't help but laugh.

"What?" He looked painfully confused. "Why are you laughing?"

It only made me laugh harder. Nerves mostly. Complete and utter relief; joy that he'd been nearby; a swell of good emotions. But it was also hilarious. This kid, no older than fourteen, scaring Tovin off and being applauded by his upperclassmen. I stopped laughing, allowing the smile to linger on my face as I observed him.

Now *that's* a main character.

"It's nothing," I said finally.

"I feel as though there's been a fundamental misunderstanding," he said, glancing around the hall.

"No, you're good. I'll explain later; we gotta run!"

"I don't like running!" he called after me as we hurried toward the south wing.

Six

"You're four minutes late." Headmaster Alrune spoke sternly.

I stood stiff as a board on the other side of his desk; I had no words. As much as I wanted to blame my lateness on Tovin, I was a hundred percent at fault. I'd been goofing around in the hymnasium showing off for someone so out of my league, I might as well be playing a different sport. I deserved whatever I had coming.

"What do you have to say for yourself?" he asked, staring daggers into my eyes.

An awkward silence descended before a smile forced itself out of the tangles of his beard. His shoulders bounced as he wheezed—his signature laughter. I laughed nervously along with him as he leaned back in his chair and ran a hand through his long, gray beard.

"What do you have to laugh about?" he asked in an annoyed tone.

My heart dropped into my stomach, and I quieted.

His face lit up, "Ha! I got you again!" He wheezed until his face was pink and motioned for me to sit down. "Tell me,

Mr. Dragstenn," he asked, smiling, "which one of us is never late from time to time?"

I sat in the chair opposite him and looked around. I had only ever been in the offices of Headmasters Rowan and Vega, and I had to admit Alrune's wasn't what I had expected of him. Given my frame of reference, I figured all of the headmasters were stuffy and uptight, but Headmaster Alrune's office was a sight to behold. It was lit with purple flames that danced in the corners—a low light accented by the haze that permeated the air. His office smelled of incense and would be relaxing were my nerves not shot. The right and back walls were lined with crowded bookshelves, while Alrune's desk was littered with scattered papers, curios, and trinkets, and several sketches of architecture, beasts, and patterns.

"Now then." He cleared his throat. "You've probably no misgivings about why I've summoned you here on your day off. Apologies for that, by the by."

"No need to apologize," I assured him. "And I'm sure it has something do with what happened in the hymnasium yesterday, right?"

He lifted his pipe to his mouth and puffed it a couple of times before closing his eyes and nodding twice. He sighed a plume of smoke and set his pipe down on his desk. "I knew you were sharp."

I remained quiet as he coughed a couple of times. He regained his composure, cleared his throat, and turned his eyes on me. "Tell me, Mr. Dragstenn. What did your eyes see?"

I was apprehensive about my answer. I didn't want to get Atlas into trouble. I thought for a moment before saying, "Well. Tovin Blackmeyer cornered him against his locker first. He was trying to intimidate—"

Headmaster Alrune furrowed his brow and waved his hand around in the haze, "No, no, no, Mr. Dragstenn. During the *duel*, boy. What did your eyes *see?*"

I sucked my lips in. They didn't care about how it started. That was for the better. After all, Atlas *initiated* the duel.

I reflected on the battle and answered. "I saw you, holding your stomach and gripping the railing."

A chuckle escaped his lips, and he nodded. "Yes. I know now the taste of the boy's power." He pointed the butt of his pipe at me. "What I'm interested in, is what it *looked* like."

"Bright," I responded. "*Very* bright. Too intense to look at directly."

"Mm-hmm," he replied as he pulled out a notebook and opened to a specific page. He pulled a pencil from his drawer and wrote. "What of Mr. Blackmeyer? Is there anything noteworthy about that spell he used? Those of us present have never seen it before."

"Um," I gripped my knees. I was worried. If Tovin found out I was snitching to them...

"Mr. Dragstenn," he said, looking up from his notes.

"I believe Atlas can shed more light on that than I can," I answered finally. "He mentioned that it made his body tingle all night long. I'm certain he'd tell you more."

"Tingling," he noted. "Anything else?"

"No, sir. It was bright, and it was fast. I wasn't able to observe the spell either time he used it."

"Indeed," he replied as he jotted down notes in. "And Mr. Grimbrooke," he continued, "how much magic does he truly possess? I've no doubt you were watching his reserves in action."

I was hoping he wouldn't ask me that.

"Why, I've not seen such a display of raw magical power in all my life," he added. "The headmasters are quite interested in the full scope of his abilities."

I sighed and relaxed my shoulders, "He used the entirety of his reserves on that one spell."

"I'm relieved to hear it," he said as he wrote.

Of all the answers I expected, that wasn't one of them. I cocked my head and furrowed my brow.

"Sir?"

"Why, I think I speak for all of us when I say the boy is plenty powerful enough. We were worried that his strength ran deeper than what we witnessed. The others will be quite pleased."

"Pleased?" I asked. "But why?"

"Dear boy," he said. "The hearts of men are fickle things indeed. The boy is young. He hasn't yet any convictions or firm principles. Do you understand?"

"You're afraid of him," I muttered, surprised.

"No, boy. Do not mistake caution for fear, strategy for cowardice, nor preparedness for pessimism. We still do not know all there is to know about magic—this incredible arcane force of nature at our fingertips. For the safety of our students, and indeed all of Galgia, we must create contingencies for our most gifted students. For Mr. Blackmeyer; for Mr. Grimbrooke; for Miss Meridia; and even for you, Mr. Dragstenn."

At that, I sat back.

"For...me?"

"That's right," he puffed on his pipe and smiled with his eyes. "You have a unique ability. There is only one other in existence who can see beyond sight. You're speaking with him right now." He wheezed with laughter and swatted the smoke away with his hand. "The point is," he went on, "we want nothing but success for our dear student. However, we cannot afford to overlook the fact that he contains within him such vast reserves of energy that if indeed he wished it..." He trailed off.

"I understand, Headmaster Alrune."

He nodded. "I knew you would. You saw what I felt..."

"For what it's worth though," I said. "I think Atlas—err, Mr. Grimbrooke." I corrected myself. "I think he's a wonderful person with a kind heart. I don't foresee you having problems with him. He's even-tempered and mature for his age."

"He's made quite an impression on you in only a day's time," said Alrune as he set his pipe down.

I only realized then how silly I sounded. Atlas had arrived at our school yesterday. It had to seem strange that I'd vouch for him after such a short time. No doubt it had a lot to do with the fact that he was a walking can of Tovin repellent.

"I pray that you're right, Mr. Dragstenn," he said. "Yesterday marks the first occasion we've had to kill a student to prevent a potential catastrophe. You may think Headmaster Anther has a heart of stone, but I assure you he is still quite shaken by the action of his own hand."

"I don't think the measure was too drastic," I replied. "The stasis field has never been tested against multiple simultaneous deaths before, has it?"

"Indeed not," he answered. "You think like a headmaster, Mr. Dragstenn."

I found myself again flattered. Headmaster Alrune was full of compliments for me today.

"No," he continued. "No, the stasis field has not withstood the brunt of mass casualties. I could not say with certainty whether it would be up to the task."

It seemed like as good a time as any to ask about it.

"Headmaster Alrune?"

"Yes, Mr. Dragstenn?"

"What...what *is* the stasis field exactly? How does it work? Who made it?" I pressed. "Does it run on its own, or do mages power it?"

His face changed. His eyes fell to the floor and then darted toward the wall. Maybe I shouldn't have asked that. But I'd been wondering about the stasis field ever since I was first revived by it. Since I'd seen *its* face for the first time.

"Thank you for your time, Mr. Dragstenn," he said with a half-smile, dodging the question. "That will be all. I've an appointment after you, and you've put me a tad behind schedule."

"Of course," I responded as I stood. I knew better than to press the issue.

"If you see him out there, do call him in for me," he said as he scribbled in his notebook.

I stepped out to find Atlas seated against the wall, sitting cross-legged with his nose in a book. He looked up and made eye contact. I stopped and jerked my thumb toward the door.

"Your appointment was also with Headmaster Alrune?"

"Y-yes," he responded, standing up and patting down his uniform. "It is. I thought I had mentioned that."

He hadn't. If he were meeting with Headmaster Alrune as well, then it stood to reason that Alrune had been tasked with handling the investigation of the duel. That meant that if Tovin hadn't met with him, then he'd probably be headed this way. I had hoped to catch Atlas after his meeting.

I looked over his shoulder at the empty hallway and clenched my teeth.

Screw it.

"Atlas," I said as I closed Headmaster Alrune's door behind me. "I know this is really weird timing, but I need to ask you something important right now."

"Right now?" he asked, raising his eyebrows.

"It can't wait."

"Um. Okay. What's on your mind?"

I stared back at him, "Atlas. When you died..."

I paused as I searched for the right words.

He watched me, and we held eye contact.

"Did you see anything...*unusual?*"

Seven

None but those who attended ENU could die and live to talk about it. Those who did caress the face of death rarely wanted to revisit the experience. It sounded unconscionable without context, but I'd been awaiting the day another student would die. I wanted to know if they saw it—that thing that had loomed in the back of my mind since the moment I was revived.

"Unusual?" asked Atlas.

I held my breath. Atlas's eyes followed the pattern of the floor tiles.

"No, I don't think so," he said at last. "I saw that light at the end of the tunnel that everyone talks about and some colors, but I don't think I saw anything I'd consider *too* crazy." He lifted his eyes to mine. "Why do you ask?"

I sighed and shoved my hands in my pockets. "No reason," I lied. "Headmaster Alrune is waiting to see you. He asked me to send you in."

"We can talk about it later if you like," he offered.

"No, that's all right," I said as I patted his shoulder on my way past. "You don't have to revisit that moment on my account."

"Well, all right then," he called after me. "I'll uhh...I'll see you later?"

"For sure." I waved without turning. I didn't know if the disappointment was hanging from my face the way it was my shoulders, and I didn't want him to feel bad about it.

After I got back to my dorm room, I locked the door and collapsed on the bed; I was emotionally exhausted. I stared at the ceiling and reflected on what had happened the day I died. It wasn't until after I had sunk to the bottom, only after that incredible feeling of loneliness, only after I was *certain* I was finished...*that I saw it.*

Eyes appeared out of the infinite darkness that cradled me. Eyes everywhere, all of them focused on me as though they all belonged to one being. As it inched out of the shadows, certain groupings of its eyes moved in tandem, like a sliding puzzle. A clear chime rang as my energy returned to me. Its eyes doted on me as though I were its newborn, and I couldn't stop myself from reaching out to it. I found the strength to lift my arm.

I remembered sitting up and everything around me changing. I was sitting in a puddle on the hallway floor, my clothes soaking wet, my arm still outstretched. I blinked several times and looked down at my hand before finding that I'd been returned to life. I looked around—everyone had left me there.

I made my way to Headmaster Rowan's office and explained what happened, but nothing came of it. That was the day I learned Tovin was untouchable. I spent the rest of that day leaning over the sink and coughing up copious amounts of water.

I had a long time to consider what I'd witnessed.

Had I seen the face of a god?

I had spent that week bringing heaps of library books back

to my room. It was the only place I felt safe, and I didn't want to leave it. Surely one of the multitudes of the world's religions could describe what I had seen. I pored through every religious text I could find, but no multi-eyed deity. Nothing even came close to describing what I experienced.

I started drifting away from my *own* religion. According to my church, I was supposed to have met with Hahnahkordia, Keeper of the Gateway—a great owl with six arms and a shining scepter.

"Maybe I hallucinated," I spoke into my empty room. "I *was* dying after all."

The experience felt so real. Like I could have reached out and touched the multi-eyed deity. I reached toward the ceiling before letting my arm fall to the bed. I wasn't uncomfortable in my uniform, but this was one of the two days a week I could wear my casual clothes.

I stripped down to my underwear and, as I was searching for my pajamas, a voice came from across the room.

"Nice underwear."

I swear my head almost hit the ceiling. I yelped and whirled around to find Fena in the doorway. My spirit left my body as I scrambled to make myself decent.

I yanked the blanket off of my bed and held it in front of me, "Ever heard of knocking?!" I screamed.

"Nope," she said as she pushed the door closed behind her with her foot.

"How did you even know where my dorm was?" I yelled as she walked toward me. "F-Fena, what the heck are you—"

She pressed her lips against mine. Time seemed to stop as I tried to piece together whatever it was that I must have missed. She placed her hand against my chest and pushed me onto my bed.

My words got caught in my throat as she ripped my blanket out of my hands and crawled on top of me.

"I've been trying to catch you alone," she said before moving her fiery mane out of her eyes and tucking it behind her ear. She kissed me again, this time pushing her tongue all the way into my mouth. Her breasts pressed against my chest as she let her hands explore.

I awoke with my lips puckered. I blinked hard and sat up. I was still in full uniform.

I hadn't realized I'd dozed off. I rubbed my eyes and looked at the clock. It was past six. I'd slept the whole day away! I let myself fall back on my bed and sighed, partly because I'd be awake all night now but mostly because I wanted to enjoy that dream a little longer.

I closed my eyes and tried to drift back to sleep, but my noisy stomach was reminding me that I'd slept through lunch. I wiped my hand over my face. I wasn't going to be able to ignore it.

I sat on the patio at The Magic Bistro, a restaurant in the west wing, and I played with my food as the rain bounced off the tin awning. My mind was swirling. I found it hard to forget my dream. But I'd known her for only a little more than a day.

What the heck is wrong with me?

Too soon to ask her out—creepy even. Maybe if I was cool about it, a super low stakes approach. If I waited too long though, she'd surely be asked by someone else. What if she said yes to that someone? I'd be crushed, though I knew I had no right to be.

Then there were the CAPE exams coming up. The Combat Analysis Placement Exam pitted student against student in one-on-one mage battles. Luckily for me, they were tiered; I wouldn't be fighting monsters like Tovin or Atlas. The school took on roughly 700 students at a time, and each was evaluated at their enrollment. Based on a number of factors, they'd be assigned a ranking. I remembered being thrilled to be assigned something like 702.

I was just happy to make it into the school back then.

"That's higher than I was expecting!"

"It's the lowest possible score," grumbled Headmaster Vegas as he looked over the file in front of him. "Your magic reserves are...tragic. On top of that you're a tome user." He looked up at me over the rim of his spectacles. "How in the world did you even make it into this academy?"

"Because I'm real good at it!" I said. "You'll see! I'll make you all see!"

I pushed a laugh out through my nostrils and shook my head. It was only a year ago, but it seemed like such a distant memory. I couldn't believe how much I'd grown since then, how much I'd changed. My parents had noticed it in me when I had visited them over the holiday. They kept asking me if something was wrong.

I'd never told them about Tovin.

If I knew my father, and I did, he'd march straight down to the university and raise hell. Ma would threaten to go to the papers, I'd be expelled, and all the negative coverage would only motivate Tovin to kill me again. This time outside the school.

It was best for everyone if I just...

My thoughts were pierced by the school bell in the distance. The bell tower signaled three times a day: once for class to begin, once for lunch, and once for curfew. Everything shut down at eight thirty, and everyone was expected to be locked in their dorms by nine. They took it seriously, too. Caught out of your dorm after curfew, and you'd be reprimanded. Caught a second time, and you'd be expelled. I didn't want to take any chances. I pulled out my money clip, tossed a tip on the table for the waiter, and signaled for a to-go container.

I cleaned my dorm top to bottom.

I got organized for the following week.

I did all I could until I was sitting at my table wide awake and bored out of my mind, watching the candles flicker. I pulled things out of my pockets before undressing, but I stopped short when I noticed something was amiss. I turned my pockets out and searched the floor.

My money clip was missing.

I broke into a cold sweat as I checked the countertop, the bathroom, anywhere else I could have left it. It had all my money for the week in it.

The bistro! Maybe I'd left it there! I looked at the clock.

11:33 p.m. I doubted the manager was still there, but if I'd dropped it...

I weighed my options. I couldn't afford to lose that much money. I'd never been in trouble with the school before. If I were caught, the headmasters weren't likely to expel me.

I had to retrace my steps. I opened the door and peered down the hallway in either direction—it was *dark*.

After night fell, little flames floated around public areas to illuminate restaurants, dorms, and walkways. After curfew, they're all extinguished. As far as the headmasters were concerned, nobody should be outside anyway. The darkness would make it a real pain to find my money clip, though, if I had dropped it.

I prowled down the hallway, my eyes fixed to the floor, searching for the gleam of the metallic clip. I made my way down the stairs and retraced my steps all the way through the western causeway. I came to the double doors at the end, which were closed after hours and opened early in the morning. A chill ran down my spine as I got that sense of "you're not supposed to be here." That feeling you get whenever you enter the back room of a store or another kind of restricted area.

I calmed my nerves and pulled the door open. It creaked like it was being tortured, and I winced so hard I could have pulled a neck muscle. I opened it just wide enough for me to squeeze through and left it open behind me. I'd be back in a few minutes; the west wing wasn't far.

I scanned the floor as I moved through the central roundabout. If I had dropped it here, then someone would have *definitely* found it. I prayed it was lying close to the bistro as I moved under the archways and into the open night air of the west wing.

All the shops and storefronts were closed and empty, like a ghost town. Before curfew, the area always buzzed with students and faculty alike. Liminal spaces always freaked me out. I centered myself and refocused on the mission. I sneaked down the main walkway, watching the ground as I turned the corner toward the bistro. The moonlight would help if I'd dropped it out here.

I made it all the way to the restaurant, but I didn't find any trace of the money clip. My stomach was in knots. I leaned against the building and heaved the heaviest sigh. I made a mental note to keep spare money in my drawer and turned to head back. I accepted defeat; the money was gone.

I stopped in my tracks.

A little girl, pale as the moon, was down the walkway aways, and she was staring straight at me. She was wearing a white dress and had long, pale locks that shimmered in the moon's glow. She wasn't moving, just staring straight ahead at me. No young children were allowed on campus. I rubbed my eyes and looked again. She stood silently with her feet pressed together and her arms behind her back.

I struggled with what I was seeing. Was she one of a headmaster's daughters? Was it *lose your kid at work day*, and I didn't know about it?

I was now staring directly at a new problem. Do the right

thing and lead her to one of the headmasters, even if I landed myself in serious trouble? Or mind my own business and be better off for it?

I gritted my teeth as I struggled with my decision. The man I was before wouldn't even question it. He'd be the hero this little girl needed without a second thought. Had Tovin really killed that part of me for good? Then, without a word, she turned around and jogged in the opposite direction.

"Dammit," I said through my teeth. "Hey!" I called after her, going from a fast walk to a jog. "Are you lost?" I yelled. "Hey, hold up! I want to help!"

She turned and looked at me out of the corner of her eye before rounding the bend toward the central roundabout. How she could run so fast on such little legs, I hadn't the foggiest idea. I turned the corner and slowed to a stop.

She'd vanished.

I scanned the walkway as I carefully continued on. She didn't have many places to hide, with all the shops closed and locked, and the central roundabout nearly fifty yards away. I put my hands on my knees and leaned forward to catch my breath.

What in the world did I just witness?

From below, a glint of silver caught my eye.

Sitting in the middle of the walkway was my money clip.

I was a hundred percent certain that I hadn't missed it the first time through. I snatched it off the ground. All my money was there. I surveyed the area one last time before deciding I'd be better off heading back to my dorm room. The only thing worse than being caught out here by senior staff would be being caught out here shouting for a little girl I couldn't prove existed.

I crept through the roundabout and back toward the heavy wooden door. I'd decided I would leave it open rather than make all that noise trying to close it. The headmasters would never know who had been here. As I rounded the corner, I found that the door had been shut tight.

Someone had been here.

Not good.

I'd only been gone for about six or seven minutes tops. I placed my hand against the door and stopped. I picked up a faint sign; so faint I nearly missed it. A magical energy signature was on the other side of the door.

I'd *never* seen someone's energy through a solid object. It was either more noticeable in the darkness, or whoever was on the other side of the door had a *massive* energy signature. Even with that, it probably wouldn't be enough since I couldn't see Atlas's energy through Headmaster Alrune's door when leaving the meeting earlier.

I could arrive at only one conclusion. The person waiting for me on the other side of the door was immensely powerful.

And absolutely furious.

EIGHT

My stomach sank as I realized that "the person" had to be one of the headmasters. My heart rate quickened. I stood still. Which one of them could exude so much raw energy? They were powerful, sure, but this? My perspective about what was possible with magic changed.

I had to move.

I held my breath and inched backward as I considered my options. Two outer hallways would take me back to the east wing. The southern and western wings were open to school tours, but the northern and eastern wings—the classrooms and the dorm rooms—were off limits to anyone not employed or attending. That meant that the northern causeway sat behind a big, heavy door, like the east. I didn't dare attempt to move it, for fear of it being as loud as the other.

That left me with only one safe way home: the south wing.

I controlled my breathing as I moved along the outer wall of the roundabout, my heart pounding like a drum. I slowly peered around the corner down the south causeway. There didn't appear to be anyone waiting for me in the dark; I'd have seen the dim glow of magical energy plain as day in the pitch-black hallway.

I rounded the corner, coming as close to running down the causeway as I could while being quiet. I was even conscious of the little cracks in my knees that surely only I could hear. I stopped at the end of it and pressed against the wall. Sweat beaded up on my forehead as I tried to steady my heart.

Here, at the entrance to the college, was where the room opened up, with high ceilings and grand architecture. Any little noise would echo and give me away. I calmed myself before poking my head around the corner.

I would have to cross the room and ascend the staircase toward hallway B. From there, I would have a straight shot to the east wing. I swept the room with my eyes. It was empty. I wasted no time. I followed the outer wall toward the distant staircase, moving past the big cutouts of happy students and creeping behind the front desk.

As I stopped at the edge of the desk, I saw something I hadn't before. A figure in a hooded black robe was standing in the corner of the room between me and the staircase. I would have run right past them had they not lifted their arm to scratch their face. I slowly moved back behind the desk.

How could I not see the energy in their body? They had to be in a special robe or something, but why take that kind of precaution? It wasn't like just *anyone* could sense or see magic. And why were they standing around in the south wing at night? Maybe one of the headmasters noticed the open door and asked someone to guard the only other way back to the dorms while he or she guarded the other. I closed my eyes and tried to stave off the panic with breathing techniques. The situation had worsened considerably. I had to think of something fast.

I couldn't summon my tome to me—speaking would announce my presence, even if I whispered. I was lucky the hooded figure hadn't spotted me, but what could I do from here? Even if I made it back to the roundabout, where would I go? The longer I waited, the greater the possibility that more faculty would join the hunt. I wracked my brain for solutions, but I came up empty. I closed my eyes and reflected on the books I'd read.

What would my childhood heroes do?

Samshir the Gallant?

No, I couldn't kick their ass.

Horrace, the Duelist?

I couldn't talk my way out of this.

Amesha the Swashbuckler?

My eyes popped open. The third book. She'd been captured aboard one of the enemy's ships.

Escaping the cage was the easy part; Lawrian craftsmanship was notoriously terrible. Lawrian *warriors* however, were a different story. Without her weapons, she was merely a fly in their web—their terribly, terribly designed web. She used the rafters above like an agile cat, the holes in the ship's interior like a crafty mouse, and the poorly disguised trap doors to maneuver around the ship like a flitting shadow. They were no match for her cunning. Her progress came to a halt however, when she came across the steps to the upper deck.

They'd perched a guard at the top of the steps. She decided to find another way up. Ships were designed to have multiple access points to the upper deck for the purpose of fire safety. It seemed however that the abysmal architecture of the Lawrian actually worked *against* her, and the guarded door was indeed the only way forward. She couldn't wait for the guard to fall asleep, or use the restroom, for as soon as her cage was discovered empty, it'd be over. She eyeballed the cups sitting on top of a nearby barrel and a smile spread across her face.

That's it!

It was a rudimentary tactic, but an effective one. It might also be my only way out. I reached up and searched the top of the desk, feeling around in the dark for anything weighty enough to heave across the room. My hand found something solid, and I wrapped my fingers around it. I inched off the desk and brought it down to inspect it.

A bottle of ink! It was perfect. I could hardly believe my luck.

It had enough weight to it that I could really huck it, and even better, it was made of glass. It would shatter when it hit the ground. The robed figure couldn't *possibly* ignore it. I peeked over the rim to make sure they were still standing there before backtracking to get behind the cardboard cutouts of the eager students. I needed to put a lot of height on this thing, so the hooded guard would have zero chance of seeing it fly from one end of the room to the other. I needed it to shatter in the entryway, so I'd have plenty of time to move. I took a deep breath and thought it over again.

If I turned myself in, I'd probably get by with a severe punishment. If I had to explain to the headmasters why I was out past curfew throwing ink bottles in the south wing, I'd be expelled for sure. I mean, I had to be one of the most expendable students at ENU. They'd let Tovin get away with this, even Atlas, I was sure. But if I messed this up...If I got caught right here...

My life as a mage was *over*.

I held the bottle and peered around the corner at the hooded figure. That massive energy signature I witnessed through the door; the little girl who led me to my money clip and pressed her finger against her mouth; the fact that this person was cloaked head to toe and invisible.

Something wasn't right.

These people didn't feel like headmasters. I had a growing feeling that if I were caught, something much worse than expulsion would happen to me. I'd heard plenty of rumors in my time here.

The student disappearances.

The Mole Eater.

The distant screams heard in the vents.

I'd assumed they were tall tales. Nobody could *prove* anything, aside from the random expulsions. Good students with high potential and promising futures were kicked out. The reasons weren't made public because, duh, student privacy, but the friends and family of the expelled often reported weird behavior and anxieties that didn't exist prior.

These sinister stories about ENU hadn't bothered me until now.

The fact of the matter was, I could be in serious danger. I couldn't afford to mess this up. I lifted the ink bottle over my head, said a small prayer to Hahnahkordia, and tossed it with what I gauged the appropriate amount of strength and height. The bottle sailed overhead in a perfect arc, just clearing the chandelier, and landed right where I'd hoped with a resounding crash.

The hooded figure rushed across the room.

I didn't wait one second. I jumped across the desk and went around the outer wall, stealing glances at the guard every time I could. I ran up the stairs, skipping every second step while I stayed low to the ground. The figure shouted. They were a male. I couldn't tell what he was saying, and truth be told, I didn't care. All that mattered to me was getting as far away from him as I could.

And just when I was in the clear, just when I thought the worst of it was over, I tripped on the last step and slammed into the floor.

The sound boomed through the room, echoing again and again. I don't know why I checked to see if he heard the noise; of course, he did. I would be willing to wager that I woke up at least a couple of students in the east wing. I picked myself up and looked over the railing. The hooded figure was moving across the room at a *hauntingly* fast clip. All the blood drained from my face as I launched into a full sprint down hallway B.

The eastern causeway was a bit different from the others, in that it was situated outside like a courtyard. It consisted of a long stretch of cement walkway with waist-high stone walls on either side. Behind those walls on both sides were grass, flowers, a couple of trees, shrubbery, etc. If I looked up, I would see hallways B and F: the two outer hallways that wrapped around the school. Both hallways have open windows along their length so the students on the eastern causeway can be seen from above.

I liked that feature—until now.

What I saw when I looked left made the hair on the back of my neck stand on end. What had been waiting for me on the other side of that door was a *very* tall, masked figure in a dark poncho, and they were racing me to the east wing. In the moment I looked down, they looked up at me. The mask appeared to be made of ivory by the way it shined in the moonlight, and it depicted an expressionless human face, not unlike a mannequin's. Dread ran through my veins as we made eye contact.

I had thought I was running as fast as I could, but the fear radiating down my spine pushed me to speeds I didn't even know I was capable of.

I looked over my shoulder. The hooded figure from the south wing was just hitting the top step. With how fast I had seen him move, I knew he'd be on me in no time. I thought about summoning my tome and icing the floor behind me, but if anyone saw it, their search would narrow to one student.

I had no options left. All I could do was try to outrun them.

My dorm was on the second story and not too far down.

I glanced again at the eastern causeway to find myself neck and neck with the masked pursuer. If we made it to the eastern wing at the exact same time, they'd still have to get up the steps to catch me.

I was so close.

Adrenaline coursed through my veins.

As I blasted through the archways and into the eastern wing, the masked figure was tearing up the steps.

I wasn't going to make it.

NINE

I slammed my door and locked it in one swift motion, my lungs struggling for air and my heart leaping out of my chest. I sped across the room and blew out the candle, shrouding the room in darkness. I leaned against the far wall next to my bed, eyes wide, holding both hands over my mouth. I waited in the silence, not moving a muscle.

In the hallway, a door creaked open.

"What the hell is going on out here?" said a muffled male voice. He sounded like Cal, my neighbor across the way.

"You heard that, too?" asked another.

More doors unlocked and opened.

I swallowed, which was painful with my throat as dry as it was. I made the quick decision to get my uniform off and replace it with my pajamas as more voices joined the conversation. My breathing was normalizing, and I was able to think. It'd be weird if I was the only one not out there. I took one last deep breath and moved for the door, unlocking it and poking my head out. I did my best to look like I'd just woken up.

Light poured out from the several open doors as students stood in the hall and discussed.

"What was that?" I asked in my best groggy voice. "Did someone fall?"

"Came from your side of the hallway," said Cal. We didn't know each other very well. He was three years my senior, generally cranky, and always had the worst smelling garbage. His blonde hair was a mess, which didn't necessarily mean he'd been sleeping.

He looked up and down the hallway.

"You see something?" I asked.

"No," he grumbled. "Probably Axle screwing around again. Kid's a nutjob."

"All right," I croaked. "I'm going back to bed then. Night, Cal."

"As if sleep is a *thing* around here," he whined as we closed our doors.

I locked mine and crawled into bed. I didn't even want to *look* at the clock. I stared at the ceiling. I had no way of knowing if either of my pursuers saw me run in here. I might wake up to find a letter with a purple seal waiting for me.

All I could do was writhe around in my bed and agonize over what might transpire in the morning. It was out of my control now.

I watched the door until the kiss of dawn began to illuminate my room. I closed my eyes and dug my palms into them as I realized I'd have to stay up all day if I wanted to get my sleep schedule back. If I took a nap, I would sleep all day. Students were leaving for breakfast, and I decided to join them. A coffee and a bagel sounded good.

"Gill!" Atlas yelled as he found me in the cafeteria. "You look terrible."

"Thanks," I muttered as I sipped my coffee.

"Are you feeling unwell?"

"Just tired."

"Ah. You slept poorly?"

"Somebody slammed their door late last night and woke me up," I lied.

If the headmasters were asking around, I'd benefit if both Cal and Atlas could corroborate my story. I was another clueless victim who had been woken up in the dead of night. I didn't lie very often, but I did lie well.

"Couldn't fall back asleep."

"I heard about that," Atlas said. "Some of the folks in line were complaining about it. Everyone seems to think it was a student named Axle."

I closed my eyes and they burned. I was *that* kind of tired.

"Axle dorms next to me," I said. "He's an avid conspiracy theorist. Pretty eccentric guy. Talks to himself in his room at night, I can hear him through the wall."

"Did somebody say conspiracy theory?" Fena asked as she walked past me with her tray and sat next to Atlas. She smelled like something delicious, and her voice was a welcome one. "Love me a good conspiracy," she added.

"Don't let Axle hear you say that," Atlas said, as though he'd known Axle for years. That brought a smile to my face, and I opened my eyes. She was the medicine they needed.

I had a new problem now, though. I didn't want people blaming Axle for last night, but they'd find it strange if I defended him. Nobody really liked him, especially those who lived near him. If he caught you in the hallway, he would *absolutely* engage you in conversation about some wild theory or another. He was such a weirdo that most of the other students hoped he'd be expelled.

But like Tovin, he was untouchable.

He was ranked number six or seven during his initial assessment. He was near the top of the school's academic list. Tovin scored beneath him once and scorched a row of lockers. Like me, Axle hadn't participated in his first Cape yet. I looked forward to seeing him compete whenever his bout was announced. I wanted to see what he could do that was so impressive that he landed in the single digits among folks like Tovin, Lana, and likely Atlas.

"C'mon," Fena said as she shoved a forkful of food in her mouth. "Hit me with one. Tell me about the Mole Eater."

"I'll also admit to a polite curiosity," Atlas added.

"It's a wild one," said Axle, appearing as though he were summoned. I nearly jumped. I hadn't even seen him sit down next to me.

"Oh boy," Atlas said.

"Oh!" Fena exclaimed. "Uh, hi. I'm Fena, and this is my little brother, Atlas."

"I know who you are," he said. "I know who everyone is. Anyways, the Mole Eater."

He had a one-track mind. I didn't need to introduce myself, as I was one of the only students polite enough to listen when he cornered me outside my dorm. He had a chin strap beard and medium-length blond hair that flipped up on the sides. He had pierced ears, and he wore a hunter-green headband with a black stripe. He also had a necklace with a talisman on it that I never saw him without.

"It all started with little Sally Ravenbeak," he began. "It was twenty years ago—twenty to the month actually! She was staring out her window on a moonless night, unable to sleep. She heard a noise behind her, and there appeared a woman with a mask. She had her hair tied up in a bun, keeping it together with a dagger. Sally awoke the next morning, assuming it had only been a dream. However, when she went to bathe, she discovered that..."

He paused for dramatic effect. "One of the moles on her left knee had gone missing!" He stared at us as though expecting some kind of reaction.

I rested my chin in my left hand and heaved a sigh.

"Is...Is that it?" Fena asked.

"Of course not," he leapt at the opportunity to continue. "Since then, several students have reported dreaming of the Mole Eater. Whenever they awaken, they've found that moles, scars, bruises, or any other imperfection below their waists were gone! Hairless, too!"

"If I may," Atlas asked, "Has anyone been able to *confirm* this? Perhaps a close friend who knew where a victim's mole was and could confirm that it had gone missing?"

"Of course!" he yelled. "Well, kinda...Not really. No," he finished. "But there have been *way* too many cases to just dismiss it."

"Well Atlas has a big ol' mole on his butt," Fena interjected as she continued eating. "If she gets her hands on *him*, I'll know it."

"Fena!" he cried out in surprise as he turned to her.

I snickered.

"What?" she asked. "It's not a big deal."

"Not a big deal?" he asked, folding his arms. "Well then, maybe it's not a big deal that you grow a big patch of hair on the small of your back like a man."

Her mouth fell open and she dropped her fork as a small squeak escaped her lips. I lifted my hand to cover my smile, but no doubt my cheeks gave me away.

"Oh, are we doing this?" she asked with wide eyes.

"Wait," said Atlas as though he knew where this was going. "No."

"I think we're *doing* this!" she yelled, slamming her hands on the table.

"Fena, I'm sorry," he pleaded.

"You guys want to know what *Atlas* has done since he was a *baby?*"

"Yeah!" Axle yelled with the biggest smile on his face.

"That's enough," I said, attempting to veil my smile. "Might as well stop while you're even, right?"

The two of them shared a wary glance before returning to their meals.

"For what it's worth," Fena said, running her hand through her hair, "I haven't allowed any back hair in years. I maintain a *very* strict beauty regimen, thank you very much."

I wanted to say, "It's working."

That's clever. Say it. Say it's working. It's still not too late.

"You look terrible by the way, Gill," Fena said.

Great.

"Axle woke him up last night," Atlas spoke up. "He couldn't get back to bed."

"I *what?*" Axle asked, turning to me.

I wanted to vanish.

"*You're* the one who's been telling people I slammed that door last night?"

"No," I said, sounding more annoyed than I meant to. "It's what people are saying. Nobody knows who slammed a door."

Axle pursed his lips and stared at me for several seconds. I glanced at him, and I started to worry. He was staring at me like he knew something.

"Are you, uhh…Just gonna let people *say* that about me?" he asked, blinking several times.

He *knew* something. I couldn't ascertain how, but he knew it was me. I didn't know what to say. Maybe he was only suspicious of me and was trying to get me to out myself.

Stay calm. Act natural.

"Well, what is he *supposed* to do?" Atlas asked. "I heard it from a group of students here. Is Gill supposed to run around all over school defending you?"

Axle shrugged and stood up. "Guess you're right."

Relief flooded my brain, but I didn't like the way he said, "Guess you're right." His tone made it sound like he knew that Atlas was not, in fact, right.

"You know, there's another conspiracy theory one of you might be interested in," he said, moving away. He leaned on the edge of the table. "It's about the *Night Watchers*."

I swallowed. Had he been watching me? I turned. He was staring right at me.

"If you're the kind of person who might *really* want to know about something like that, you know where to find me." He walked away, leaving us with that.

"*Do* we know where to find him?" Fena asked, with a confused but comical expression before digging back into her breakfast. I turned. Atlas was eyeing me. He knew I was the only one who knew where to find Axle. I'd told him we were neighbors. He was putting it together.

This wasn't good.

TEN

“Gill,” Atlas said as I drank the last of my coffee. “Your hands are trembling.”

“Yeah, I'm tired,” I shot back.

I let the silence linger.

“My eyes may not be as good as yours,” he said, staring me down. “But I can see that something is wrong.”

“Is everything all right?” asked Fena, looking up from her food and glancing between the two of us. She tilted her head, “I feel like I'm out of the loop; what's going on?”

“There's no loop,” I growled as I stood up and gathered my things. “It doesn't have anything to do with either of you. Just drop it.”

I left, tossing my trash in the bin before making my way to my dorm. If Axle knew something about what happened, I needed to know *exactly* what it was. More importantly, I needed to make sure he kept his mouth shut, even if I had to pay him.

I didn’t fear expulsion so much as I worried what would happen to me if I had seen something that I *really* shouldn't have. The headmasters are powerful. Headmaster Rowan is rumored to be a High Priest of Galgia.

Just what had I gotten myself mixed up in?

The money didn't seem worth it. I could have explained what happened to my parents, and they surely would have sent me a little to get by.

"Hey, mister," Fena said voice in a no-nonsense tone from a distance. At first, I thought I'd imagined it; I imagined her voice kind of a lot. I turned. She was marching across the cafeteria; y'know, the kind of march where there's a strong possibility that you're about to get smacked. She stopped in front of me, staring into my eyes.

"My little brother considers you a friend," she said, venom dripping from every word. "He's not good at making friends. He's *worried* about you, you absolute ass."

I was caught off guard. "I...I didn't..." I stammered.

"I'm not the type to trust someone easily," she went on. "But my little brother has good eyes for *people*. He's got a big heart of gold, and I swear on the gods if you step on it," she trailed off, piercing me with her emerald gaze.

I didn't realize how cold I had come across. I didn't consider Atlas a friend yet, much less the type I would worry about when they weren't around. Deep down though, I understood. If I had difficulty forging bonds with people, I'd be protective of the ones I had. He was a fair deal younger than me, too. He always seemed so logical and composed that it made it easy to forget that.

"I'm sorry," I said finally.

"Not to *me*, you're not," she responded, not backing down an inch. She was scary when she was mad. Beautiful and scary. Weird combination. She had a point, though. I didn't want to leave Atlas with hurt feelings.

"All right," I conceded. "Let's go get him. I'll tell you guys what's going on back at my dorm, but not a second sooner. It's not a public conversation."

We grabbed Atlas. I apologized to him with Fena breathing down my neck. After convincing him that his big sister had nothing to do with the apology, we trekked back to my dorm. I closed my door behind us, and I locked it. Probably shouldn't have, that's what serial killers do. They didn't know anything about why I was anxious yet.

I heaved a sigh on the way to the kitchen, sitting in the one chair I owned.

"You can sit on my bed," I offered. "I'm sorry there isn't better seating in here; it's usually just me. The sheets and comforter were just cleaned, I promise."

"You keep it real tidy in here," Fena said as she looked around.

"Yeah, I like to keep things clean." The place had been a disaster before last night.

"Take notes, Atlas," she said. "This is what a made bed is supposed to look like."

"Yeah, yeah..." he muttered as the two of them sat.

"Actually," I said as I stood up. "I want to stand. I don't feel like sitting right now. I'm just...I'm on edge," I admitted. "And you're about to know why."

"So, something really *did* happen?" Fena asked with concern in her tone.

"Gill," Atlas said reassuringly. "You can tell us."

He really did consider me a close friend. I swallowed, tracing the floor with my eyes before opening the can of snakes that had been twisting in my guts all night long.

"Yesterday," I said, "I...I messed around in the hymnasium with you guys for too long."

"That's right; you were late to your meeting," Atlas recalled.

"Are you in trouble?" Fena asked. "How much trouble could you be in for being a couple of minutes late?"

"No," I said, "let me talk for a few minutes."

The two of them exchanged glances before turning their attention back to me.

"I ran back here and got dressed really fast. I ran out the door and straight into Tovin. He and I have...a history," I said.

"Did he bully you?" asked Atlas.

I sighed, lifting a fist to my mouth. I chew on my knuckles whenever I'm nervous or uncomfortable; a habit I've had since I was young.

"Atlas. Fena...Tovin *killed* me."

"What?" Fena yelled, standing up.

"Shh!" I shushed her. "Not so loud."

"Like by accident?" Atlas asked in a hushed tone. "In training, maybe?"

"No," I said grimly. "He was pissed off at me...and killed me in the hallway."

Atlas's eyes widened. "Tovin *murdered* you? Out of spite?"

"When?" Fena asked, sitting back down, and leaning forward attentively. "When did that happen to you?"

"In my first year here," I answered. "I don't want to talk about it. It doesn't matter to the story other than for you to understand that seeing him now is emotionally draining for me."

"Yeah, no shit," Fena interjected. "That would be draining for anybody. How is he still allowed to attend if he attacked another student on purpose?"

"Murdered," Atlas corrected her, flames on his tongue. "He *murdered* another student."

"It's a long story; I'll tell you later," I said, doing my best to rush past it. "What matters is that I ran into him, we had a small altercation, and I was late to my meeting. The headmaster, gods bless his playful heart, scared me into thinking I was in a ton of trouble and my nerves were shot by the time I got back here."

I sat down again. "I took a nap to clear my head...and I slept the whole day through. I woke up around six, I think."

"Hate it when I do that," Fena said, rolling her eyes. "Stress can wear you out."

"Well...I ended up going out to the west wing for dinner. Magic Bistro."

"Oh, I've heard of that place." Fena said with a smile. "You should show me where that is sometime."

"I've got a map of the west wing I can lend you; I don't need it anymore." I said, trying to keep the conversation on track. "In any case, I dropped my money clip, and it was real late when I figured that out, and it had all my money in it, so I..."

I closed my eyes. "I snuck out of my dorm past curfew."

They were new, so they had *just* been read the riot act about how strict curfew was.

"They take that seriously here," said Atlas. "How much money are we talking?"

"Enough that I took the risk," I answered, leaning forward. "I snuck all the way out to the west wing and..."

I thought about telling them about the little girl, but I decided she wasn't important to the story. I also didn't want to seem like an insane person to my newest friends.

"On my way back, I ran into...Well at *first*, I thought they were headmasters. These tall figures in dark robes. One had a long gray beard and wore some kind of cloak that concealed his internal magic reserves from my eyes. The other was tall...Taller than any of our staff here, now that I think back on it."

"Hold on," Fena stopped me. "Patrolling the hallways at night? What time was this?"

"Past midnight, at least," I said, rubbing my eyes. "But that's not the worst part."

"Did they catch you?" asked Atlas, visibly captivated by the tale.

"They *tried*," I responded, eliciting gasps out of both of them.

Atlas's eyes were wide. "You *ran* from them?"

"You don't understand, Atlas," I shot back. "One of them...I could see their magic energy through a thick wooden door."

I explained how that shouldn't be possible. Why I felt like I was in danger. I also went back and included the little girl. I took them through everything from the figure wearing that creepy mask, to the ink bottle distraction, and then finally the chase.

"I slammed my door behind me," I said. "It woke everyone up. I didn't know what to do but lie about it. I was...and still *am* scared for my life. What if they saw me come in here? What if they come back tonight?"

"If you didn't look as haggard as you do right now," Fena said, "I don't think I'd believe you. But that's real stress on your face, no doubt about it."

"Everyone heard that door slam," Atlas added, turning to his sister. "I can't think of a reason why Gill would lie to us. He gains nothing and has everything to lose."

"I get it now, Gill," Fena said with a sympathetic look. "It makes sense why you wouldn't want to tell us something like this. It's serious business, and you don't know us well enough to know if you can trust us like that."

"For what it's worth though," Atlas chimed in, "I'm glad you told us."

"Not *me*," Fena lifted her hands. "If I get asked about it, then I've got to *lie*."

I looked at her with surprise. "You'd lie for me, Fena?"

"Of course, we would," Atlas smiled. "That's what friends do."

"And also, my little bro and I have a 'no-snitch' policy that we've honored since we were kids."

It was totally heartwarming. I had an expectation that they wouldn't tell anyone, but I'd never expected them to cover for me.

"Thank you," I said, smiling at the two of them. "Really. Thank you. It feels good to tell someone. I *still* feel like I'm a little out of my mind."

"I would too," Fena responded. "I think any mentally healthy person would. Because we're still in the dark about this situation, I guess the next thing to do is go see if Axle really *does* know anything about this."

"You're going to encourage his delusions?" asked Atlas.

"Conspiracies, legends, myths," Fena responded. "Those things all originate from a kernel of truth. You can't dismiss stuff because it doesn't seem plausible. It's important to challenge the way we think from time to time, and it doesn't hurt to see what Axle knows about these Night Watchers."

"I agree," I nodded, exhausted. "I was planning on speaking to him, if you guys want to come with me."

"Uh, I'm *invested* buddy," Fena said with a no-nonsense expression. "If masked freaks are running around in the hallways at night, I want to *know* about it. I just started here; it's *not* too late for me to pick a different college."

We shared a much-needed laugh, cutting the tension. We walked next door to see what kind of information we could pry out of Axle. Before last night, I never gave any credit to the wild stories surrounding the grand halls of the university. But seeing is believing, and now I need to know anything and everything I could. I lifted my hand to knock on Axle's door and it swung open before my knuckles even made contact.

"Oh!" I recoiled, as Axle's excited mug appeared in the doorway.

"Come on in!" he shouted excitedly, stepping aside, and holding his hand out as though he were a circus ringleader presenting his new attraction.

I have to admit, I was hesitant. But I was the closest to the door, and I didn't know how to back out after how excited he looked to have company. His room was as strange as he was. He had painted warding runes all over all four walls and his ceiling. He had broken up his bedframe, and his mattress was on the floor. Carved wooden effigies were on his dresser, kitchen table, and countertops. His window was barricaded, and the boards had warding runes carved *and* painted into them.

"Stop!" he shouted.

I whirled around to find him with his hands pressed against Atlas's chest.

"You never *ever* enter a room with your left foot first!" Axle cautioned. "You always enter *and* leave with your *right foot*."

Atlas shot Axle a bewildered look, and then turned to me as if *I* had answers. I grimaced and shrugged. He stepped back, re-entering with his right foot, and making sure Fena did the same as she came in behind him. She lifted her shoulders and tucked her arms as though she feared Axle would touch her.

"Good," Axel said, closing the door behind her. I wasn't surprised to find wardings painted and carved into his door. I *was*, however, surprised to see seven latch locks of different sizes and colors on his door, all of which he got to work on.

The three of us exchanged worried glances. *Definitely* something serial killers did.

"Uhh, Axle?" I piped up.

"Yes," he called back as he worked the fifth lock.

"This looks like a mage trap."

He finished sliding the seventh latch and turned to face us. "Oh this?" He gestured at the room. "This is a cautionary measure. You never know *what's* going on at this school."

"Uh-huh," Fena responded. "These aren't magic runes. These look like..."

"Correct," he smiled. "You have good eyes, madame. These are for evil spirits, devils, demons, phantoms, ghosts, etcetera etcetera. You know how it is," he added, moving past us into the kitchen. "Would any of you like anything to drink? I've got frog juice, bladder water, spider milk..."

I dry heaved at spider milk.

"I'm just joking," he said after a long pause. "I've got purified water."

"I'll take a glass of that," Atlas called out.

"Same," I said. My throat was dry.

"I'm good," said Fena as her eyes wandered the room.

"So then," he said as he brought the glasses to us. "The Night Watchers."

"Perhaps you should let Gill tell you what he saw last night first," Atlas said.

"I was listening through the wall," he said. "I heard everything."

"How thoughtful," Fena remarked, rolling her eyes.

"Before you begin, Axle," I interjected, "I have to know something first. How did you know it was me? Were you still awake last night?"

"Moreover," Atlas spoke up, "your jab at Gill this morning in the cafeteria seemed to suggest you knew these Night Watchers were pursuing him. How could you have known that? Were you hiding in the walls or something?"

Axle didn't seem bothered by the interrogation. In fact, I'd say he was proud; he looked like he wanted to say, "Wouldn't *you* like to know." He leaned against the column that stretched from his kitchen counter to his ceiling and folded his arms.

"Yes, I was awake. No, I wasn't hiding in the walls, though there are some *seriously* good spots in there. I'll show you sometime. As for how I *knew*..."

He made eye contact with each of us as he savored the moment. *"I can read people's minds."*

"Very funny," Fena said, clearly unamused. I felt the same. I hadn't come here for jokes. I was dealing with a genuine crisis.

"Truly?" Atlas asked. "You can read the minds of others?"

"Absolutely," Axle nodded. "Well, kinda. Not really. No," he finished as he scratched the back of his head and averted his gaze.

"I get the feeling you exaggerate a lot," I said, resting my head in my hands. I wasn't feeling playful, and I was verging on the cusp of irritation.

"Guilty," he admitted. "But there's truth there, too, about me reading minds. That is. I *can*, but I don't get to choose whose mind I read or when. I'll explain it to you, but if any of you tell anyone, I'm gonna blab *all* about Gill's midnight outing. This is my super-special secret."

"Sure," I agreed. "And if you tell anyone about me, I'll blab about your kinda-maybe-mind-power."

He smiled in a way that made me a tad uneasy.

"It's a deal, Gill Dragstenn."

Eleven

"It started when I was a little kid," Axle began. "You ever heard of 'Magnolia, the Magnificent Medium?'"

"Ugh," Fena groaned. "That lady is such a hack. She suckered my brother and me into a reading once at the Koldt County Fair."

"I remember her," Atlas added. "We pooled our finances for the reading."

"Her readings weren't expensive," Fena continued. "But we were little kids. We only got money on our birthdays or for the solstice season. She fed us some crap line like, 'Don't worry about what you're worrying about.' That was all we got."

"*Were* you guys worried about something?" I asked.

"Worried about getting ripped off," she said, leaning to one side. "I've warned everyone I know to stay away from her. I hope I saved a lot of folks some money."

"So, the medium," Atlas steered the conversation back on topic. "How does she fit into your story?"

"She's my mom," Axle answered with a worried smile.

Fena's eyes turned to disks.

"How's that foot taste?" I asked her with a cocky grin.

"Axle, ohmigosh." She held her hands out. "I'm *so* sorry!"

He averted his eyes and forced a smile, "No, no, it's...It's all right. You're not exactly the only person angry with her."

"I'll never talk ill of her again," she said. "Atlas either, right?" she asked her brother, hitting his chest with the back of her hand.

"But I didn't even *say* anything," he said, just above a whisper.

"Guys, guys, it's okay," Axle reassured us. "What I'm trying to tell you is...It wasn't *her*. She wasn't the mind reader." He paused. "It was me."

"You?" I asked in surprise.

"Mm-hmm." He nodded. "When people are near, I hear fragments of their inner dialogue. I almost never hear a complete sentence. I have to piece it together with context clues, and even then, it doesn't always make sense."

"For real?" Atlas asked, his eyes glowing. "You're a real life medium?"

"I think mediums claim to speak with the dead," Fena interjected. "I think the term psychic is more appropriate."

"Do they ever stop?" I asked. "The voices?"

"No," he said, appearing more sullen than before. "The voices are only silenced when no one is near. Living in the city, that means never. Here at the college where people sit in their room and study? It's a circus, sometimes."

"That sounds...miserable," Atlas said despondently. "So, your mother used your gift for fame?"

"I won't dispute that," he responded. "I was sitting under the desk behind the thick tablecloth, jotting down what I was hearing on paper. It wasn't always right, and it didn't always make sense, but when it landed, it *landed*." He picked his head up and his face brightened. "The wonder in their voices as they tried to figure out how she did it. It was my favorite part of the job."

"Did she pay you at least?" I asked.

"No," he shook his head. "So long as I made her money, I got to eat."

"Forgive me for saying," Atlas spoke up, "but that sounds kind of cruel. I'm sorry she took advantage of you like that."

"It wasn't always bad," he came to her defense. "Whenever I made her a lot of money, she'd buy something delicious for me."

"So, the reason she retired recently," I said, trailing off.

"You heard about that?" Axle asked with a tinge of surprise. "Yeah. It's as you suspect. I received a letter of acceptance here and refused to be part of her act anymore."

"Well." Fena shrugged. "It was nice of her to let you come here and follow your dreams at least."

"Wrong," he wagged his finger. "She told me...to never bother coming back home. Called me a freak. Haven't talked to her since."

"By the gods," Atlas muttered in apparent disgust. "How heartless can one be?"

"Can I give you a hug?" Fena asked, "I'm gonna give you a hug."

She slid off the bed and threw her arms around him. He lifted his hands as though he didn't know what to do with them, and then brought them up to her shoulder blades. His eyes wandered and then closed. It meant a lot to him.

I didn't know Axle had it like that. I felt bad for all the terrible things I'd thought about him. Oh jeez, what if he *heard* them?

What if he's hearing these *thoughts right now? Or am I just a voice in a crowd, like he said? What a strange and stressful ability.*

"So, your mom deserted you," I spoke up, partly to halt my internal dialogue. "What about your father? Was he all right with that?"

"He left when my mom started doing the medium thing," he responded as Fena sat back down on the bed. "I don't know if it was a coincidence or not. I was too young to understand, and mom refused to talk about him. She wanted me to forget him, like he didn't exist."

His story just got worse and worse. I couldn't imagine my mom using me to make money, my dad skipping out on me, or going to a school where everyone thought I was a freak. All things considered though, he seemed well adjusted—harmless, at least.

"Anyways, that's my ability. I can hear the thoughts of others fade in and out as they pass me in the hallways, or as they walk past my room."

"I get it now," I said, thinking back on his behavior. "Why you stay locked in your room on the weekends."

He nodded. "Yeah. Almost everyone spends their time off in the west wing. Makes it nice and quiet around here."

"Now that I'm thinking about it," said Atlas, "that explains why you were in the north wing yesterday. That *was* you, wasn't it? You walked past us in the hallway."

"Now that you mention it," Axle said, pondering, "that really was the three of you, wasn't it? Yeah, I passed you guys on your way to the hymnasium."

Kind of embarrassing. I hadn't noticed him. My eyes had been glued to Fena that whole morning. I felt like a creep when I thought about it that way. I shifted my gaze over to her as Atlas and Axle conversed. I wasn't a creep—there just wasn't anything nicer to look at on almost every occasion.

"I like to hang out in there on weekends because it's nice and empty," Axle went on. "Two students were in there yesterday though, eating snacks and shooting the breeze. Their thoughts didn't bother me, they were just...loud."

"We saw them in there," I recollected. "Now that we understand your ability, your behavior makes a little more sense. You're not weird; you're just coping with the constant mental voices of everyone around you."

"I think that's the nicest thing anyone has ever said to me," Axle said sarcastically. "I've come to grips with my power. I can tune it out when I'm in the zone, studying, reading, or concentrating hard. I can also, with the help of a handy little spell, zero in on a single person. But even then, their voice fades in and out of my head like an ocean tide. For some reason, it's stronger when they're under emotional distress."

"That's crazy," Fena spoke up. "I one hundred percent believe you."

"It adds up," I admitted. "And on top of that…It would explain why he heard me so clearly last night. I would say with great confidence that I was pretty damn emotionally distressed."

"That, and everyone else was asleep," Atlas chimed in. "Not many minds speaking that late, I'd imagine."

"Clear as a bell," Axle affirmed. "You were pretty freaked out. I wanted to help, but…I didn't think you'd even give me the time of day—err, night."

"To be fair, I wouldn't have answered that door for *anyone*," I said. "In fact, I'm starting to think I need latches on my door like you've got on yours."

He set his glass of water down on the countertop and looked at me with a serious expression, "Gill, let me ease your mind about something."

We all quieted.

"They didn't see which dorm you ran into. They don't know which student was walking the halls last night."

I breathed a sigh of relief, and a rush of soothing chemicals flooded my brain. That was the best news I'd heard in a long time. Tension lifted from my shoulders in real time.

"How do you know?" Fena followed up. "Could you hear their thoughts, too?"

"Not just that. I was awake, and my dorm room is on the very corner near the stairwell. I heard the commotion right through my kitchen wall." He turned to me. "Two of them pursuing you. One from hallway B, and one from the east wing causeway, correct?"

"That's right," I said, a smile creeping across my face. "Amazing."

"You must have been running this way from hallway B because I could hear the pursuer from the east wing causeway ascending the stairs."

"Right again," I confirmed.

"Well, the two of them collided at the top of the steps next to my dorm. They fell over one another, from the sound of it. One of them yelled at the other for their clumsiness, and when they made it to the hallway you were gone."

"What insane luck," Fena said with a laugh as she smiled at me. "You hear that? You're in the clear, good buddy!"

I laughed with relief and fell back onto the mattress. I couldn't stop chuckling as I placed both my hands over my face and wiped them over my chin. I sat up. If I could bottle this feeling and sell it, I'd be a rich man. "Thank the gods."

"As you should," Axle said in a darker tone. "Your pursuers weren't thinking about capture. I think they intended to kill you, Gill."

Something inside of me already knew that. I wasn't shaken when he said it. I may not be able to read minds like Axle, but I definitely had that gut feeling of imminent danger.

"They were going to...*kill* him?" Atlas asked, his face drained of color. "But...why?"

"The Night Watchers are the dark masters of this school. They drain students of their essence and use it to power the Moon Monocle, a magnifying laser where they're gathering energy to bring the moonfolk here to Galgia. They travel via light, you see, and they need a bridge to get here. It's going to be their ultimate weapon against the Diesel Empire."

Axle read the room.

"Well, that's how the myth goes anyways," he added. "Look, I'll just tell you what I *know*. I know that they go by a few different names. The Night Watchers, The Shadow Folk, The Hall Monitors, the—"

"*That* one," Atlas interrupted, glancing at us. "I like that one. It's less scary."

"Sure, we'll call them the Hall Monitors then," Axle nodded. "But I feel like Night Watcher is a cooler name." He wiggled his fingers. "Night Watchers!"

"I'm sorry, but what do you find *cool* about cloaked men running around the halls at night trying to kill students?" asked Fena. "Do the headmasters know about this?"

Axle looked surprised before looking at the floor. "I guess...I guess I thought they were kind of cool before," he answered sheepishly. "But now they've attacked my friend, Gill, and that means they've made an enemy out of *me*."

I couldn't help but notice that he casually said we were friends. I didn't know the guy that well. I guess I *was* the only one who talked to him. There probably wasn't a single soul at the university to whom he felt closer.

"The headmasters deny their existence," he continued, looking up. "As far as they're concerned, it's just a fairy tale students have been telling for decades." He paused. "And as for the *men in cloaks*, as you put it...I'm not certain that they're human, at least not all of them."

"Not...human?" Fena asked, as taken aback as the rest of us.

"Yeah," he responded. "The Hall Monitor chasing Gill down hallway B had some scattered thoughts. That's not uncommon. I'll do my best to simulate what I was getting from him," he said, clearing his throat and deepening his voice.

"If he saw the procession wal......hen he has to die. Word absolutely *cannot* get ou......we're discovered, the other three colleges, including the high priests..." Axle stopped, with a look of concern. "That's what I was getting from the person on Gill's tail," he said. "But the other one...He was repeating one word over and over and over." He stared at the floor again. "He was saying...Kill kill kill kill kill kill kill."

We all sat there in stunned silence. I was more confused and concerned than before.

"And there's more to it," Axle continued. "His voice didn't sound...Well, it didn't sound human."

"I don't understand," Atlas interjected. "How does one not *sound* human? Do you hear their thoughts in their own voices?"

"Sorry if I forgot to mention that detail. Yes, I hear your thoughts in your own voices. I can't explain why it didn't sound human. I think it's partly because humans don't think like that. To add to it, it repeated the word in the same tone and inflection every time, perfectly spaced apart. People don't *do* that, guys." He sounded flummoxed and a bit frustrated.

"And then there's what the human Hall Monitor said to the other one when they collided at the top of the steps..." He took a deep breath and shook his head. "He called it a *clumsy miscreation.*"

He looked back up at us. "Does that sound like something one human would say to another?"

TWELVE

"Clumsy miscreation?" Fena asked with renewed concern.

"He's right," Atlas said just above a whisper. "Humans don't talk to each other like that."

"I don't want to jump to conclusions," I said in direct defiance of what my gut was telling me. "Some humans are weird."

"Who's jumping?" Fena asked. "Based on what Axle has told us, it's hard to argue with his suspicion."

"Based on what Axle has *told* us," I repeated lifting my gaze to Axle.

"Are you *accusing* me of something?" he asked, standing up straight.

"Maybe I am; maybe I'm not," I said, watching him. "You have to understand how crazy this sounds. It's hard to believe, and I hardly even *know* you, Axle. Try to think about this from my point of view."

"Gill, I'm *hearing* it from your point of view," he shot back. "You don't believe what you're saying. You're in denial."

I stood up, balling my fists. "Stop reading my mind!"

"I'd stop if it I could!" he raised his voice.

"Hey, guys!" Fena moved between us.

"Gods be my witness as I say this," he yelled over her shoulder. "I would. I would if I could," his voice cracked. He swallowed. He was holding back tears; he was as shaken up as we were, even if he'd managed to keep a cool demeanor. I sat back down on the bed and leaned forward with my elbows on my knees. Axle sat in his chair and Fena glanced at the two of us before sitting back down herself.

"I'm sorry, Axle," I said.

"I'm sorry too," he said, his voice quivering. "I'm not an easy person to get along with. Folks have a right to the privacy of their own thoughts, y'know." He let out a deep breath. "It's like living with a mind burglar who keeps taking and taking."

"Was he right, Gill?" Atlas asked. "*Do* you believe him?"

I nodded hesitantly. "Yeah," I admitted. "The thing in the mask...It didn't move naturally. Even that night, before any of this," I gestured around the room. "I was wrestling with the idea of whether that thing could have been human."

"If it's not human," Atlas asked, "then what *is* it?"

"There's only one other dominant race on the planet," Fena piped up. "And they're an ocean away and too big to walk these halls. There aren't any bipedal animals outside of myths and legends. If it wasn't human, and it was walking on two legs, then perhaps it's an elemental?"

"Elemental creatures don't have thoughts the way we do," Axle interjected.

"They're more like semiconscious forces of nature," Atlas concurred. "Have you ever read the thoughts of an elemental, Axle?"

"No," he said as he rubbed his chin. "It's a good place to start, though."

"Lana," I said, looking up. "She found the frequency to the plane of elementals last year. She can sing them over."

"You're right," Axle said, a smile forming on his lips.

"Lana?" Fena asked.

"Lana Meridia," Axle answered before I could. "She started here at the same time as Gill and me. She's a talented melodic caster."

"She's got good reserves, too," I added. "She can sing into our realm all by herself monsters that would normally take two people harmonizing."

"She's a high rank," Axle tagged back in. "Somewhere in the teens."

"The problem is her attitude," I said through a sigh.

"Funny how often that becomes a problem, the higher up the rankings you go," Axle noted.

"So how do we get her to sing in an elemental for us?" Atlas asked.

"We don't," Axle shot the idea down. "Singing troll class monsters into the school without supervision is prohibited. There's no faster way to be expelled."

"That can't be right," I said.

"It's true," said Fena. "It's in the handbook. Singing in troll or devil class monsters without express permission from the headmasters is grounds for immediate expulsion. If you sing in anything higher than devil class, you'll also go to prison —if you survive the experience."

Elementals fell within troll class. Monsters don't naturally occur in our world, but there are lower planes and gap dimensions that, through the use of magic, can be accessed by melodic casters. Where exactly they pull the monsters from depends on the pitch and frequency of their voice, as well as how much magic they're willing to expend in the process. The more magic used, the deeper the plane a caster can pull from.

Creatures summoned will obey the caster until they're returned home either by banishment or by release. Why the creatures bewitched into service don't turn on their summoners is not fully understood, but it's been known to happen with devil class creatures and higher.

Monsters come in five categories and are ranked: Imp, Troll, Devil, Dragon, and Leviathan. Imp level creatures are small, mischievous, and easily manageable by any adult. Imps, goblins, spiders, void slugs, things of that sort. Troll class monsters can overwhelm a group of unprepared mages, and they include trolls, lycanthropes, cyclopes, elementals, and larger threats of that nature. Devil class creatures are considered potent threats, capable of damaging an entire school wing. Among monsters of this class, you'll find demons, giants, young dragons, or older vampires. We know of only a few Dragon class monsters, hence the name of the class. Dragons, hydras, wyrms—anything that could destroy the college while taking out any resistance. The final grouping of is known as Leviathan class threats. These are monsters that could wipe out our entire nation. We've never seen one, but we're aware that they exist. We haven't placed a single monster in that category yet, but they'd be akin to gods.

New monsters are discovered all the time and are catalogued into one of these tiers by the supervising headmaster.

"So, we're at a dead end," Atlas muttered.

"It may be for the best," Axle answered. "Look, I *love* myths, legends, conspiracies, all that stuff, believe me, but this? This is *real*. This is close to home, and I'd say we're lucky that we're walking away from this without being expelled." He used air quotes around "expelled."

"So, what, we just pretend like there aren't madmen running through the halls at night?" Fena asked.

"That's *exactly* what I'm saying," Axle answered. "This is bigger than us. I say we just keep our heads down and our eyes open."

"I agree," I said. "Let's shelve this for now. Lana's got to take the Cape, same as Axle and me this year. Maybe she'll summon an elemental, and Axle will get the chance he needs to see if that's what we're dealing with."

"Hey, that's right!" Axle grinned. "I didn't even *think* of that."

"But then what do we do with that information?" Atlas asked.

"One step at a time," I said. "For now, let's be thankful things went the way they did this time, and be more mindful of the curfew."

"Uh, yeah," Fena said. "I didn't need *you* to tell me that. I'll be in bed by *dinner* from now on."

"I'll be careful too," Atlas agreed.

"If you guys see anything else," Axle said as went for the door. "Call a meeting. We should meet in here because I've warded the room." He started undoing the latches as the rest of us stood up.

"And for the love of all things holy," he added as he opened his door. "*Don't* be caught outside of your dorm after dark."

I managed to make it all the way through the day without taking a nap, but now that it was time to sleep, my mind didn't want to shut off.

Friday had been orientation. Learning where all of our new classes were, meeting the professors and going over the syllabi.

Tomorrow was the start of the new year. Several of my professors used the term, "hit the ground running," so I was in for a whirlwind in the morning. My class schedule consisted of Battle Tactics, War Theory, War History, Phys Ed, Lunch Break, Philosophy, Magic Arts, and then my elective. I chose World Religion in the hope that I'd stumble upon information about my experience with death. I thought about that creature every night; about what awaited us after death; if we were pissing it off by defying it.

I fell asleep to visions of its many eyes watching me as they rearranged themselves on its face.

———

I was sitting down as the clock tower chimed in the distance. I wasn't late to class, but I wasn't early either, and I got stuck sitting at the very front of the classroom. I hated being between the professor and everyone else's eyes. Professor Wuthrand walked in with a stack of papers under his arm and closed the door behind him. He was tall; it was possible he'd be looking over my head all year.

"Good morning, everyone!" he called out through his expertly trimmed but full and bushy beard. "Take your seats, take your seats."

He strode over to his desk and set his papers down. He unrolled some kind of scroll and set paperweights on its opposite corners to keep it open. He gazed at the class, standing with his arms behind his back. The chatter dulled to a murmur, and I turned around as people walked down the aisle toward their seats. It was one of the larger classes I'd ever seen —at *least* fifty students.

"Thank you, thank you," Wuthrand said, the murmur breaking beneath his deep gravelly voice. "Welcome to day one of battle tactics. For any of you who missed orientation, we'll be discussing old war tactics as well as how they've evolved. But first," he almost shouted, grabbing everyone's attention. "It's upon *me* this year to talk to you all about your Cape Exams."

I shifted in my seat. This year would be the year I would

test myself against another student in real combat. I was both excited and terrified.

"Now!" he continued. "All of you were assessed upon your enrollment and given a ranking from one to seven hundred and four. I want to be the one to tell you that your ranking doesn't define you. The fact that you're walking these halls means you're the best of the best, and if we didn't see potential in you, you wouldn't be sitting in this classroom."

He smiled at me.

Dammit.

"The scores you have right now are meaningless, I assure you. Students in their second year, that's you," he gestured at us with both hands. "Earn the chance to show what you're made of. But we're doing things a little differently this year," he smiled and nodded while looking around as whispers permeated the classroom. "You may have heard, but first year students will be competing as well!"

What? I leaned forward, wondering if I'd truly heard that correctly.

"We've observed a pattern of students who are initially ranked very low upon their enrollment being bullied, ostracized, or isolating themselves. The headmasters decided that first-year students will be allowed to test their mettle against you lot."

Gods. They changed the entire procedure for Atlas, didn't they?

"We've got some promising new blood on campus this year, and we're all very excited to see them in action."

No doubt about it. The headmasters could hardly hide their jitters when Atlas triumphed over Tovin last Friday. This was bad news for a low rank like me. The pot just got a lot thicker. Damn Atlas and his protagonist status.

Wuthrand picked his stack of papers back up and tapped them against his desk to align them before handing them to the student at the end of the first row. "Pass these down," he said, moving back to his desk.

"These," he said, turning around, "are the rules for the Cape Exams. They've changed a bit this year from last year, so make sure to read over them."

I took one of the papers and passed the stack.

"We're going to go over these together," he said. "You in the back," he pointed to one of the students. "Let me know when you've got your copy in front of you."

He looked down at his scroll and ran his finger along it as though he were reading something. I took the opportunity to read the rules for myself.

- **Rule #1:** Obey the observing headmaster's instructions at all times.
- **Rule #2:** All items brought into battle must be catalogued and approved by the observing headmaster.
- **Rule #3:** No black magic.
- **Rule #4:** Students are not allowed to surrender.
- *Not allowed to surrender? What the hell are they thinking?*
- **Rule #5:** The match will not be stopped until one combatant is resurrected by the stasis field.

My hands trembled as I stared at the page.
Battles to the death? Whose idea was this?

Other students were finding rule five around the same time. The classroom buzzed with worried voices.

"You all need to remember," Wuthrand said in a serious tone, "that you are all here preparing for potential *war*."

"What kind of crap is this?" someone shouted from behind me.

"Fighting to the *death?*" hollered another student from further back.

More voices joined in, and the class erupted in protest.

The door to the classroom was wrenched open, and through it walked Headmaster Rowan and Headmaster Huede. They were prepared for this kind of backlash. Had they been waiting outside the door in case things turned ugly?

Why the sudden shift from safety to a warlike mentality? Had the Diesel made a move? As the headmasters worked to restore order, my stomach turned. Something strange was going on. I wondered if it had anything to do with Atlas. Surely, they wouldn't have changed everything for one student.

A third person entered the classroom after Headmaster Huede.

My heart fell out of my ass.

Tovin marched to the center of the classroom and stood behind the headmasters, his feet shoulder width apart and his hands behind his back. His glassy black eyes swept the classroom like a predator until they landed on me. After resting his eyes on mine, he stared straight ahead.

The part of me that wanted to be a mage was being tested.

I was starting to hate this school.

THIRTEEN

Headmaster Rowan took a couple of steps forward, just ahead of Tovin.

"Good morning students," he said with a chuckle. "I think I've met some of you before."

He was the head of the admissions department. If you were to apply to ENU, he'd be the first person you'd meet if your application were to be accepted. He decided whether you were a fit. Nobody walked these halls without his say so.

The oldest of the headmasters, he walked with a staff and a hunch, and he had a long beard that all traces of color had left long ago. He wore a pointy purple hat and a long robe to match—attire indicative of the era in which he grew up. At one time, his garb was the height of mage, or rather wizard fashion, as they were then known. Now, it identified him as a relic of an age that few other than him remembered.

"I would like to formally congratulate you all on making it to your second year here," he spoke in short bursts divided by half-second pauses as though forcing his speech through shallow breaths. "Year one was about making sure we are all on the same page, so to speak. I am certain there are those among you who found some of your year-one classes to be rather repetitive."

I *had* heard a lot of whining in my first year. We went over a lot of stuff that we learned in Magi School. I was appreciative of it; I found it a nice refresher that allowed me to start off with a spectacular GPA, strong enough to take a hit if I struggled in a future semester.

"But you must believe me when I say," he coughed into his fist, "that we, the headmasters, were preparing you to hit the ground running."

There it was again. When I'd heard it the first few times, I figured it meant that we wouldn't be slowing down for students who felt left behind. But after reading the rules, "hit the ground running" might mean running for our *lives*.

"Now that you've had a chance to look over the rules for yourselves," he said, gesturing widely toward us, "I'd like to take just a (cough) just a brief moment to explain to you all why we've changed things a bit in regard to the Cape Exams." He turned and shuffled over to the professor's desk, precariously placing his staff against it as he again turned to face us. He leaned forward on the desk, the wood creaking in harmony with his old bones. "This scroll unfurled in front of me...is intelligence from our divination specialists—our forward scouts in the ongoing effort to keep Galgia safe from the Diesel Empire."

The classroom was swallowed in a fog of murmurs and whispers.

"The Diesel?"

"War?"

"So, it's happening again."

"Are they on the move?"

"I'm not ready for this."

"Everyone shut the hell up!" Tovin barked. "Act like you're soldiers, gods damn you!"

It was crude, but it worked; silence settled over the class. I watched Tovin closely. His magic was all riled up. No doubt he was seeing us as a bunch of unreliable weaklings. I swallowed and remained still—I wanted to stay under his radar if I could.

"Mr. Blackmeyer," said Headmaster Huede quietly; only those of us in the front row heard him. "That's quite enough. There will be time for that later."

"Right, then." Rowan reclaimed the students' attention. "The enemy has been spotted at our borders. Troop movements, scouts, new mechanisms, and the like. We cannot say for certain if they are preparing for an advance." He looked at us through his long white eyebrows. "But we cannot dismiss the possibility that Galgia may be bathed in the flames of war once again, and far sooner than we had hoped or imagined."

The students murmured at the possibility of all-out war once again. Tovin's face twisted up, but before he could yell at us again, Headmaster Huede rested a hand on his shoulder. He took the hint and held his comments behind his clenched teeth.

"Fear not!" Headmaster Rowan lifted his staff in his wobbly hand. "Eye of Newt University and the other three colleges have well-trained and capable junior and senior classes."

"We'll be going over how our military functions later in today's lesson," Wuthrand cut in. "But to clarify for Headmaster Rowan, juniors and seniors will be the tip of the spear against the Diesel. Freshman and sophomores will see their share of the fighting, but on smaller battlefields against softer targets."

"Correct," Rowan nodded with a smile. "And allow me to reiterate (cough) that we are *not* raising the alarm. War, as it stands, is not upon us. However, we are watching and taking measures to ensure the safety of our students and our nation."

"That means toughening up our freshman and sophomore classes," Headmaster Huede spoke up. "And we're starting that *today*."

"Headmaster Huede will take it from here," Rowan said as he turned and ambled toward the door. "I have business to attend to. Please, give Headmaster Huede your absolute respect."

"Thank you, Headmaster," Wuthrand said as he strode past the old wizard and held the door open for him.

"Listen up," Headmaster Huede announced. "Many of you are shocked. But it's more important than ever that you learn what it feels like put your life on the line, and even more important," he paused, "what it feels like to *take a life*."

I sighed, looking down at the rules again. It was no joke; they expected us to fight to the death. I had to admit that it made at least *some* sense. And it explained why they were including the first years.

"As is tradition, we've brought the number-one ranked student in to speak with you all before you participate in your first Cape Exam. Your aim is to be standing where he is next year. Go ahead, Mr. Blackmeyer."

"Thank you," he responded. "You all know who I am. I'm the student who kicked those doors open on my path to greatness and obliterated anyone who stood in the way." He lifted his arms, "With these two hands, I punched through every obstacle. I'm supposed to stand up here and tell you all that you can do it, too, but the truth is, some of you were born to be failures."

He turned and stared at me.

"Like Gill Dragstenn, here."

I shriveled up inside. My face got hot as a hundred eyes settled on the back of my head.

"He was born with pathetically small magic reserves, and timidly walked through the front door of ENU holding a tome. A *tome*," he repeated for emphasis. "That he could *ever* stand where I am right now is nothing more than sad delusion. I give him credit; he's probably never even dreamed of being ranked number one. He doesn't have what it takes, and he damn well knows it."

Just kill me already. It would be less painful than this.

"Mr. Blackmeyer." Headmaster Huede nudged him.

"Everyone told him he'd never amount to *anything* from the day he was born."

Not entirely true Tovin, jeez.

"He can't do real magic like the rest of us," he scoffed. "He needs his little book and a *sword,* for crying out loud." He shook his head.

To my chagrin, a few of my classmates laughed.

I buried my face in my right hand. This was actually happening.

"And what the fuck are any of *you* laughing about?" Tovin snarled.

The classroom went silent.

I lifted my eyes.

"Gill was essentially born magic disabled, and he's attending classes at the most prestigious magic academy that exists. None of you are better than him. In fact," he chuckled, "you're worse. What's *your* excuse, huh?" He cupped his hand around his ear and waited for an answer. "That's exactly what I fucking thought. If *any* of you had the drive, the vision, or the guts that Gill has, you'd be ranked a lot higher than you are. Not one of you in this class is higher than rank three hundred, and that's *disgraceful.*"

Everyone was stunned, but nobody more than I. In a mean-spirited and unintentional way, Tovin had *complimented* me.

"I'm here to tell you that things are about to get *real.* You either get your shit together or you end up an unidentified corpse on an unknown battlefield. The choice starts now," he said, turning and walking away.

We all watched him leave in stunned silence.

"Uhh," Headmaster Huede stammered. "I uhh...I suppose that was as rousing of a speech as we should have expected from Mr. Blackmeyer."

It coaxed nervous laughter from the students. The headmaster had changed the mood, returning it to where it was before, albeit a bit lighter. We were still confused and anxious about all the sudden changes. Tovin had done little to help that.

"I'm sure in his own way," Headmaster Huede continued, "he was saying to work hard and stay focused, and good luck in the exams. Oh, and one more little thing I nearly forgot to mention."

He paused, looking around. "As you all know, you take a Cape Exam every year after your first, and each school conducts their own exams. The high priests asked that the other three schools take their exams on our campus this year."

The other schools are competing with us? This whole thing keeps getting worse.

"They believed it best to allow the other students to go all out in the only place where death is not a factor. It will also make it easier for the exam proctors to match each of you with an opponent of similar skill. The final, and in my opinion, most important reason we agreed to this, is to forge brotherhoods among the colleges rather than rivalries. You may find yourself fighting alongside the talented mages of the other schools soon."

Yeah. Good luck with that.

The colleges Huede is referring to are Brightroot Elemental Academy (BEA), Attainment & Conflux University (ACU), and the Augury Institute of Magi (AIM). The rivalries among them are *fierce*. Each school is situated within a separate province in Galgia, and they might as well be in different countries.

BEA's school colors are green and white, and their teaching philosophy is progressivism. Theirs is a more student-based approach to education that's rooted in pragmatism and real-world situations, rather than in the broad strokes of segmented study. Brightroot's students are more eccentric, unusual, and free thinking.

ACU's school colors are black and blue, and their philosophy of education is romanticism. They don't have a class structure with exams, grades, and set curricula. Instead, students decide what they want to study, and they are matched with experts in their field who can nurture their curiosities. The Conflux value individualism, instinct, and inspiration, and they'll follow that inspiration wherever it takes them.

AIM's colors are red and white, and their students are taught according to the perennialist philosophy. They value critical thinking and rationalism, and they focus on lessons that transcend the ages. These timeless lessons, they believe, prepare them for any situation they might face. They hang on the words of wise men long dead and can often be found with their noses buried in classic texts. Augeries are organized and disciplined, and, above all else, they seek eternal truths.

ENU's colors are blue and gold. We are taught under the philosophy of essentialism. Our school day is structured, and we go to classes where our professors lecture us. The difficulty of the material increases as we move into our second, third, fourth, and fifth years. Newts are well-rounded students with a broad knowledge of many subjects, rather than mastering one or two.

Depending on the colors you wear, people are *going* to treat you differently. The four schools are considered the height of magic expertise, and the mages who attend them are Galgia's answer to the Diesel Empire's machines.

Graduate from any of them, and you're a total celebrity. Fame, fortune, prestige—the oligarchy sets you up for life. But when the call to war comes, you'd better be ready to answer. Graduates train throughout their lives, preparing for the day the empire returns to finish what they started.

"The battles will not take place in the hymnasium this year," Huede continued, "but will be held in ENU Stadium. The event will be open to the public. You'll find out who your opponent is as soon as we've matched everyone."

The classroom came alive again, almost too loud to hear the headmaster. "Keep an eye out for the postings; we'll be pinning them to the cork board in each dormitory hallway. Thank you for having me in your classroom this morning, Professor Wuthrand. Good luck, students! Address your questions and concerns to Headmaster Vega's office."

Only as he was leaving did I realize my mouth was hanging wide open.

Public matches to the death among all four colleges? Were they out of their minds? By the gods, my *parents* were going to attend this! This was going to be the must-see event of the century.

Oh... They're gonna monetize the hell out of this, aren't they?

"If your families ask," the professor yelled over the commotion. "We don't yet know when tickets are going on sale. Please ask them to be patient."

Of course. It all made sense now. I wondered how much of that brotherhood crap was true as it dawned on me how much money the colleges stood to make on this. The weird surrender rule made sense now, too; if people were paying for this, they'd want to see a *fight*.

I suppose they had to pay our wages somehow, but this? I

was *already* nervous about my Cape, but now my fight would be watched by thousands? I missed only worrying about cloaked figures stalking me at night.

We spent what little remained of class going over how the exams would be scored. We each would fight only one battle where we would be scored on a 1–10 scale in several categories. Raw power, intelligence, adaptability, stamina, and resilience. The scores would then be put through some kind of formula based on hidden factors, and we'd be given a new ranking. In addition to pitting students of similar ranking against one another, the headmasters decided that first-year students would only fight other first-year students, with a few exceptions based upon how they were initially ranked.

No doubt they wanted to see Atlas fight Tovin again. In fact, I'd bet my life that Tovin marched down to Vega's office and *demanded* it. He wanted to destroy Atlas in front of everyone.

My blood boiled thinking about it. Tovin was ruthless; I don't think he'd ever been bested before. He didn't want to beat Atlas; he wanted him to suffer.

"We had more planned for today, but we'll just have to pick up the slack tomorrow morning," the professor announced. "Headmaster Rowan isn't a very fast speaker," he said, coaxing a laugh out of the students. "I'll see you all tomorrow bright and early; have a great rest of your day."

As people left, a few stopped to offer me pity, which stung more than it helped. I kept my eyes to the floor and skulked into the hallway.

The day had only just begun, and I wanted to go to bed.

"Hey, Gill!"

I turned. Fena was walking down the hallway. It was like she was moving in slow motion. The light from the windows seemed to set her fiery locks ablaze as she smiled at me. Just like that, I felt a hundred times lighter.

"Did you have any trouble last night?" she whispered when she got close enough. "You know with the Hall Monitors," she said with a cheeky smile that manifested her dimples.

I laughed and shook my head. "Nah, I tossed and turned, but once I finally drifted off, I slept good."

"Ugh, I know what you mean," she said as we turned and walked together. "My nerves were everywhere last night. I really needed somebody to talk to."

"I recommend reading," I said with a smile. "I've got some great books."

"Hey, guys!" Axle's voice came from behind us. He shoved his way through the crowd.

I sighed. I'd hoped to have spent a little more one-on-one time with Fena.

"Good morning, Axle," Fena said in a cheery tone.

He threw his arms around her, and she reciprocated.

My heart skipped a beat.

After they separated, he looked at me with his goofy grin.

I forced a smile.

They were *hugging* already?

All my alarm bells started singing.

FOURTEEN

At my desk in class, I rested my head in my hands. I was trying to pay attention, but I couldn't focus on anything the professor was saying.

"The continent of Aurii consisted of six civilizations before the 'War of Red Rust.' The Tauri, The Lang, The Galgians, The Hanouru, The Diesel, and The Raeche. The Diesel, unlike the other nations, were obsessed with progress and put science above spirituality, culture, their citizens' welfare and happiness, and the very environment that nourished them."

Am I missing something? Are Axle and Fena hanging out without me? Am I waiting too long? Should I try to get closer with her now?

"The Diesel Empire is governed by Ruth Martha Whitlock. She was democratically elected once, and she became the Diesel's supreme empress. All who have run against her have died. The Diesel seek progress above anything else. Their society is a magicless blend of smog, heat, and whirring machinery. They choke the minerals and resources out of every piece of land they settle on, and they only stopped expanding when their science failed to understand the power we Galgians wield at our fingertips."

Should I try to hug her? No, that would be way too weird after what I just saw. She'd totally catch on. What's worse is that I'm not safe in my own head with Axle around. I've got to be careful to not think about this stuff while I'm close to him... And I live right next to him.

"The Diesel Empire runs on two resources. The most important is a mysterious liquid known as oil. They use it to power everything from their factories to their war machines. We don't know where they're getting it; our spy network has found nothing. So cutting off their supply lines, a tried-and-true war tactic, isn't possible."

Who am I kidding? It's not like I'm ever going to make a move. Even if I did, she's drop-dead gorgeous. She could go out with any guy she felt like. She's hanging around with me because I'm her little brother's friend. Axle is handsome and has a neat power. More useful than being able to see magic.

"The second important resource is electricity, which we at least understand, albeit to a lesser degree. They've managed to harness it and use it to power their civilization, much like we power all our appliances and gadgets with magic. How they've captured literal lightning from the sky is anyone's guess. Scholars believe they may be pulling static electricity from fabric, like the kind that shocks you when you move around under the covers. How one would even go about storing it, however, is a mystery in and of itself."

I need to settle down. It's a hug. It's probably nothing. Maybe he's a huggy guy, and I misinterpreted the whole thing. Incredible how something so simple can destroy my focus. I can't remember a thing we talked about in War Theory last period. I've got to forget about it. That's it! From here on out, I don't care. I'm not the guy beautiful women want. They're looking for strong men. Men who are ranked insanely high, like Axle or Tovin.

"The Diesel Empire has managed to contain lightning in glass bulbs, illuminating their walkways, roads, and dark buildings. Although these miracles may seem attractive, the Diesel are crushing any civilization who stands in their way. We'll talk more about the civilizations that existed before the 'War of Red Rust' tomorrow. Read chapters one and two tonight, and come prepared for a quiz tomorrow."

Maybe Tovin was right.

Maybe I'm...

"Class dismissed."

Those last two words pierced my consciousness as everyone packed up their things. I sighed and did the same. I hadn't heard a word of the lecture. Not like it mattered; we'd been learning about the Diesel since magi school. I'd heard it all at this point.

I filed out of class with everyone else and made my way to my locker to put my books away and grab my gym clothes. PE was next, and I was pretty thankful. Exercise was a great way to flush out excess anxiety.

Inside the boy's locker room, I got changed and did stretches while everyone around me buzzed about the Cape Exam. Everyone seemed to be at an extreme: excited or horrified. I was in the latter camp.

"Gill?" A voice came from behind me.

I turned. Axle had his arms out and was wearing a goofy smile. "What? We're in Phys Ed together?"

Shit. I mean! G-Great! This makes me super happy! Happy, happy!

"Hey, how about that," I tried to sound excited.

"Wanna be gym partners?" he nearly yelled.

"You-you read my mind," I said with a half-smirk as we clasped hands.

"Ha!" he laughed. "You're a clever fella, Mr. Gill. C'mon, let's get out there."

I sighed and followed him out to the floor; I didn't see any way out of it.

The gym teacher was a young woman. She was short, with a freckled face and her blonde hair tied back in a ponytail. She wore some kind of headband and was dressed in gym attire, like the rest of us. A silver whistle hung from her neck, and she was resting her foot on a rubber ball.

"Line up!" she called out.

We all fell in on the hymnasium's long side. I did my best to think about *anything* else, but I was failing. Axle and Fena's hug was such a stupid thing to obsess over. I was embarrassed by how much I cared. So what if they were together? She didn't *belong* to me or anything.

Psychos think that way!

"You may call me Coach Hanley!" the gym teacher called to us. "I will be your physical education instructor this semester." Her voice echoed. "Today, I'm going to observe you all playing a little game." She looked down at her clipboard and ran her finger down it as she moved her foot around on the rubber ball.

"I'm going to call two students at random up here to be team captains." She paused as her eyes moved up and down the clipboard.

"Gerard Johnson," she called out. A student to my right walked out to the coach's left and turned to face us. He was dark skinned, tall, and wore glasses. He was lean and muscular at the same time. He had a round afro and thick sideburns that ran down past his ears and toward his jaw.

"And let's have...Fena Grimbrooke."

Had it not been for the slight echo, I'd have needed her to repeat that for me to believe it. Fena trotted out from somewhere down the line and turned around to face us, standing to the right of the coach.

"What?" Axle whispered. "The three of us? Wow, what luck! I didn't know we had first years in here."

Fena did a double take when she saw us, smiling and waving discreetly.

I was doomed. No way would I make it through the entire class without Axle picking up on it. My stomach twisted into knots.

Why couldn't I be normal, like everyone else? How do I tie myself up into pretzels like this?

"Take turns picking students until you have full teams," Hanley called out. "Ladies first."

"Ummm," Fena hummed as she looked over us.

I wonder who she'll pick first. Wouldn't blame her for taking Axle early; he's at least seven hundred ranks higher than me. He's the most gifted student in the class, now that I'm thinking about it. I'm fine with being picked second.

"You!" She pointed at someone at the end of the line.

"What?" Axle hissed. "C'mon, the three of us need to be on a team."

A tall and muscular student trotted over to stand next to her. I had to admit, I was surprised she hadn't picked one of us. I mean, we were friends, right?

"I'll take that guy," Gerard pointed, and another built student joined him.

"You," Fena pulled another stocky individual out of the crowd.

The two of them went on until it seemed no easy picks were left. Gerard was looking up and down our ranks.

"Hmm...You," he pointed. A student on the smaller side rushed out, and I died a little on the inside. I had muscle. I had worked a forge most of my life, and my arms had nice definition. Swinging a hammer all day was hard work.

Fena's finger finally found me, and my heart leaped.

"Axle!"

His name seemed to echo around me as he cheered and hurried out. I had even taken a half step. I felt like dying right then and there out of sheer embarrassment. And I really hoped she didn't see that.

"You," Gerard pointed at me.

I didn't move. I hoped he meant someone else.

After a couple of seconds, his face changed. "I said *you*, c'mon!" I glanced to my left and right before stepping out of line and shuffling toward him.

"Sorry, Gill!" Fena said quietly.

I didn't look at her. I was actually pretty upset. The worst part of it was, I had no reason to be. She'd done nothing wrong, Axle either. I was just caught up in my own head about my feelings for her. Still, we were just playing a game. I had no right to be so caught in the feels.

But I *was*.

When all the students were picked, Coach Hanley walked a few feet away from us, leaving the ball in the center of the room. She turned and surveyed us.

"Looks like we got even teams," she said with a cocky smile. "Good. Now then, on to what we're doing today."

She widened her stance a tad and took a deep breath before singing a beautiful melody—one we wouldn't have expected from her. Most of us recognized it. Through the open maw of the void slipped an imp, and then she shifted one key lower. Another void opened and out slid a void slug.

In case you've never seen an imp, they're small—about the size of a young child, with an intellect and temperament to match. They've got two bat-like wings, spindly arms with claws at the ends, and a thin tail with a little hook at the tip. They came in many colors: red, blue, dark green, black, and even yellow. Void slugs are easier to imagine. Just picture a dark violet slug about the size of a corgi with a curvy gray stripe down the side. Black flames blaze on their backs, and although they're not fire, they *are* an irritant to the skin if touched. Void slugs also leave behind a slimy trail of goop that, if ingested, would pretty much glue you to the toilet for the rest of the day.

Hanley said something to the imp, and it did a loop de loop before flying off to the other end of the hymnasium. It rummaged through a closet before scampering out with two rubber balls. It ambled across the floor on its reverse-jointed legs, attempting to fly now and again, but only fluttering a few feet at a time.

"We're going to be playing dodgeball today!" Hanley announced as she took the balls from the imp. She tossed one to Fena and one to Gerard. "But here's the *twist*. I've instructed the imp to tag players from both teams in an alternating order, starting with your team," she said, pointing at Fena.

"What?" she whined, getting a chuckle from the students.

"Ladies first, right?" Hanley said with a smirk.

"Oh, I *like* her," Gerard said with a big smile, earning a bigger laugh.

"If the imp touches you, then you're out. If you're struck by a ball, then you're out. If you catch a ball, then the student who threw the ball is out. The void slug will be wandering around the hymnasium. If you step on the slug, fall on the slug, or bump into the slug, then you're out! It'll be leaving slime all over the floor, making it slippery. You'll need to watch your footing, and pay attention to what's going on above you, below you, and in front of you. No *offensive* magic is allowed. No *melodic* magic is allowed. Understood?"

"Yes ma'am!" a few students answered.

The imp tapped around near Hanley's feet, baring its little fangs. The void slug slid across the floor. Hanley backpedaled with her whistle in her mouth and pointed left, then right, indicating that we should separate and prepare.

"You guys ready to win?" Gerard asked with a smile as he and Fena walked to the center of the court. The two put their balls down and moved.

Axle and Fena high-fived one another as they took their positions. I was overcome by an interesting feeling. No doubt it was jealousy—my id had been showing its ass lately. I couldn't overcome the butthurt.

Why was I being left out?

My determination grew. I would show her why she was wrong; why she should have picked me. My spirit ignited. I wasn't going down without a fight.

"Ha-*tôn*!"

My tome fell into my hand, and everyone on my team turned to look at me. A few snickers, eye rolls, and hands over mouths. Whispers abounded.

"Is he gonna hold that thing while we play?"

"Oh my god, that's the tome kid."

"Really? Of everyone in the school, we got the tome guy in here?"

I took a deep breath and forced it out.

"Everyone listen up," I said. Only a couple of people gave me their attention, some still in their side conversations. "This is a team-building game. The reason we're expected to be able to keep an eye on the sky, the ground, and in front of us is because she wants to see *teamwork*."

"Hey," Gerard yelled. "Everyone shut up; he's making sense over here. Team meeting, gather up."

Everyone quieted and turned to face me. I nodded at Gerard and continued.

"First thing we need is someone who is responsible for warning the team when the imp has tagged a member of the other team."

"That's a good idea," Gerard said, with surprise. "I'll do that. I'll just yell *imp*, all right?"

"Imp," a couple of people repeated and nodded.

"Everyone listen for Gerard's call, okay? Stay spread out. If you're going to catch a ball, don't reach for it. Let it fall right into the breadbasket."

"Breadbasket?" asked a girl to my left.

"Try to catch the ball with your whole midsection," I clarified. "It's harder to drop it like that. Aim at their legs when you throw; they'll find it more difficult to catch a ball like that."

"Who is *this* guy?" Gerard said with a wide smile. "You some kinda dodgeball pro?"

I smiled back. "It was my extracurricular in magi school. I wasn't great at it, but I remember the tactics. Throw together and take out the strong players first."

"*Hell*, yes!" Gerard said, placing his hand in the middle of the group. "Everyone in! One two three, go team!"

Everyone reached for the center and shouted in unison before spreading out across our side of the hymnasium.

"*Loving* the team energy over there," Hanley called out, holding the whistle close to her mouth. "You guys ready?"

I stared ahead at Fena. At Axle. I thought of Tovin, too.

I'm not giving up. I'm not a loser. I'm not useless.

"Hey, man," Gerard called to me. "What's your name, anyway?"

I stared straight ahead.

"I'm Gill Dragstenn."

"Begin!" Hanley shouted and blew the whistle.

FIFTEEN

I let the faster students race for the balls in the middle of the hymnasium. My legs were still sore from Saturday night's chase. I don't think I'd ever sprinted such a distance.

I needed to conserve my magic for crucial moments and rely on my eyes and reflexes for as long as my cardio lasted.

Gerard was the fastest to the middle; it wasn't even close. Not only did he scoop up the first ball, but he whizzed it at the closest opponent, nearly taking their legs out from under them. He then grabbed a second ball and used it to deflect a ball thrown at him. From that point forward, it became absolute chaos. The magic rose within my opponents, bodies glowing as they prepared a multitude of spells. The shrill sound of Coach Hanley's whistle nearly tore my attention from the game.

"Out!" she yelled.

The imp ascended from the other side of the hymnasium as a dejected student wandered toward the sidelines. I had lost my focus just long enough to completely miss an incoming projectile. Gerard appeared in front of me and caught the ball before it tagged me right in the face.

"Look alive, Gill!" he called back to me.

The coach blew her whistle again. "Out!"

"Imp!" Gerard warned before hurling the ball back. The little creature appeared overhead, searching for a target with a mischievous smile. When it chose its new victim, I refocused on the game.

Coach blew her whistle a few more times in rapid succession as rubber balls whizzed around the field, students slipped in the slime, and the imp picked off one after another.

"Out! Out! Out!" Hanley yelled. "Don't argue with me; you touched the slug. Out!"

I swallowed. I was finding it more difficult to pay attention to it all than I expected. Plus, my tome *was* cumbersome. I wouldn't be able to catch a ball while holding it, nor would I be able to throw one with all my strength. My gym clothes didn't have the clip on the hip I'd fashioned for my uniform.

"Yes, you did; the void slime is still on the side of your shoe! You know what, time out! Time!" Hanley yelled before blowing her whistle. "Everyone time out! Let me explain something to you. My rulings are final."

The imp fluttered over, landing next to her.

Gerard jogged over to me. "Hey, Gill. You good? You looked lost, man."

"Y-yeah," I admitted. "I need my tome on my person to be able to cast. It's a spellcasting conduit. But it's hard to play dodgeball with one arm, y'know?"

"I got an idea if you're all right with me taking your shirt," he said. "Is that cool?"

I blinked a couple of times. "My *shirt?*"

"Did I stutter? Give it here, c'mon."

"A-all right." I set my tome down and pulled my shirt over my head.

"What the hell," he said as he looked me over. "My man got abs!" he yelled to the others with a smile before laughing and taking my shirt. Everyone kind of laughed with him, and I'm sure I blushed. I didn't consider them abs. I was thin enough that my muscle showed through.

He then tore my shirt.

I dropped my shoulders and sighed. I hadn't given him permission to do that. He folded it, twisted it, and tied it in a manner I had difficulty following.

"Momma had three of us at the same time," he said as he worked. "Triplets run in our family. Her momma taught her how to make one of these, and she taught *us* how. It's how you carry three babies with only two arms."

He draped the remodeled shirt around my neck and over my shoulder before picking the tome up. He had turned my shirt into some kind of shirt-satchel, like a toga.

"Hope this works," he said as he pushed the tome into the shirt and twisted it once. I looked down at myself, surprised. The shirt was comfortable, the tome was secure, and Gerard had made it in seconds.

"Gerard!" I smiled big. "This is amazing!" I said, jumping a couple of times. The tome didn't jostle around. "You've gotta teach me how to do this!"

"I'm surprised you don't know how to do something like this *already*, tome-boy," he responded as he made his way back toward the frontline.

"Arguing with my rulings will result in an automatic out! Everyone get back in your positions. We're starting again in three, two, one..." Hanley blew her whistle. I lowered my stance and smiled.

All right. Time to show 'em what I can really *do.*

I took a mental snapshot of our situation. We were down four players, and they were down three: six on seven. They had two balls on their side of the court. Someone on our side was holding a ball. The imp was chasing someone on their side. The void slug was behind me somewhere. One of their players was using magic to enhance her speed. A green flame was dancing around another opponent; I couldn't ascertain the spell's effect by looking at it.

In that moment, I formed my plan. I needed to make myself an enticing target for the speedy girl. She'd be almost impossible to hit, but my eyes would make her easier to track. If I caught the ball she was holding to get her out, then we'd be able to get one of *our* players back.

It was time to use it.

I applied Fortify to myself. Then I envisioned the symbol for Jetstream, and the raging waters bubbled beneath my feet. In that second, I shot toward the front of my team. I stopped short of the dividing line and broke left. Miss Speedy headed in my direction just like I'd hoped. I'd caught her attention. She hurled the ball at me, and I maneuvered backward to gain time to assess its trajectory.

"Slug!" Someone behind me shouted.

I looked over my shoulder. The void slug was sliding across my path. I didn't have time to think about it, really. I could only hope that I could open my legs wide enough to miss it. As I widened my stance, I failed to maintain even water pressure on both feet, sending myself into a spin.

It all happened in slow motion. I somehow not only swiveled around the void slug but caught the ball at the same time. I righted myself and slid around the hymnasium's perimeter, some of my teammates cheering as I passed by.

I couldn't do that again if my life depended on it, but nobody else had to know that. The coach blew the whistle and called an out as I picked my next target. I whipped the ball at his knees. He couldn't react in time, and the whistle sounded again.

I glided left down the dividing line, and I found Fena

among the five remaining opponents. Her eyes were wide, and her face was about as red as her hair.

Ha. She has to be mad *to look at me like that. Good.*

She deserved every bit of it for counting me out. One of our players tagged back in, making it seven on five—a quick reversal of our fortunes.

"Hell *yeah!*" Gerard boomed from somewhere behind me. "Woo! That's what I'm *talking* about!"

The ball I'd thrown bounced back into our area, putting all three in our possession.

"Remember to throw together!" I yelled as I slid between everyone. "The void slug is over there right now; you're all clear!"

"The imp is still chasing 'em too!" Gerard called out. "Let's end this!"

He led two of our players toward the dividing line, aiming their shots as the other team gathered in a huddle.

They're clumping up? I thought. *That's* never *a good idea in this sport. What are they doing?*

Not only had they moved together, but they had moved behind Axle. He wore a confident smile as my team wound up to throw. Something was up, but I had no idea what. Axle's body glowed, and he moved his arms in a pattern that forecasted a kinetic spell.

My team had to be running into a trap. I lifted my hand to warn them, but the words wouldn't come out. As they hurled the balls, Axle leaped forward and threw his hands up. A translucent barrier appeared in front of his team, and as soon as the balls made contact, it lit up and sent them right back.

The balls struck all three of them in the chest and sent them flying backward onto the floor. I ended my Jetstream and stumbled a few steps as I did the math. Four on five now, their favor. Hanley blew her whistle three times.

"Out, out, out!" she shouted. "Brilliant!"

I gritted my teeth as I locked eyes with Axle. He smirked and accepted low fives from his team as they backed away from the dividing line.

Damn you, Axle. What kind of spell was that? It not only protected his entire team, but returned the balls with extra force.

My teammates were struggling to find their feet. They'd had the wind knocked out of them.

Fena stared at Axle with admiration glimmering in her eyes. I sighed and relaxed my shoulders. I wasn't about to let him show me up. No matter the odds, I was *not* about to lose.

"Out!" the coach yelled again after blowing her whistle. The imp lifted into the air, giggling into its claws as one of their players left the court.

"Four on four," I called out to my remaining teammates as they scooped up the balls. "The imp is after us now, too," I said, taking up the onus of imp-caller. The little creature floated over to our side, choosing its target.

"Let's wait until it chooses," one of my teammates called out. "We've got all three balls; we can take a second to wait."

"Slug is headed this way," another warned.

The imp's eyes passed over us one by one. Finally, its eyes lit up and it dove toward its perceived prey. She tossed the ball to me before turning and ducking under the imp's claws. "I'll keep it busy for as long as I can!"

I nodded toward the other two boys, and they nodded back.

"We're gonna do that again," I called out.

"What?" One of them yelled. "What makes you think that'll work *this* time!"

"I don't think he can cast that again," I lied. "His magic reserves look low."

"You can *see* his magic?" asked another student.

"Hate to break it to you, Gill," Axle called to me. "But I've got more in the tank than you think."

I observed his riled magic reserves and I smiled. "He's bluffing, guys."

"I don't *bluff*," Axle retorted. "But if you want to test me, then test me."

I smirked, looking back at my teammates. "Trust me."

They exchanged glances before turning their wary faces to me and nodding.

"All right, Gill," said one of them. "We're trusting you then."

I bounced my ball twice. "All together now," I said. "Let's go!"

The three of us shot forward and the four of them gathered back together. Axle moved his arms. The three of us hurled our balls toward them. Right on cue, Axle leaped forward to finish the kinetic component of his spell.

I wasn't about to miss the moment. I swept my arm as I brought the pattern for Sleet to the forefront of my mind. Below him, the floorboards iced over. As he landed, his feet came out from under him, his eyes popping open as he toppled over. Against the warded floor, the ice dissipated as fast as it had appeared, but it had done its work. Their eyes widened as the balls sailed over the top of Axle and tagged all three of them.

The coach let out excited laughter before regaining her composure and blowing her whistle three times. "Out, out, out!"

Fena stomped once in anger before making for the bleachers. I didn't know if it was my ball that had struck her, but I secretly hoped. It was a vindictive thought, but it was mine.

Our entire half of the hymnasium roared. It was four against one now, and—

"Out, out!" Hanley yelled before blowing her whistle again. I turned. The student the imp had been chasing was pinned to the floor by the imp, and the void slug nibbled on the shoe of another player.

He looked down at the slug and then up at me with wide eyes, and it was all I could do not to facepalm.

"Look out!" shouted our last player as he lunged toward me. He pushed me to the floor and caught a dodgeball hard on his cheek.

"Out!" Coach blew her whistle.

I lifted myself by my hands. I had messed up taking my eyes off of him. From across the room, Axle was hurling another ball in my direction. I rolled out of the way, the wind blowing my hair back as I just narrowly avoided it. The rubber may have actually just grazed my forehead.

I got to a knee and steadied my breathing. He was out of ammunition. All three balls were rolling around on my side of the court.

"That was pretty clever, Gill," Axle said. "Got to admit, I've underestimated tome casting," he went on. "The ability to cast a spell with no warning, no tells, no signals…That's damn annoying."

I got to my feet, remaining silent as I contemplated my next move. I had three or so spells left in me.

The imp floated off the court and returned to Hanley's side.

"It's down to one on one," she called out. "The imp and void slug will return to me. From here on out, it's student versus student."

I exhaled and gathered up the balls as our teams shouted words of support. I was thirsty. My mouth was so dry, it hurt to swallow.

Across the room, Axle moved his arms in a symmetrical motion. His magic roused. I stepped back as he clasped his hands together, one over the other.

Then, just like that, his magic settled back down, dimming

in his midsection. I lifted an eyebrow and kept my guard up as I watched him carefully.

What is he doing?

"C'mon, Gill," he called out. "Are you scared of me?"

I held onto the ball, probably overthinking things as I stared quietly.

Maybe he's activating a barrier, like the one I saw before? No, that's not possible. I'll see it, even if it's invisible to everyone else.

"Or maybe you're afraid you're going to lose...And let your entire team down," he said with a cocky smile.

I'm not the one who's going to lose. No way in hell. I've got all the balls right now. This thing only starts when I start it.

"Well, are we going stand here all day, ball master?" he called to me.

That was cocky of him. Is he reading my thoughts?

I glanced at all the students cheering on the other side of the hymnasium.

No. It isn't possible. There are too many people here. His mind-reading ability should be pretty scrambled right about now. Calm down, Gill. This game is yours to lose. I've got to let down Fortify for a second. If I toss the ball I'm holding and use Jetstream to launch the ones by my feet, I can catch him off guard. I'm gonna have to be quick, though.

I tossed the ball up in the air once before winding up and heaving it with all my strength. Without hesitation, I activated Jetstream under both feet at maximum strength, sending myself into a back flip and kicking both balls toward him.

I landed on one knee as he leaped into the air and turned himself sideways, avoiding all three projectiles in a spectacular flourish. The whole hymnasium exploded with screams and cheers as I pounded the floor with one fist.

"What," I said out loud. That was *beyond* lucky.

He landed on one knee and paused for a moment before getting to his feet.

"Thanks for the balls," he said before gathering them up.

The tables had turned. I reactivated Fortify and felt a pinch—my reserves warning me that I was about half empty. But I couldn't stop using Jetstream now when it mattered most. I needed to figure out a way to take him down with one or two spells.

He walked back to center court with two balls under his arms, stopping with one underfoot.

"Breathing heavy there, champ," he said, staring me down. "Your tiny magic reserves starting to get the best of you?"

W-what? He's making fun of me now!

"She's watching you know," he said, just loud enough for me to hear over the noise my team was making.

My eyes widened. My pulse quickened. I balled my fists and gritted my teeth.

Without another word, he whipped the first ball at me. I activated Jetstream and broke left, only to find the second ball on trajectory to hit me. I shifted diagonally backward, only to find myself in the path of the third ball.

I couldn't stop in time. It was too low for me to catch it. If I widened my legs, it'd bounce and hit me anyway. I couldn't believe what I was seeing.

How is he doing this? Is this checkmate?

The only way I could think to avoid it wasn't going to be pretty. I deactivated Fortify once more, allowing the Jetstream to send me horizontal. I think it touched my shirt, but if *Hanley* didn't call it, then *I* wasn't about to.

I landed hard, shoulder first with a thud that caused everyone to wince. I rolled over and picked myself up, leaning back on my hands as I stared at Axle. Those throws were *insanely* accurate. He had to have played before. The edge I thought I had was lost.

"No resting!" Coach called out. "C'mon, this is meant to get your blood pumping. Off your keister!"

I gulped in air as I gathered the balls again. I came to the dividing line and stared at him as I held a ball.

He lowered his stance. "You'll never touch me, Gill. I'm telling you, it's *pointless*."

Something swelled inside me as I seethed.

How has it come to this? You insert yourself into my life. I consider us friends, then you steal Fena right out from under me. You're the freak, the nutjob, the psycho conspiracy theorist nobody likes. Fena seemed afraid of you when she met you, and now...

She was standing on the sidelines cheering for him.

I won't let it happen. I won't! You're not better than me because of some number the headmasters gave you. I'll show you! I'll show everyone!

I summoned my fury and whipped the first ball out, reaching for the second without hesitation. Before I could throw it, something I didn't expect happened.

The ball struck his hip and bounced away. He stood there, stunned, staring at me.

My teammates rushed the court to celebrate with me, but I wasn't celebrating. That didn't feel like a victory at all. In fact, if I was certain...

Axle *chose* not to move.

With the way he dodged three balls at once earlier, there was no way a simple toss like that would have been enough. He looked forlorn as his teammates attempted to comfort him, patting him on the back and rubbing him on the shoulders.

He stared at me with the saddest eyes ever, and it hurt my heart to see it.

"H-hey," I called out to him as my team jumped around me.

"We have a winner!" Hanley called out before blowing long and hard on her whistle. "Get changed and get to lunch!" she said, banishing her void slug and commanding her imp to retrieve the dodgeballs.

Axle left the court quietly. Fena watched him go with a concerned expression. She then turned and looked at me as if for answers—answers I didn't have.

I won, but...

Why do I feel like I lost?

Sixteen

s the commotion eased, I wondered what exactly the game had meant to him. Maybe he had something on the line, too. No way he heard what I was thinking with all that noise. He let his guard down for a moment, and I capitalized on it...Right?

No.

I was ignoring the fact that he let himself be struck by the ball. He could have moved, but he didn't. And with how much trash he was talking, there was no chance he was about to let me win. He stood there, staring at me like I'd announced his expulsion.

"Gill!"

Fena's voice cut through my inner dialogue. In the dissipating crowd, she walked toward me. Her brow was wrinkled with worry.

"Hey," she said, as she tucked her hair behind her ear. "Umm...Has Axle said anything strange to you lately? Not like conspiracy stuff, I mean anything that would...y'know, worry you?"

"No," I shook my head. "Why?"

"Well," she turned her head, and I followed her gaze toward the double doors; Axle was leaving with his gym clothes over his shoulder. "We all came out to tell him that he did great, but..." She turned to me with sad eyes. "He said that it'd be best if we didn't hang out with him anymore."

A knife went through my heart.

He'd heard it.

Somehow, some way, he'd heard what I was thinking.

It was after that: The ball struck his hip and then bounced slowly away.

But it doesn't make sense. How could he single my *thoughts out?*

Maybe it was just a coincidence. Maybe he'd lost his focus and got tagged. But that wouldn't explain what he'd said to Fena.

"Oh, Gill, do you think it could it have been something I said?" she asked, clasping her hands.

"No," I said straight out. "I think it might have been something I *thought*."

"What do you...oh." She stopped. "Were you thinking something mean?"

"Uhh..."

"Gill."

"I have a tendency to...get competitive." It was a half-truth. "I don't always talk trash, but I *do* think it sometimes."

"Oh, that's all right; I do too," she said.

"Really?" I asked.

"I'm *really* competitive," she admitted. "It's why I didn't pick you first. Sorry about that," she said, folding her arms.

"Um. What?"

"Yeah, I picked the bigger guys first because I wanted to *win*. I picked Axle before you because he's so sensitive. You were next on my list though," she said, punching my arm. "I won't let it happen again, though! You *killed* it! I didn't know you could play like that; where the heck did *that* come from?

I scanned the floor as my mind went crazy. All of my anxiety had been for literally nothing. I let my own thoughts drive me insane.

"I didn't know he was...sensitive," I said.

"Yeah, the two of us hung out after we all parted ways the other day. He spilled like his whole life story. The guy's been so socially backed up that he wanted to talk till his tongue gave out. I was happy to listen, but man, I had to make up a reason get out of there. I was so hungry," she said, laughing.

"I noticed you guys seemed closer today," I admitted. "I thought maybe...you guys were going steady or something."

Her expression went blank for a moment. Her cheeks filled with air, and she busted out laughing.

I forced a smile as she got herself together.

"Gill, you dummy," she wheezed. "No," she clarified as she took a breath. "No, we're not an item. Gill...Axle isn't exactly into *girls*."

I stared back at her. "Wait...what?"

"Yep," she chirped.

I laughed with relief. "I...Wow. I did not know that. Sorry. You were hugging and stuff, and..."

"Oh man, that's the *sad* part," she interrupted. "The other day when I hugged him. Remember that, in his dorm room?"

"Yeah?"

"That's the first time he's been hugged." She grabbed my shoulders. "*Ever.*"

"You're joking," I said.

"No," she shook her head. "He told me it felt really nice, and he asked me if we could do it more often. He totally broke my heart into a million little pieces, and I agreed to be his huggy-buddy."

"By the gods," I muttered as I realized what a dirtbag I'd been.

"I know," she replied. "That's why I found it so strange that he friend-broke-up with me a few minutes ago."

I'd made a terrible, terrible mistake.

"Well, he thinks a whole lot of you, so maybe you'll get through to him," she said. "Let's walk to lunch, and we'll figure out how to cheer him up."

The knife in my gut was twisting.

"I'm gonna go change," she called out as she jogged away. "I'll meet you in the hallway!"

Everyone had left the boys' locker room already. I paced across the floor and sat down on the bench that bisected the room. I pulled my shirt-satchel off and set it next to me before leaning forward and holding my head in my hands.

I'd never felt lower. Axle's life had been mostly terrible. His father was absent, his mother used him, everyone thought he was a total weirdo.

And then, when he found a group of friends...I mean, he put himself out there when he sat at our table that day. That took courage. He welcomed us into his room and shared everything he knew—even his secret ability.

I stood up, rinsed off, and changed back into my uniform. I clipped my tome to my belt checked myself in the full-body mirror.

I loathed what I saw.

A destructive, jealous, and insecure child who assumed the worst of people. He wasn't trying to steal Fena from me. I might have crushed a totally innocent friendship.

But how could he hear me like that? His ability...

My eyes popped open as I remembered what he'd said yesterday. He could also, with what he called "a handy little spell," zero in on a single person. The pieces began to fit together. That spell that I thought didn't do anything—it *did* do something.

And all the trash-talking he was doing...He wasn't trying to piss me off for no reason—he was trying to read me more clearly.

I banged my fist on the mirror and pressed my forehead against it.

"Dammit, dammit, dammit," I said through my teeth as I thought about what he must have heard me think: *How has it come to this? You insert yourself into my life. I consider us friends, then you steal Fena.*

I felt nauseated as I recalled the mental tirade: *You're the freak, the nutjob, the psycho conspiracy theorist. Fena seemed afraid of you when she met you, and now...*

Tears welled up when I imagined how much that must have hurt him. I was such a fool.

"Gill?" Fena called into the locker room. "You still in there?"

I looked at myself one final time, curling my lip in disgust as I left.

The two of us walked toward the cafeteria, but I didn't feel like eating. I felt like finding Axle right away and explaining everything. I only realized she was speaking to me halfway through a sentence.

"—nd I don't know what you thought at him, or if it's something else entirely, but you might be the best person to talk to him in either regard." She glanced at me. "He says you're the only person on campus he could stop and talk to."

I couldn't swallow all the guilt in my throat...I stayed silent.

"You're a good person, Gill," she said as we rounded a corner.

I stopped in the intersection.

She stopped and turned to look at me, "Gill?"

"I...I don't think I'm a very good person, Fena," I said, staring at the ground.

"What? Why? Because you thought something mean and it hurt his feelings? He was trash-talking you like mad! He deserved it for provoking you and looking into your mind." She turned to face me. "Our thoughts are meant to be private, Gill. Actions are what make us."

I looked up at her through bleary eyes.

"I think terrible things all the time," she said, with a shrug. "I don't *say* them, but I can't help that I *think* them."

In her own way, she was right. Still, it didn't soothe my guilt. The other hallway led to the central roundabout. I wondered if he was in his room.

"Even so," I responded. "I think I've hurt his feelings. Whether I meant to or not, it doesn't change the fact that he's in a lot of pain. I can't not do anything."

I looked her in the eyes. "I'm going to go see if he's in his dorm room. If it's all the same to you, I'd like to go alone."

"Oh, okay," she said, holding her clasped hands to her chest. "And I didn't mean we should *ignore* his pain, by the way. I think you're doing the right thing. I'll be in the lunchroom with Atlas. I'll see ya," she said with a wave.

"Hey, Fena," I called after her.

She stopped and turned.

"Thanks," I said with a smile.

She gave me a cute little salute before leaving. I made my way to the roundabout and up the stairs into the empty hallway. I walked to the first door on the corner. I took a deep breath and knocked twice.

"Axle? It's me, Gill. Hey. Can we talk? Please?"

I stood in the silence and listened. No sounds came from within.

I swallowed and knocked once more, "Axle? Can you let me in? If you're in there, I want to apologize for...anything you might have heard. I know I'm probably the last person you want to see, but..." I trailed off. "I'm just...I want to say I'm so sorry. That's all."

Silence.

He wasn't in there.

I heaved a heavy sigh before shoving my hands in my pockets and heading to lunch. I took a couple of steps before I heard a noise behind me.

I smiled as a comical number of latches slid open.

Seventeen

The door slowly creaked open revealing Axle's sullen face. I could tell from the redness in his eyes that he'd been crying. He sniffled and wiped his nose with his wrist, but maintained eye contact with me.

I suddenly realized that I didn't know how to begin. The two of us stared for a second longer before I gathered myself and broke the silence.

"Axle...Can I come in please?"

He scanned the floor a moment before turning and walking away, leaving the door open for me. I closed the door behind me and turned to face him, shoving my hands in my pockets. He turned his chair at the kitchen table around and sat in it backward, gesturing toward the bed as he did. I took a seat on the mattress before clearing my throat and leaning forward on my knees.

"Axle...Look. I'm not sure where to begin. So I'm going to start by saying I'm sorry. It took me longer than it should have to realize it." I met his eyes for half a second before he turned away. "You were very *clearly* reading my mind."

He swallowed audibly and rested his chin on his forearms.

His right heel was bouncing rapidly. He pressed his lips together as though he wanted to say something but couldn't figure out how.

"But you *have* to know," I continued, "that because someone *thinks* something doesn't necessarily mean that they *mean* it."

"I know," he answered in a melancholic tone.

"People are flawed," I added. "We can't help what we think. Only what we say. I was talking to Fena. She told me some things about you, Axle. You've got to understand that I didn't know."

We sat in the silence for a moment before I took a deep breath and let it out.

"Ha-*ten!*"

My sword fell into my hand.

Axle picked his head up in surprise.

"This is my sword, Axle," I said, as I laid it across my hands. "My dad came home with an ingot one day, a block of wood, and some leather." I tilted the weapon, the iron shining in the light. "Like our thoughts, the metal had to be refined before the world could see it. My thoughts were unrefined, Axle. But they were just as sharp."

"It's okay, Gill," he responded, clearing his throat. "Really. I was never mad at you," he said, heaving an anxious sigh. "I was just—" He stopped, closing his eyes as he tried to keep himself together. "I started to think that I had found a place in this school, y'know? Friends. Real friends."

"And you have!" I said louder than I intended. "Look, Fena told me you seem to think a lot of me, but...Axle, I'm not a very good person. I'm jealous, possessive, selfish, *super* insecure—"

"You're *human*," he interrupted me. "And I happen to think you're a damn good one."

I sat up in surprise.

"I know, Gill," he said softly. "I know that peoples' thoughts are supposed to be private. Unfortunately for me, I'm a sporadic thought thief. When I pried into your mind back there..." he trailed off. "I guess I thought yours would be a safe mind to read. Me getting myself hurt and all...Nobody to blame but me."

"Not true," I interjected. "Some of the stuff crossing my mind..."

He swatted at me and smiled at the carpet. "C'mon, Gill. It's in the past."

"I don't *believe* any of that stuff...I only thought it. Can you forgive me?" I asked.

"No need, partner. I told you already. I was never mad at you."

His mood had brightened considerably. As far as apologies went, it seemed to be a success. I leaned my sword against his bed, standing, exhaling, and opening my arms. He smiled at me before pushing his chair out of the way on his way over. He wrapped his arms around me tightly and we hugged it out.

"Good game, Axle."

"It *was* a good game, wasn't it?" he responded, his smile evident in his voice.

I let go and smiled back before patting his shoulder and making for the door. "Now c'mon, ya doofus, I'm hungry. And leave your wallet. Food is on me."

"Nuh-uh!" he called out as he snatched his wallet from the counter. "Today was *your* victory! It's on me! Say, where'd you learn to play like that?"

———

The line was short. Almost everyone had gotten their food already. We sat with Atlas and Fena and discussed the insane dodgeball game. Atlas was mad that he wasn't in our class with us and lamented missing out on the fun.

Axle made it a point to hug all three of us before we parted ways after lunch. Atlas stared at me as Axle picked him up and bear-hugged him. I could tell by the expression on his face that he was itching to know what he missed.

Fena demanded to know how my conversation with Axle went, and she followed me all the way to my philosophy class to hear the full story.

"That sword analogy was nice," she said with a big smile that revealed her dimples.

I really loved her dimples. They made her already gorgeous face somehow sweeter.

"Thanks," I said. "I'm not super good at apologies. I had to think fast."

"Are you kidding me?" she said with an incredulous expression. "That's one of the best apologies I've ever *heard!* I'd say you're a natural! Sheesh, I need to get mad at you now to get one of those for myself," she laughed.

I had no idea how to respond.

What would a cool person say?

"Darn skippy!"

It wasn't that.

"Is this your stop?" she asked as I stopped in front of a doorway.

"Yeah, this is me."

"All right, well, I'll catch ya later," she said, pulling me in for a hug.

The world stopped. Time froze. Everything inside of me broke and repaired itself in the same second. My breath left my lungs, and my heart sang.

"Thanks for clearing that up with Axle," she said, just above a whisper.

I had three pairs of uniform pants. Two of them fit, but

the third was a bit too tight. I was too polite to say anything at the time. I'd never regretted that decision more than now as I walked in holding my tome in front of my pants.

The rest of my classes blew by. I did pay *some* attention, but my head was dancing with my heart in a high-tempo salsa of celebration. That one hug dangled in the forefront of my mind, interrupted every so often by the words she said in my ear and the heat of her breath on my neck.

I had been struck by a bolt of lightning, and static lingered in my veins.

I rode that high through the entire school week. It seemed Atlas, Fena, and Axle would be my primary friends for the rest of the year. I knew when I could stop and chat with them, and we always met at the same lunch table.

I'd made a name for myself in Phys Ed, and the story of the dodgeball game had spread. At one point, Tovin stopped me in the hall and reminded me that the only reason people were talking about it was because everyone had assumed I wasn't capable of anything. I didn't need Axle's ability to know that Tovin was jealous of the spotlight.

I found myself going to bed earlier than everyone else for two reasons: first, I never wanted to be late back to my room. If I ever saw a Night Watcher again, it would be too soon. The second concerned Axle. Fena was often my last thought when I closed my eyes. She had a powerful grip on me, and if I'd had half a sack, I'd say something. But I was scared, and I didn't want Axle to accidentally eavesdrop on my most private thoughts. If I got back early enough, I could fall asleep before everyone else did and hide my ideas in the static.

———

When I opened my window on Friday morning, the birds were singing, and the air was cool, indicative of fall. I strolled over to my closet to get dressed when something caught my eye—a letter in my mail basket stamped with a purple seal. I changed course. My need to know outweighed my need for clothes. I knelt down and unwrapped the envelope.

Student: Gill Dragstenn

You've been summoned by Headmaster Rowan. You will report to him in the conference hall located in the south wing at 9:45 a.m. This is a disciplinary action. You may wear attire that is most comfortable for you.

—Vice Principal Wharl

I read it over and over again to make sure I understood it correctly.

A disciplinary *action? But* why? *What did I do this time?*

I racked my mind for answers but came up short. I snapped my head toward the clock. The meeting was a whole hour away. I had planned on breakfast, but I'd lost my appetite. For forty-five minutes, I paced patterns into my carpet before hurrying down to the conference room.

I hadn't been there since orientation, but I was pretty sure I knew where it was. I made my way to the headmasters' offices through massive main hall of the south wing. I turned into a hallway that led to the conference room. The double doors at the end loomed.

Someone stood outside with his arms crossed. He wore a dark brown cloak, and his hood was drawn. As I drew nearer, I couldn't shake the feeling that I'd seen him somewhere before. He was tall, had a medium-length gray beard, and eyes that seldom blinked.

It took everything I had not to stop in my tracks when it struck me.

I searched for the signature of magic in his midsection but found nothing. It was *him*. The man who chased me back to my dorm. I subdued the chill that forced its way down my spine as he reached over and opened the door.

What the hell is going on? Why is he here? Am I walking into a trap? Should I run for my life?

I had to stay calm. Axle assured me that they had nothing, and I believed him. It had to be something else. I had to relax and not seem suspicious. But I had never seen the guy on campus before. Then I find him lingering around the building after dark—and now outside of my meeting with the headmasters? Who was this guy?

I moved through the doorway into the room. The conference room had no windows, as it was in the center of the building. Instead, a grand chandelier hung overhead lighting the room with a warmth not unlike a fireplace. A long table was situated in the center and every headmaster was seated at it, with Headmaster Rowan at the end.

He was standing.

"Come on in, Mr. Dragstenn," he croaked. "Please, have a seat."

The door closed behind me, and I turned to see the cloaked man walking toward me. He pulled the chair out, and, with a small degree of hesitation, I sat. He scooted me in and stepped back, blocking the exit. My heart pounded like crazy as I tried to remain as calm and innocent-looking as I could.

"Mr. Dragstenn," Alrune spoke. "Is there anything you'd like to tell us."

I looked around at their faces and swallowed.

"Uhh…Thank you all for inviting me?" I asked with a tilt of my head. "I'm sorry, but did I read that this was a disciplinary action?"

Seven of them remained silent. Rowan leaned forward on his staff and took off his pointy hat. He set it on the table and looked me square in the eyes with a ferocity that I hadn't thought him capable of.

"We *know*, Mr. Dragstenn," he said. "We know that it was *you* in the south wing after curfew that night."

Eighteen

h-what?

I stared at the headmasters across the table, and they stared back, their eyes dead serious. The tension was pulverizing as I searched desperately for anything to say.

"There's no use denying it," said Vega, the second-youngest headmaster. He had brown hair with faint streaks of gray along the sides, and he wore it in a short ponytail. He had bushy black eyebrows and striking, pitch-black eyes. "We've spoken to your friends. In exchange for their continued enrollment at ENU, they've given you up."

How is this possible? Fena seemed serious when she said she'd lie for me, and I got that sense from Axle, too. It couldn't have been Atlas. Nobody else knows the truth either.

"Sneaking around the halls at night is one thing," Vega continued. "But destruction of school property. *Running* from Inquisitor Imandr when he commanded you to stop," he pounded his fist on the table, "that is *unforgivable!*"

I turned to look at the cloaked man.

He's an inquisitor? What's an inquisitor doing at ENU?

"Your behavior," Rowan said, "is unbecoming of a student at this prestigious institution. Expulsion is the only proper punishment."

I felt like I was about to cry. My heart raced. Pins and needles were poking me from all directions. I thought I had gotten away clean.

My breathing quickened as I raced to defend myself. "Wait, hold on!" I stammered.

"Silence!" Vega screamed, now pounding on the table with both hands. "You've made a mockery of our university and its rules!"

How is it they know? Beyond a shadow of a doubt, at that?

"If I may," said Alrune.

"You have the floor," Rowan muttered.

"Mr. Dragstenn shows incredible potential. He is unusual. Although he has not reached his full potential, I believe his expulsion from our university would be a detrimental blow to the future of our nation." He turned and smiled at me. "I see great promise in him. Can there truly be no other way?"

All eyes turned to Rowan. He closed his red-rimmed eyes and stood for a moment before sitting and laying his staff across the table.

"Does anyone else agree with Headmaster Alrune's motion?" he asked with a sigh that rattled in his throat. He lifted a hand to signal the voting had begun.

Vega sat back and folded his arms, shaking his head in disapproval.

Norah's hand lifted from the table.

"I have spoken with Miss Hanley," she said. "She remarked that Mr. Dragstenn's magic control is peerless. She spoke at length about his tremendous potential." She turned her eyes to Rowan. "That woman does not hand out compliments. For this reason, I would see that Mr. Dragstenn remain enrolled."

Norah was the youngest of the headmasters and the only

female. She was the daughter of a high priest and a talented verbal caster. She wore her bleached blonde hair in braids that ran alongside her temples, had glacier-blue eyes, and carried her chin high. She *was* beautiful, and I never thought that more than I did now.

"Hanley said that?" asked Edwin as he rubbed his chin. Edwin was the only other one who could be considered young. Between last year and this, his mustache had turned gray, and he'd chosen to shave his head rather than watch his hairline recede. It did make him look years younger. "Hmm… Very well. Then I too support his continued enrollment." He lifted his hand.

I didn't know Hanley had pull like that. Even the gym coach at this school was an incredible person, it seemed. I glanced among the undecided.

I needed only one more vote.

Movement on my right. I turned to see Huede, who was seated nearest to me, lift his hand above his shoulder before slamming it down on the table.

"I will support Mr. Dragstenn's continued education within these halls," he announced before turning and staring into my eyes. "*If* he provides us with a full confession as well as his reasoning for being out after curfew."

A confession? Why would they require a confession if they knew I did it? Some kind of power play?

That didn't seem like their MO. Why did it take them an entire week to bring me here and coerce a confession out of me? It didn't make any sense no matter how I thought about it.

"Very well," Rowan said as he lifted his eyes. "Mr. Dragstenn. Your confession will protect you from expulsion. Do not misunderstand, however. You will still be reprimanded. Let us hear it then, boy. Why were you traipsing around the school after hours?"

"And what did you *see?*" asked Vega as he watched me intently.

That sealed it. They didn't know if it was me or not. If they were looking for a confession, then that was one thing. But Vega wanting to know what I saw? That lined up with Axle's intel about "the procession."

I glanced at the headmasters.

Something isn't right. Would Axle lie about something so important? Would they give me away if it would put my life in danger? No. No they wouldn't.

This is a trap.

"Well, Mr. Dragstenn?" pressed Vega.

I stood and placed my hands against the desk.

"Respectfully," I said, "I don't think you've got the right person."

"Nonsense!" Vega shouted. "We offer you a once-in-a-lifetime deal and you spit in our faces?"

"I-I apologize," I said, my voice cracking under the stress. "But whatever you've heard...It's n-not true. I've never been out past curfew. I know how strict that rule is, and I'm so thankful to b-be a part of this university. I'd never risk b-being expelled." I tried to stay calm, but I still stammered through the entire speech.

Alrune audibly sighed with relief and leaned back in his chair.

"Vega," Norah said. "I tire of this. I do not think we're going about this the right way."

"I agree," Alrune responded. "At this rate, we will only scare a student into falsely confessing. What good does that do, I ask you?"

Vega stood up abruptly and left his seat at the table. He marched past me and out the door without saying a single word.

I looked around, confused.

Rowan shook his head in apparent disappointment. "My apologies, Mr. Dragstenn," he said, standing and leaning on his staff. "Allow me to explain," he coughed a few times into his sleeve, struggling to free the mucus from his throat.

"May I?" Anther asked, speaking for the first time and resting a hand on Rowan's shoulder. He had a surprisingly clear voice for how old he appeared to be. He was the tallest of the headmasters. He wore his dark gray hair long and braided but preferred his face clean shaven.

"Mr. Dragstenn, what Headmaster Rowan is trying to say is that this was a little bit of a ruse on our end," he said casting me a sympathetic look. "I'm sorry if that was frightening."

"I don't understand," I said with a tinge of annoyance in my tone. "Why?"

"Watch your tone," Huede warned.

"Is he not justified in his anger?" asked Norah.

Huede rolled his eyes, but he held his tongue, possibly out of respect for a fellow headmaster. Anther glanced among his colleagues before clearing his throat and continuing.

"A student was out of his dorm after hours. About your height, about your build," he said. "Inquisitor Imandr is certain of what he saw. The student was asked to surrender himself, but instead he fled. He ran all the way down Hallway B and disappeared into one of the dorms near yours. We've been calling students in here and attempting to goad a confession out of them."

"Because of the curfew rule?" I asked, looking around at them. "I'm sorry. But doesn't that seem a little extreme?"

"Indeed," Norah answered in an annoyed tone.

"It is not up to us," Rowan interjected, "to debate the integrity of the archbishop's commands. He has sent an inquisitor. We must only comply."

The archbishop sent the inquisitor? But he was already on

campus that night. The inquisitor had to have been sent for a different reason. They were still lying to me.

"I...I understand," I said. "Does this mean that I'm excused?"

"It does," Rowan nodded, "after *this*, of course."

The inquisitor wrapped his fingers around my neck. I jerked back in surprise, but his grip was tight. I struggled to breathe as I glanced at the headmasters. Why in the world were they allowing this? They had all either turned their heads or closed their eyes—abandoning me.

"Tenatuse Ghalrion Kindu brauchded ke molinor tasticus," spoke the inquisitor as he stared into my eyes.

I gripped his forearm—it was *massive*. I struggled as a burning sensation overcame my esophagus, and I inhaled. I saw symbols and characters floating in a violet void as my vision darkened. I took one last look at the headmasters before the light faded, and my consciousness slipped away.

Nineteen

He released his vise-grip hold on me, and I fell back into my chair. I inhaled on impact , coughing and holding my burning throat. Inquisitor Imandr stared down at me with an unnecessary amount of disdain in his eyes and tone.

"You will not *speak* of this meeting," he instructed. "You will not *write* about this meeting. If you attempt to convey to another student the details of what happened here, you will find yourself mute. Only an inquisitor, one of my order, can restore your voice, should this happen." He narrowed his eyes. "It would be in your best interest if we never speak to one another again."

I looked around at the headmasters. Their hands appeared to be tied. They were outranked. I locked eyes with Imandr one more time before he pointed to the door.

"Leave," he commanded.

I scurried back to my dorm without another word. I couldn't believe all that had just happened. I sat on my bed and ran my hands through my hair as I tried to process everything. My mouth was dry; I needed water. I stood up to move for the kitchen and froze in place.

My furniture had been moved. My cupboards were open. Someone had been in my room while I was being interrogated. The investigation was far more serious than I could have imagined. There was something happening outside of our dorms that night that I really, really wasn't supposed to see, so much so that the archbishop himself had dispatched an inquisitor to the school.

On top that, I was sure the headmasters didn't know either. They didn't even seem to want to be there. Looking back, only one of them cared—I could *see* it. Vega's aura had swelled immensely during the meeting. Unlike his fellow headmasters, he seemed to be emotionally invested in finding the culprit.

The question was why. Why only him?

I closed my window before peering out at the front lawn. The worst part of all this was I wouldn't be able to warn the others. I didn't want anyone going down for a false confession. No doubt that was why they needed the inquisitor for this.

They weren't planning on letting me go if I confessed, at least not Inquisitor Imandr. He had the touch of a rapist. It wasn't hard to imagine that he had probably killed people in the past. I caressed my throat. Never had I heard a verbal spell with so many casting words. Almost an entire sentence! I wondered if he blocked keywords or phrases—verbal landmines that I'd have to tiptoe around.

I closed my curtains and sat at my desk to organize my thoughts.

The archbishop had sent an inquisitor to look for something. Something at night? Then he, no doubt, found that door I'd left open, and he and his partner, human or not, waited for me to walk into their trap.

Then the headmasters wanted me to believe that the

inquisitor was sent because of that incident. But even the headmasters seemed like they were annoyed by the investigation process. Something insane was going on at ENU, and I'd somehow inserted myself right into the middle of it.

A knock came at my door. I swallowed and stayed seated until I heard a call from the other side, "Hey, Gill, it's Axle. Open up!"

I hesitated for a second before making for the door. "Gill, lemme in," he said urgently, shoving his way inside. He locked the door, then turned and stared at me. "You want to explain to me what the heck is going on?"

"W-what?" I asked.

"I picked up on strange thought patterns near our dorms recently. I couldn't make sense of it until I ran into Cal about a half hour ago. He looked seriously spaced out. He was practically screaming in his head. I could hardly make any of it out, but I caught some keywords. Keywords you're screaming in *your* head."

"In my head..." I muttered. "Holy crap, that's it!"

He curled his lip in confusion. "Huh? What's it?"

"Axle," I said as I took a few steps back to get my thoughts in order. "I need you to use that spell on me. The one from the dodgeball game."

"Can't you just tell me?" he asked with a shrug.

"No," I responded, lifting my hands. "I *literally* can't. Please trust me on this."

He narrowed his eyes in confusion before shrugging and clasping his hands together toward me. His magic riled within him and then receded as he peered into my thoughts. I closed my eyes and tried to convey as precisely as possible everything that happened.

"I think I've got a pretty clear picture," he said as I opened my eyes. "Now I get why you can't speak. That man in the cloak was an *inquisitor*. They use a spell to silence people from spilling their secrets. It's colloquially called *Censor*, but only mages of their order know how to cast it."

"I don't know a whole lot about the inquis—uhh...*those guys*," I said, trying to avoid any specific buzzwords. "Just that they're government investigators."

"They're more than that," Axle warned. "The inquisitors are a dangerous arm of the government. They answer only to the archbishop. They investigate people and places of interest. During the War of Red Rust, they were given legal immunity. At the time it seemed reasonable—we were at *war* after all."

He folded his arms and leaned against the wall. "But after the fighting ended, they retained that power. They walk around with total impunity. I saw it for myself firsthand when I was younger. They took my mom right from her bed. No explanation or anything. She was gone for several days. Our neighbors took me in until she was returned."

"What?" I asked. "They abduct people like that? I mean, I've *heard* they do that, but I thought they were conspiracy theories, boogeymen, y'know?"

"There's a reason you think that," he responded. "Anyone who sees anything is *Censored*. If it weren't for me, you'd have never been able to tell anyone what happened. I would never have known what happened to my mom either if I couldn't have read her mind. The inquisitors' minds are like thick safes."

I fell back onto my bed, staring at the ceiling. Why Axle was a conspiracy theorist made sense now. He'd seen one happen and watched people mock it.

"It sounds like rainfall inside their heads," he added. "I have no idea why."

"I may have failed to say this," I interjected. "But I can't see their magic."

"I wouldn't be surprised if they took precautions," he said, sitting on the bed next to me. "I imagine that's why they took my mom. If she really had the stuff, they'd likely have employed her. I never want to be one of them. But if they found out what I was capable of, I'd probably have no choice. If they couldn't have me, then they'd want to get rid of me."

I was putting that together as he was speaking. A power like Axle's would be a big problem for anyone who wanted to keep a dangerous secret. It made total sense why he wouldn't want anyone to know about it.

"Wow, Axle," I said finally. "Yeah, come to think of it, you'd make a *great* inquisitor."

"If I really put my mind to it, yeah," he admitted. "But I don't want to live that way. I don't ever want to be ordered to take a child's mother from her bedroom like that." His face soured. "I *couldn't*."

"Hey Axle."

"Hmm?"

They're going to call you into that room probably tomorrow. Do you think you could try to figure out what Vega is thinking?

"Vega? I could try," he replied to my thought as if I had spoken it out loud. "You think he's up to something?"

The other headmasters seem disinterested. They were ordered by the archbishop to conduct that interrogation. But Vega's magic was restless. He wanted to know who it was. I want to know why it mattered so much more.

"But...they're going to censor me like they did you," he countered. "I won't be able to tell you *anything*."

I stood up and made my way to the kitchen table, grabbing my planner and a pencil as I did. I flipped it open to the last page of the year—nobody ever used it.

"What are you doing?" he asked as he followed me to the table.

"I'm going to make a list of theories and possibilities. When you get back, I want you to point to anything you can confirm."

"I guess that could work," he said, leaning on the table. "What are your theories?"

I wrote them down:

- The headmasters are corrupt.
- Headmaster Vega is doing things of which one or more of the other headmasters aren't aware.
- Inquisitor Imandr is investigating the many rumors about this school.
- We're all in grave danger and need to leave somehow.
- The curfew situation has nothing to do with this.
- We're better off not prying any further.
- I couldn't gather any concrete information.

"Is this sufficient?" I asked.

He looked over the questions. "Yeah, but let me add a few.

- The headmasters know about the moon bridge.
- Expelled students were sent to a dungeon off campus.
- Bug people.

"Bug people?" I looked at him.

"I mean, wouldn't you want to know?" he stared back at me.

An unexpected knock at my door caused us both to jump. I closed my planner and tossed it on the kitchen counter.

"Answer it!" Axle hissed.

"Well, yeah," I said, laughing to myself as I walked across the room. I didn't know what Axle expected to happen in broad daylight.

I opened the door to find Atlas standing in the hall. "Hey, Gill!" he said in an unusually cheery tone.

"What's up Atlas," I greeted him.

"The postings are up," he announced.

"The wha—" I shook my head.

"For the Cape Exams." He lifted his arms over his head in excitement. "Everyone's seeing who they're paired against. C'mon, let's go!"

The Cape Exams! In all the commotion from today I'd forgotten about them.

"Hey, Axle." Atlas looked past me and waved.

"I hope none of us have to fight each other," said Axle as he pushed past me out the door. I put my shoes on and followed them to the corkboard. People crowded around the postings as they struggled to read the fine print.

"Is Cham Dunley in this hall?" someone called out, looking to meet their opponent.

"Tera Kingsly?" yelled another.

We made our way through the crowd and eventually got close enough to the board to see the postings. It looked like each name had a ranking attached, as well as a little symbol containing the colors of their school.

I traced the list for Dragstenn and found it not far from the top of the page. I was squaring off against someone named Tanz Hauley. I'd never heard of them, but their little badge indicated that they were from the Brightroot Elemental Academy. They were number 300 in their school's ranking system.

Someone had decided that I was better than my ranking reflected. If I could win, I'd jump several hundred rankings. I smiled at the thought—no longer dead last. My name lost in the jumble rather than sticking out at the ass end of every list.

My smile faded when I stumbled upon another pairing below mine.

Tovin Blackmeyer vs Fena Grimbrooke.

"W-what?" I yelled over the noise. "Fena is fighting *Tovin?*"

"Looks like it," Axle said as I stepped away from the board. I couldn't believe it. My hands began to tremble.

Tovin had to have fixed the fight. He might have wanted to be sure he wouldn't have to fight Atlas again, but he still wanted to get back at him. Killing his sister right in front of him would be the perfect payback.

"Well, how about that," Atlas said. "And here I was hoping for a rematch."

"How are you so *calm* about this?" I yelled at him in confusion. "Your sister is fighting Tovin Blackmeyer! Why aren't you panicking?"

He turned his eyes toward me and smiled.

"Because, Gill, my sister is *strong*."

TWENTY

“Okay, look,” I said as I pulled him away from the crowd. “Your battle with Tovin is not indicative of his true strength. He's a hell of a lot better than you think.”

“I could say the same of my sister,” he retorted, his smile disappearing. “On what basis do you believe she can't defend herself?”

“That…That is *not* what I'm saying!” I argued.

“I agree with you,” Axle interjected. “Don't get me wrong, Tovin is a *monster*. But the proctors thought she'd be a match for him. Isn't that enough?”

“No,” I turned to him. “Tovin is ranked number one, but it's a long way to the second-highest student. He's in a league of his own. We've got to *do* something!”

Atlas folded his arms. “I'll tell you what we do. We have faith in Fena.”

My arms fell to my sides as I realized I wasn't getting anywhere. I pushed my way back through the crowd. I had to have made a mistake. I found the listing again, and I traced my finger from his name to hers. Then I noticed her ranking; it was displayed right next to her name the same as Tovin's.

No. 1 Tovin Blackmeyer (ENU) vs. No. 4 Fena Grimbrooke (ENU)

She was ranked number four? Right out of the gate as a new student? Just how terrifying was she that they would rank her that high without seeing her in actual combat?

I scanned the list until I found Atlas's pairing.

No. 9 Atlas Grimbrooke (ENU) vs. No. 5 Leo Torre (ACU)

They had ranked Atlas number nine after he destroyed Tovin on the first day? I shouldn't even have been surprised. Tovin was ENU's golden boy. On the other hand, Atlas wasn't good at controlling his magic. I'd yet to *see* him in action. I rubbed my chin as looked for Axle's pairing.

No. 18 Axle Auddle (ENU) vs No. 16 Lana Meridia (ENU)

I blinked twice. Axle was paired against Lana? A small smile took my lips as I turned and found Axle conversing with Atlas at the other end of the crowd.

I pushed back through and interrupted them. "Hey, hey, hey." I placed a hand on Atlas. "Sorry to interrupt, but did you see who you were paired against, Axle?"

"Hm? Yeah, Lana," he responded before his eyes popped open. "Oh. Oooh!"

"The one who summons elementals." Atlas caught on and smiled at the both of us.

"By the gods," Axle smiled. "The investigation. It's not over!"

"Talk about luck," I laughed with him. "We shouldn't talk about this out here, though."

"Want to head back to my dorm?" Axle asked. "I'd say we needed to call a meeting anyway, considering..."

"Considering what?" Atlas asked urgently. "Did we learn something about the Hall Monitors?"

"Can I just say," Axle said, with an expression of pleasure on his face, "it's *so* nice that you're as excited as I am about all this."

"Heck yeah!" Atlas said in an excited tone. It seemed Axle was rubbing off on him.

"Have you seen your sister?" I asked, scanning the hallway. "She'll want to hear this."

"Ugh," Atlas's head fell back and he rolled his eyes. "I knocked on her door, same as I did you, but you know women," he whined. "They've gotta drag their feet doing *everything*. First, they gotta wash their face, then they gotta put on their makeup, then she's gotta put on some stupid zit cream, and this is all before her *hair!*"

A growing crowd of girls was forming behind him as he went on.

"Uhh, Atlas." I attempted to warn him.

"And then it's the pee!" he yelled. "Always with the *peeing!* It's like every thirty minutes with them!"

"Atlas," Axle asserted as Fena appeared behind him.

"Then, when you ask 'em why they're taking so long, they act like you're the unreasonable one. Nobody cares about your nails but you! If you spent as much time training as you did worrying about your—"

Fena cleared her throat.

Atlas must have realized that the hallway had gone silent. It settled in on him before he turned to find many female eyes on him. I have to admit, it was amusing watching him die inside.

"W-wait. Fena! I—"

She picked him up by his ears, and I winced as he hollered. The girls laughed, and my face grew hot from secondhand embarrassment. After forcing him to vomit a slew of apologies, she set him down and smiled at the two of us.

"Sorry I'm late."

"You look great," I said.

"Hmm?"

"I said you're late," I lied. "You *are* late."

"I have a morning routine," she said, flipping her hair. "You guys look at the pairings already?"

"Uh, yeah," I answered. "About that."

"Fena Grimbrooke," came an unfortunately familiar voice from down the hall. The crowd parted as if they were in on it as Tovin sauntered down the hallway. "I have to admit," he said, "I didn't expect to be paired with someone ranked less than two."

"Oh," Fena muttered just loud enough for us to hear. "Him?"

"Him," the three of us said at once.

She sighed, folding her arms in a stance that said, "I just woke up and I'm done with you."

He lifted his arms in an exaggerated shrug. "You know, it's too bad. Your first year here, and you have to start it with a humiliating defeat in front everyone in Galgia."

Rage ran from my head to my feet as I balled my fists.

"You know, if you ask nicely," Tovin added with a cocky grin, "I might make it look like a close fight to save you the embarrassment."

Atlas took a step, but Fena grabbed him by his shoulder.

"Oh, are you going to *try* something, Atlas?" he asked. "I heard about your little *problem*. Next time you cross me, you're—"

"Hey," Fena said in a commanding tone that somehow captured everyone's attention. She strode toward Tovin with all the blue-blooded fury of a queen slighted.

She put her face inches from his. "Everyone in this room saw the fear on your face when Atlas nearly decorated the walls with your sorry ass." She narrowed her eyes. "As plain as the smog in your soul."

He took a step back, struggling to maintain a tough façade. It seemed she'd hit him where it hurts.

"If you thought my *brother* was scary, you're not ready for what's behind door number two. It *will* be close, and not because you're nice," she said, making her way back to us. "In fact, the rules require me to hold back. Thank your headmasters for giving you a chance."

The crowd droned on as Tovin's face shriveled with rage. "Y-you *bitch*," he seethed. The crowd drowned out the rest of his hate-fueled diatribe as she breezed past us.

"Come on," she called to us.

We exchanged glances and hurried after her.

Where did all of that come from? And what did she mean when she said the rules were limiting her?

"Shut up!" I heard Tovin yelling as we walked away. "I said shut up, all of you!"

I couldn't stifle my smile—a contagious phenomenon among the four of us.

———

Back in Axle's dorm, he explained everything that happened in my meeting with the headmasters, including the fact that I'd been Censored.

"I can't believe they did that to you," Fena said, concern in her tone.

"I can't believe you didn't break down and confess," Atlas added with a laugh. "That all sounded really stressful."

"I have to be careful what I say," I replied, silent for a moment after as I considered my words. "But I think it's safe to say that without Axle's information about the Hall Monitors, I'd have cracked."

"You're lucky I was in the cafeteria that day," said Axle.

"That wasn't by accident, was it?" Fena asked with a smile.

"Guilty," Axle nodded. "He was screaming about it in his head all night. I hardly slept."

"Let's get back on track," Atlas said, steering the conversation. "Vega was acting fishy. We've got an inquisitor on campus who was worried about Gill *seeing* something he wasn't supposed to see. Something that they were willing to kill him over."

"Well," Axle shrugged. "I don't know how else to interpret 'kill kill kill kill kill.'"

"Not just that," Fena spoke up. "But, as Axle said, Inquisitor Imandr seemed worried about repercussions from the other colleges—even the high priests."

"What I don't understand," Axle ruminated, "is why an inquisitor would be worried about that. I mean, they work for the archbishop and the archbishop works alongside the high priests. An inquisitor on official business wouldn't be worried, would he?"

"That's a solid point," Atlas agreed. "So, we're left with two possibilities. Either the inquisitor was *not* sent here on official business..."

"Or he's not an inquisitor at *all*," Axle surmised as we exchanged glances in a moment of silence. Both of those prospects were worrisome for different reasons.

"You guys think I should test it?" I asked. "The spell."

"No," said Axle quickly. "Don't. It's not worth it. If he really *is* an inquisitor..."

"...He could kill you," Atlas cut in. "For good."

We sat in the seriousness of that for a moment before I made a decision. "If Axle goes into that meeting and doesn't pick up game-changing information...I think we should just drop this whole thing."

"What?" Axle and Atlas yelled in unison.

"He's right," Fena jumped in. "We're lucky this hasn't gone wrong yet. If you ask me, we shouldn't dig deeper. In case you guys have forgotten, we've got enough to worry about with our schoolwork, not to even mention the Cape Exams."

"But..." Axle retorted. "We're so close to blowing the lid off this thing..."

"We don't know what's under that lid," I cautioned him.

A second silence fell over the four of us.

"All right," Axle conceded. "Then I guess I'll have to focus tomorrow," he said with a confident grin. "I've stumbled upon a real honest to gods conspiracy. I can't let it end here, not when we're so close."

"Don't forget you've got Lana to worry about," I advised him.

"Right." He tightened up his jaw and lowered his eyebrows. "Just leave it to me."

"That reminds me," Atlas turned to his sister. "You didn't see whom I was paired against, did you?"

"Hmm? No, I never looked at the board," she said in an annoyed tone. "Tovin was up my ass before I got the chance, and I didn't want to stick around. Guy makes my skin crawl."

"It's Leo," he said in a serious tone.

Hey eyes widened and her lips parted. "...You're kidding," she said just above a whisper.

"I wouldn't kid about that," he looked at the carpet.

"There's...there's got to be someone we can talk to," Fena reasoned.

"No," he said in a deep tone. "I want this."

"I saw that pairing," I spoke up. "Leo Torre. You have a history with him?"

"That's *one* way of putting it." Fena sighed. "We should alert the proctors about a grudge."

"A grudge?" asked Axle.

"Yeah..." Atlas looked up at us. "Leo and I go all the way back to magi school. I don't want to talk about it. I'd like to have a good day today."

"S-sure." I lifted my hands. "By all means. Let's skip it."

"Another time," he said with a nod. "Promise."

"You never have to tell us if you don't want to," Axle said. "But we're here for you."

That forced a smile out of Atlas, and he turned his head.

"Is anyone else starving?" asked Fena.

———

"Thanks for finally bringing me here," Fena said as we sat down at our table.

"You've never been to Magic Bistro?" Axle asked with a 'get outta here' kinda smile.

"We're pretty new here," Atlas countered.

"That's no excuse!" said Axle, making numerous suggestions down the menu.

The Magic Bistro was an outdoor restaurant with about fifteen tables on a large patio with a fancy black iron fence that ran along the edge of its property. Some of the trees had started to turn color, and I was admiring their orange hues when I noticed seven boys wearing the same colors—green and white—walking down the main hallway. They were loud, laughing, shoving people out of their way, and making a terrible first impression.

They were from the Brightroot Elemental Academy.

"What are they doing here?" Atlas asked, taking notice.

"Being dicks," Axle replied.

"They're here on a sanctioned visit," came a new voice from the other end of the table. Our server was holding a notepad and watching them as they drew near. "The boss told us to expect heavier traffic than usual this weekend. The Auguries and the Brightroots will be here today and tomorrow, and the Conflux will be in next weekend. They're touring the campus before the Cape Exams."

"I hadn't heard anything," said Axle.

"Me either," I added.

"I imagine they're restricted to the south and west wings," said Fena as they bullied their way toward us. "They're going to be on campus all day long on the day of their exam."

I hadn't considered that. They'd likely send everyone whose fight was scheduled for the day over on one train. What would those who weren't fighting do while they were waiting for their match, other than hang around the restaurants and attractions?

"You'd better order before they get here," our server warned us. "You're going to want your food started before I send a big group back there."

We placed our orders as they walked up the path through the gate. I sighed as they moved tables together on their own.

"How about some beverages!" called one of the boys.

"Hungry customers!" yelled another one, laughing as they took their seats. I rested my head in my hand as they made fools of themselves. I almost pitied them; they probably thought they were cool.

"Hey, baby!" one of them yelled to our table. "You lookin' for a *man*, hot stuff?"

Axle turned to us with a half-smile. "You think they're talking to me?"

"No," Atlas said, burying his face in his hands. This was something he was used to.

One of them strutted over to us. He had short brown hair —almost a buzz cut—a pierced left ear, and an impressive beard for our age group. He had a scar over his right eye and his eyebrow separated around it. He looked like he'd been in a lot of fights and lost all of them.

He leaned on our table with one hand and stared at Fena, who glanced at us with wide eyes, as if to ask, "Are you seeing this shit?""Hey, cutie pie," he said, "why don't you ditch these kiddies and come sit at the adult table?"

Before any of us could respond, Fena did. "Why in the *world* would you think that would work?" She looked at us, "What woman has that *ever* worked on?"

He glanced at the rest of us before he returned to his table. Between their noise, rude gestures, and carrying on we could hardly talk to one another. The server asked them to keep their voices down, but they ignored him. The few other students at the tables around them got up and left.

"I'm going to say something," Atlas said as he scooted his chair out.

"No," Fena said, pushing his chair back in. "We don't need any trouble. Ignore them."

"How?" I asked in a dejected tone. "I can't even hear myself think."

"I can't hear you think either," Axle said tossing his napkin on the table in exasperation.

"How about we take our food to go and move to the cafeteria," offered Fena.

"Now *that's* a plan," Atlas smiled. "Good thinking, Sis."

That was when I noticed a new variable. "Uh-oh," I said, lifting my finger. They all followed my gaze to Tovin, who was walking our way.

"For fuck's sake," Fena said through her teeth.

"You think he's following us?" asked Atlas.

"I don't know," Axle said in an annoyed tone, turning to face me. "He hates Atlas, enjoys picking on Gill, and Fena just humiliated him in front of everyone in the hallway. I don't think I've had much interaction with him, now that I think about it. How does he keep popping up?"

"Believe me," I groaned, "as the one person in this school of seven hundred students I avoid, he's somehow *everywhere*."

"Hey!"

We all turned to see Tovin was at the entrance to the bistro. The obnoxious visitors halted their conversation and stared at him.

He appeared to be speaking to them. "This university is the treasure of Galgia," Tovin yelled over the gate. "Under normal circumstances, filth like you would *never* see the inside of these prestigious halls! Do everyone in the west wing a favor and *shut your fucking mouths*. Act like adults, gods damn you!"

For once, I agreed with Tovin. He'd taken the words right out my mouth, if ever I had intended to say them.

All of them stood up, the magic within them radiating in their midsections.

"Oh yeah?" one of them called, pushing his way to Tovin. "Are you gonna *make* us?"

Twenty-One

My butt cheeks clenched as Tovin stared back at them with a blank look. His deadpan stare—the harbinger of coming disaster. That ominous calm before the winds blow and the birds seek shelter. Behind his black eyes billowed the thunderous clouds of a looming storm, and I couldn't tell whether the visitors from the BEA were skilled privateers or children playing pirates. Everyone who'd been milling about nearby had stopped as though frozen in time, all eyes on Tovin.

"Do any of you," Tovin spoke in a voice trembling with fury—and a tinge of excitement, "*think* you're a match for me? Or maybe," he chuckled to himself as he stepped past the gate. "Maybe you assumed I would walk away, as though a stern talking to was enough. Is that it?"

"Take one more step and I'll *fry* you," said the student standing closest to him.

"No, no, no, no, tsk tsk tsk tsk," Tovin said as he stared them down. "No, your school is too relaxed. Progressivism is a flawed teaching philosophy. It lacks the structure and etiquette of essentialism. Now I'm going to teach you some respect...the painful way," he growled as he took another deliberate step. "Class is in session."

The foremost mage whirled his arms in a circular motion, embers dancing around him as he gathered a mass of fire near his midsection.

"Hit the deck!" someone shouted before the mage threw his arms ahead of him, unleashing an impressive gout of flame. Tovin took a few rhythmic steps before bringing his arms up high while simultaneously speaking words of power. I leaned in; he was casting *two spells at once* by combining the arts of verbal and kinetic casting.

A spout of water leapt from his feet, intercepting the flames with a mighty hiss and coating the area in a thick cloud of steam. His verbal spell then collected the steam into a boiling cloud around his opponent. The bloodcurdling screams from within the steam were hair-raising.

"Boyde!" they screamed as the steam cloud dispersed and their friend tumbled out. His skin was crimson and bubbly. He appeared to have passed out from the pain.

Tovin strode through what remained of the steam cloud. "Is it sinking in now?" he asked. "The extent to which we train here? What magic can do when you're not holding back? This is what war looks like when it's on your doorstep."

"Get him!" shouted the bearded one we'd spoken with earlier.

The six of them fanned out around him and the four of us put some distance between ourselves and the coming battle.

"Did you guys *see* that?" Axle asked as we backed up to the gate. "He boiled that guy alive!"

"Not just that, but he used the spell cast against him to enhance his attack," Fena added.

"And he prepared two spells at once," I said. "I've never even thought to *try* that."

"It's even more impressive than you're making it out to

be." Atlas weighed in. "He knew the spell that was coming before the magic manifested. He knew from his enemy's *movements* what spell was coming and selected two to counter it without hesitation. He didn't stop to think about it; he knew them seemingly by muscle memory."

Atlas cast me a nervous glance. He understood what I'd been trying to tell him in the hallway.

Tovin was more than the No. 1 ranked student. He was a once-in-a-generation *genius*.

The students began casting. Some shouted words of power while others made motions to launch their spells. Fire, water, wind, ice—all manner of attacks were thrown his way, and he stepped around each one while molding his own kinetic spells. It was like an elaborate dance as he pierced one through the chest with a fiery javelin and sent another barreling through a table with a heavy beam of light.

The most popular offensive spells among mages are those of the natural elements. In ascending order of difficulty: wind, fire, water, ice, earth, and lightning. More difficult are light, shadow, force, and beam spells. Light spells scramble an opponent's mana by overloading them with more of it. Shadow spells drain the target of their mana reserves, but the caster runs the risk of having their own mana eaten as well. Force spells are impossible to track with the human eye and hit hard, though they're extremely mana intensive to cast. I couldn't cast the weakest force spell with all the mana I possess. Beam spells, pure concentrated magic energy in its rawest form, are the most destructive kind of spell one can wield, but the casting costs are out of this world. Not only are they taxing on one's mana, but they also weaken your maximum mana reserves. You might take days to fully recover. During the war, they were the only spells capable of penetrating some of the Diesel's most durable machinery.

Tovin was struck by a force spell, sending him stumbling back into the front gate of the bistro. All of us were surprised to see it. Tovin dodged a light spell and deflected a stream of fire onto the gate on his right. The iron bars bowed, glowing red and yellow from the intense heat.

They had him on his heels. He backed out of the bistro as they launched attack after attack, but it was the one who was sneaking around the side who caught my attention.

The bearded one with the scar over his eye.

I quietly left the group and hopped the gate, followed the student around the side. I wasn't about to let him attack Tovin from behind like a coward. It was five versus one, and although I disliked all parties involved, I despised dirty tactics.

A crowd had gathered at this point, but they weren't cheering. They were screaming and calling for headmasters as Tovin fought at parity against four mages. He had regained his footing and was beginning to attack back again, but he'd lost track entirely of the sixth mage. He skulked through the crowd, and I followed, careful not to lose sight of him.

Why am I doing this? Why do I care if this guy gets one over on Tovin, of all people? Gods know *he's had it coming. I don't understand why, but I despise* this *guy more than him. I don't like how he disrespected our school; I don't appreciate the way he spoke to Fena; I don't like being belittled in front of her, either. Even so, am I making the right decision?*

I didn't have another moment to think about it. He moved out of the crowd as Tovin narrowed his battle to a two-on-one fight. His movements had slowed, his breathing was labored, and he was too focused to notice the danger behind him.

I bolted from my place in the crowd.

Time seemed to slow.

I didn't know why I was doing it—only that I *was.*

The bastard moved in preparation for a kinetic spell. As he turned to wind up, he noticed me out of the corner of his eye.

Tovin had finished his opponent and had begun to turn, but he wouldn't be fast enough.

I didn't have time to summon my tome.

The only thing I could do was get there in time.

In the assailant's distraction, he misplaced a step and found himself off-balance. In that moment, I connected with him and the two of us tumbled to the ground. He ended up on top of me, and stared into my eyes with unbridled, fiery rage. He cocked back and brought his fist down on my face with all his might.

My ears popped.

I was shellshocked. He had a good arm on him, and it dizzied me to such a degree that the noise from the crowd drowned away and the world turned watercolor.

Although I expected another strike, my face was sprayed with a warm liquid.

The world took form again, and when my vision returned, I found the student on top of me. He had a bewildered expression. Blood fell from his chest in pools. He looked off into the distance as though in a trance before he slumped off me and onto the cobblestone walkway.

Tovin appeared above me and stared down at me with a mixture of scorn and irritation. From the way the sun was positioned behind him, and my dizzying stupor, I almost mistook him for a god. I wanted to explain myself, but I couldn't form the words.

He picked me up off the ground with both hands, lifting me into the air by my shirt.

I winced in pain.

"I didn't *ask* for your help," he growled.

Our eyes met.

I put in a lot of effort to avoid him all the time: trying to stay out of his way; keeping myself hidden from his line of sight; glancing down hallways for good measure before taking them.

And here I was, held above him, our eyes locked onto one another. It was a sobering moment that brought me fully back to my senses.

He set me down in front of him, looking at me with disgust, "That *your* blood, or his?"

"B-both, I think," I managed to say.

We stared at one another for a few seconds longer before he turned to the bodies that littered the area. I think it began to sink in for him just what exactly he had done. No permanent deaths on campus, but word *would* get back to the Brightroot Elemental Academy.

I was unsure if the headmasters could overlook this, even for Tovin.

"Go clean yourself up," he said just loud enough for me to hear. "And Gill..."

"Yeah?" I asked.

"If any of the headmasters ask you," he looked at me over his shoulder, his tone serious. "You were *never here*. You got that?"

I managed a nod before turning and hurrying into the crowd. The others joined me in my dorm as I cleaned the blood off my face. They were right to accost me for what I'd done. I couldn't even explain it to them because I only halfway understood it myself.

"I don't know why I helped," I said as I held the cold cloth over my face. "I just did. I *know* it doesn't make sense. I hate Tovin as much if not more than the rest of you."

"Well," Atlas sighed, "what's done is done. But I never got to eat, and I've got studying to do if I want to pass my test on Monday. I'm going to grab something from the cafeteria and hit the books. Try and stay off your feet awhile, Gill. I'll maybe see you guys tomorrow."

"I was about to say something similar," said Axle as he followed Atlas to the door. "I'll see you all tomorrow. I would stay out of Tovin's way for a while. That goes for you too, hun."

"Yeah, yeah," Fena said, not taking her eyes off of me. She peeled the cloth off my face as they left and winced at the damage. "Gah-*lee*, did that guy clock you," she said as I turned away from her and leaned on my kitchen table. My head was pounding.

"I should probably study, too," Fena said.

"Yeah. I'll see you around," I muttered.

"Gill?" she asked.

"Yeah."

"Can I ask something of you?"

"Of course."

She sat on my mattress, "It's just that...Look, we haven't known each other like, *super* long or anything. But in the time, I've known you, I've got to say. You have just one of the biggest hearts of anyone I've met."

I remained silent.

"But you're so *reckless*. I mean. It's been one thing after another, y'know? The watchers, getting choked by an inquisitor, that incident just now. I mean, that's a lot in such a short time."

"I guess so," I responded.

"I guess what I'm trying to say is...I don't want to see you picking any more fights. Gill, you're a sweet guy; I *mean* that. But compared to some of the other students, you're not..."

My heart raced to the bottom of my stomach.

"I was worried that jerk was going to kill you," she said, changing course. "I know there's a stasis field around the school and all, but I don't *ever* want to see you die."

"Am I that easy to kill?" I asked, unable to mask my anger.

"That's not what I'm saying!" she corrected herself as I turned to face her.

"Am I really so fragile that a single punch is gonna do me in?"

"Ugh," she rolled her eyes. "Sometimes I forget you're a *man*."

Something inside of me broke.

"You have man-brain," she continued. "You guys turn everything into something else. I wasn't saying that a punch was going to kill you, *nor* am I trying to say you're a fragile little flower. I'm just saying that I don't like seeing you in pain."

I sighed and tossed the cloth onto the kitchen counter. We stared at one another for a moment before she averted her eyes and placed her hands in her lap.

"I'm sorry if I offended you," she said as she stood and started toward the door. "I'm gonna go study. I suggest you do the same."

"Yeah," I muttered as she closed the door.

I stood in the cadaverous silence of my dorm and reflected on everything that had transpired for a moment.

A knock came at the door. I swallowed. I was too inside of my own head to answer it. It was a painful place to be. I wanted to be alone.

The knocker persisted, this time faster.

I wiped my hand over my face before pulling the door open

Fena stepped in, threw her arms around me, and pulled me in close.

All of my pain washed away. My head cleared as my worries floated away on bubbles of bliss.

"Forgot to give you one of these," she said. "Do me a favor and don't be so reckless, ya goof. 'kay?"

"O-okay," I said as I hugged her back.
"See ya," she said as she let me go, turned, and left.
"Take care," my voice broke as I called after her.
I closed the door before leaning against it.
Smiling like an idiot.

Twenty-Two

The following morning, the "battle at the bistro" was all anyone was talking about. I sat at the table in the cafeteria and watched the rain come down as I listened to the rumors fly around the room.

"I heard the Brightroot Elemental Academy is pulling out of the Cape Exams!"

"Tovin is getting expelled for sure this time."

"I heard there were riots in the Basandra province."

I took a swig of my coffee as Axle approached with an egg sandwich. I acknowledged him with a quick nod, before turning back to the window.

"Lemme see it," he said as a parent would to their child.

I sighed and faced him.

"Yikes," he said, curling his lip. "That bruise is green in the middle, my man."

"Yep," I responded. "It was hard to sleep with this thing."

"I bet," he said, taking a bite of his sandwich. "You think the headmashters gonna exchpell Tovin thish time?"

"I did at first, but now I'm not so sure," I said, plumbing the depths of my mug. "I don't believe *any* of the rumors I've heard. I'd bet you money the whole thing gets swept under the rug."

He took a drink of his milk and wiped his mouth with his sleeve. "Really? You think the Brightroots will just let this whole thing go?"

"I do," I replied, swirling the liquid around in my mug. "Think about it. Both schools look bad for this. If the story gets out, the public is going to learn that the seven Brightroots were destroyed by a single ENU student. The tension between the Gohblu and Basandra provinces would worsen—might even lead to fights in the streets."

"Huh," he said taking another bite of his sandwich. "I guessh I never thought about the political ashpect like that. Impresshive deductive reashoning there, Gilly Billy."

"Thanks, and don't call me that." I finished my lukewarm coffee and stood up.

"Got plans today?" he asked.

"Yeah, I'm spending the morning studying. I'm not confident about my tactics test tomorrow; a few strategies feel counterintuitive to me. How about you?"

He reached into his breast pocket and produced a letter with a purple seal on it.

"Oh," I said.

"Yep," he tucked the note away. "Looks like it's time."

"Don't do anything too reckless, Axle," I warned.

"You're one to talk," he shot back. "I'll be fine," he added with a smile. "If you find yourself with free time tonight, Atlas and I are gonna hit the bathhouse around six thirty. You're welcome to join us."

"Bathhouse is closed for cleaning on Sundays," I reminded him as I grabbed my tray.

"Exactly," he pointed his fork at me. "But they finish their cleaning around five and leave. I hang out in there by myself all the time, nobody checks. It's nice and quiet."

"Really?" I asked. "Huh. Guess I can count on you to know where nobody's gonna be."

"I have my uses," he remarked with a sly smile.

"I guess, yeah, I'll see you guys tonight then," I said, as I headed out. "Good luck with the meeting."

"Good luck with your studies," he called after me as I walked away.

More rumors about the fight surfaced as I made my way back to my dorm. Everyone seemed to think there were going to be expulsions.

"Tovin is G-O-N-E *gone*."

"Good riddance. Guy's a nightmare."

"Bet you those seven Brightroots are done for, too."

I kicked my shoes off in my dorm room, grabbed the appropriate books, and took my place at my kitchen table. I studied for about twenty minutes before I got a knock at the door.

I finished reading the sentence I was on and scooted out of my chair. The knock came again as I made my way to the door. I wondered if it was Fena, and my heart swelled in my chest. We didn't have any of the same classes, but I wondered if she'd be interested in studying with me.

I was thinking of something cool and snappy to say as I undid the deadbolt and pulled the door open.

Where I expected to find Fena's sweet and smiling face, I found Tovin Blackmeyer glassy eyes burrowing deeply into mine. Dread ran down my spine. My mouth opened but no sound came out. I began to backpedal out of sheer instinct and he strode through my doorway after me. He kicked the door shut behind him and started toward me.

"T-Tovin," I said in surprise.

"Shut up," he commanded.

My back hit the wall, and he wrapped his fingers tightly around my neck. I was too petrified to react. Fighting him wasn't an option. My trauma had me by the throat, and I couldn't think of anything to do but accept whatever was about to happen.

"Aeroastra," he said, and in an instant all the air was ripped from my lungs. My entire chest burned as I fell to the floor and squirmed. It was a pain unlike any I'd felt—*far* worse than drowning. I turned to my side and looked up at him as my vision doubled.

"You were never there," he said before turning and walking away.

I lifted my hand toward him, begging for mercy—a scene I had hoped I would never have to relive. He stole one glance at me over his shoulder before leaving. I hoped Axle was back in his dorm by now, that he would hear my suffering and come to help.

I had no hope that he would be able to save me.

But dying alone was awful.

My last thoughts before my vision darkened were about what I'd done to piss him off so much. After what he'd said to me that day, I had almost fooled myself into believing that everything was behind us.

My body began to shut down. Everything darkened like a theatre closing the curtain.

So dark.

Cold.

Then suddenly, warmth.

The darkness now felt familiar. Welcoming even, as though I had walked into my childhood home after years spent away. An anticipation of something good to come, as though I were five years old, and my birthday was around the corner. I felt the sensation of my worries sloughing off of my body like a slinx shedding its skin. Then the darkness relented only a little.

A dim light winked into existence somewhere far from me.

I walked toward it without thinking. Whatever was on the other side of it was tantalizing, and every instinct in my body compelled me forward.

Then, slowly, the light was eclipsed by a large figure. I slowed to a stop as several eyes opened on and around the object. I understood that I was seeing it again—the thing that had kept me up countless nights; the thing that I scoured the old texts for; the thing that I felt I shouldn't be seeing, as though it weren't meant for my eyes.

The mystical entity stared at me as we floated in the infinite darkness together. The eyes, as they had done before, moved on their own in an almost mechanical way around its main body. Each remained transfixed on me, no matter their position. The air vibrated around my entire body.

"Be...not...afraid..."

It spoke in a garbled voice that I took in not just through my ears, but through my entire being. It was as though it were speaking to me from underwater or through some sort of distortion field. The light glowed like dawn behind its form and swallowed the darkness around us. It was soon blinding beyond sight, and I shut my eyes tightly. Everything trembled...and then there was nothing but tranquility.

Someone's heart was beating in my ears, and when I opened my eyes, I was staring at my ceiling. I immediately filled my lungs with air; my chest felt like it was on fire. Pins and needles coursed through my entire body. I turned over and coughed a few times before lifting myself off the floor. I stumbled to my dresser and held myself up as my senses returned to me one at a time.

My hearing was still a whirlwind when Vice Principal Wharl arrived at my door. His face was red with rage, and as his lips moved, I tried to make out the words.

Another figure appeared behind him. Tall and muscular with a thick mustache that hid his lips. A member of the staff. I recognized his face, but I'd never learned his name.

Blood rushed in my ears. "Mr. Dragstenn!" Wharl was nearly shouting now.

"Yeah," I squeaked out.

"That's 'yes, *sir*' to you," he shot back. "Are you going to come willingly, or must we *drag* you?"

"Wait, wait," I said as I stood up straight. "What's this all about? Wha—"

"Silence," he interrupted me.

The unnamed man pushed past the vice principal and started toward me. I lifted my hands, sobering up by the second. "No, no. I'll...I'll come. Just...gimme a second."

I breathed as I gathered myself and took my first step. It was awkward at first but soon became natural as the static in my feet subsided.

"What's the matter with you?" asked Wharl, his voice coming down an octave.

"Nothing," I said, coughing again. "Please, lead the way."

He wore a dubious expression, looking me up and down before turning and leading me out of the room. I followed him, and the other staffer stuck close behind me. It was Sunday afternoon, and most students were either in the west wing or in their dorms studying. My perp walk was a private one.

The creature lingered in my mind as I followed the vice principal down the big staircase.

Be not afraid. That's what it was saying to me. It was clearer this time than last. I can probably draw it now. The words it spoke...I can ask the librarian about that. Maybe that'll be the key to finally busting this thing open.

I was taken once again to the conference room. Although Inquisitor Imandr was standing outside the door as he had been last time, he declined to follow us in. I made accidental eye contact with him as he opened the door for us.

Once again, I stood before all the headmasters.

Wharl and the other staff member that had been accompanying us left at Rowan's signal—a wave of his bony hand.

They were seated the same way they were the first time, with Rowan standing at the head of the table, clinging to his cane as he watched me through furious eyes. The tension in the room was tangible. I felt as though my senses were still coming online one after the other, but it didn't take much to know I was in serious trouble this time.

"Mr. Dragstenn," he said, "do you mind telling me why a fight broke out in the west wing yesterday?"

I studied them for a moment and cleared my throat. "I-I don't know how that happened."

"Liar," Vega spat as he pounded the table. "Four students said they saw you causing trouble! One of them *named* you, and the other three described you in fine detail!"

"Mr. Dragstenn," Huede said firmly. "We do *not* allow such behavior on our campus unsanctioned."

"I didn't," I stammered. "I didn't have anything to do with that! You've got the wrong guy!"

"Doesn't *that* sound familiar," mused Vega.

"I will read from the written statement," Huede adjusted his glasses and read the paper in front of him.

"Gill tackled one of the visitors from the Brightroot Elemental Academy He wrestled him to the ground and a scuffle ensued. Gill was struck hard in the face, and Tovin stepped in to rescue him. Gill seemed to be unconscious. Had Tovin not intervened, he may have been killed."

He took off his glasses and turned his fiery gaze at me. "Mr. Dragstenn, is that how we behave here at Eye of Newt? This is not your personal playground. Those students were our esteemed guests! Do you have any idea what you've done?"

My throat had turned dry as a cobblestone street in the middle of summer. I swallowed and tried to speak but managed to only stutter and stammer. I was certain of one thing: someone had cooked the books.

The witness managed to conveniently miss the entire fight between Tovin and the Brightroots. They also completely overlooked the bodies littering the campus. This felt like a hit piece designed specifically for me.

"And then, to involve Mr. Blackmeyer," Rowan added. "You are quite lucky he was around to protect you."

"That-that's not how that happened!" I yelled, losing my temper.

"Mr. Dragstenn," Rowan interrupted. "I have heard *quite* enough." He looked around at his fellow headmasters, "I hereby move to expel Gill Dragstenn."

My heart dropped. This couldn't be happening again. And with such flimsy evidence?

I had to be dead still. I had to be dreaming.

"All in favor?"

Vega lifted his hand, Huede right after him. Anther followed suit.

"Wait," Alrune interrupted.

He was eyeing me as he stroked his beard and stared at me through narrowed eyes.

"Why have you halted the vote, Headmaster Alrune?" asked Rowan.

"Well," he began. "If the events in the witness testimony are to be taken seriously—"

"They *are*," Vega interjected, venom in his tone.

"Then certainly, young Mr. Dragstenn would have something to show for it. Would he not?"

The headmasters exchanged glances as Alrune walked around the long table toward me. He lifted his old hand to my chin, using it to guide my head both left and right.

"Surely one who was knocked unconscious would have bruising," Alrune noted. "At the very *least* a single mark... Would you not agree?"

The headmasters murmured among themselves as I stared at them in disbelief.

Were they all completely blind? The bruise on my face was green in the middle, according to Axle. How could they possibly miss it?

I lifted my hand to my cheek and felt around. *Nothing*. No pain, no swelling, no discomfort of any kind.

"Allow me to read that record," commanded Norah.

Huede passed the paper across the table to her as Vega made a new case for expulsion. "Mark or no, can we agree Gill is a problematic student? Would we not be better off without him? It was a mistake to even accept him here to begin with."

Norah looked up at me and pursed her lips, "No, this doesn't make sense. I agree with Headmaster Alrune. The facts aren't lining up well enough for me to be decisive in this instance."

"In light of this oversight, I retract my vote," spoke Anther. "I see no damage from the kind of strike described in the witness testimony. Perhaps the witness was mistaken."

"We should scour the grounds for a student with a healing wound on their face," Alrune noted as he moved back to his seat.

"B-but," stammered Vega. He looked around the room wide-eyed in disbelief.

I was in an equal state of confusion. How could they not see the bruise? Could it have healed that much in so little time? How long was I out for after Tovin—

Then I remembered. Tovin had stared me dead in the eyes and told me I was never there. Then he killed me. It began to make sense. The entire reason for his visit.

So, then the stasis field...It's the same as Atlas's broken nose. All my unhealed injuries are repaired, including the bruise.

I remembered him glancing at me over his shoulder as he left the room. He knew exactly what he was doing all along. It wasn't a senseless murder. My death had a purpose this time.

He knew somehow that they were coming for me. He knew right after the battle, probably. The headmasters'll forgive him, but they'll need a scapegoat. They'll want to show the Brightroot Elemental Academy that they've taken disciplinary measures.

"Until investigated further, I will vote for no such measure," Edwin announced.

Rowan breathed a frustrated sigh and averted his eyes as Huede cursed under his breath. Vega stormed out of the room just the same as he had before.

Norah rolled her eyes and rested her head on one hand as she made eye contact with Alrune. His shoulders bounced with a silent chuckle, and he lifted his pipe to his mouth. He really got a tickle out of pissing off Headmaster Vega.

"I..." spoke Rowan after a long silence. "Defer this meeting until further evidence has been reviewed," he said, taking his seat. He sounded down about me staying.

"You're excused, Mr. Dragstenn."

I didn't need to be told twice. I made for the door.

"Tell Inquisitor Imandr we're ready for Mr. Auddle," Rowan added as I pushed the door open. I stepped out, coming face to face with Axle. He glanced at the inquisitor and then back to me.

"They're uhh...They're ready for you two," I said, stepping aside.

Imandr grabbed the door and waved Axle in. He looked at me one last time before he moved. Imandr followed him in and closed the door behind him.

I could hear their muffled voices as they began the charade.

"Mr. Auddle, is there anything you'd like to tell us before we begin?"

I did not expect them to start without Vega present. This was bad. Axle wouldn't be able to ascertain *anything* from him if he didn't come back soon. I could only hope that one of the other headmasters knew something about that night. Anything that could give Axle a clue.

I was lost in my thoughts as I moved down the hallway.

"How'd it go," asked a voice from behind me.

My heart jumped. Tovin was leaning against the wall outside the administrative hallway where the room opened up to the south wing. I swallowed. I was becoming mentally scattered. My instincts were cringing. I needed to say something —anything.

"It...It went fine," I said in a shaky voice.

"I trust you're still enrolled here, then?"

"Y-yeah," I nodded. "They said they needed to reexamine the witness."

"Era Gardener," he said. "And she won't be saying *anything* else. I made sure of that."

The way he said it, there was a chance there were *two* murders on campus today.

"Oh," I said turning to face him. "How did you—"

"I know people," he interrupted. "Information gathering is easier for me than most. Call it a perk of being number one around here."

"Of course," I said. "Makes sense, I guess."

He stared at me for a moment, moving his weight to his other foot. "Gill."

"Yeah?"

"Why did you do it?"

"Um. Why did I do what?" I asked.

"Tch," he turned his head away from me and pushed off

the wall, heading for the roundabout. "Never mind," he called back to me in an annoyed tone.

He disappeared around the corner, and I let out all the air in my lungs. That was the most pleasant interaction I'd ever had with that guy. Not being killed was a plus.

I turned and made my way back to my room as I thought about what had just happened. Tovin had *covered* for me. He killed me, so the stasis field would heal my bruise. Without the mark, I could maintain plausible deniability.

Tovin had been thinking several steps ahead of them from the beginning. But why did he help me like that? I thought he *hated* me.

As I came closer to my room, I stopped.

My door was *open*.

I stopped just short of the door frame. Vega was standing in the center of my room staring at me.

And he was holding a bloodied damp cloth in his hand.

Twenty-Three

The two of us stared at one another for a few moments before he lifted the bloodied rag and pointed at it. "What is this?"

I was frozen.

"Nursing an injury, were we?" He pushed my bathroom door open with one boot. "Couldn't help but notice your sink has a pink hue to it. I don't suppose you were washing off makeup, were you?"

As I entered, I took a deep breath, relaxed my shoulders, and cleared my mind. I could talk my way out of this. I needed to think on my feet; something I wasn't half bad at.

"What are you implying, Headmaster Vega?" I asked in my most respectful way.

"*I'm* the one asking the questions here, you *worm*," he said, seething as he marched toward me. "Why do you have a bloody cloth in your room? Answer me this instant!"

"It's been getting cold out, Headmaster," I answered. "When that happens, the staff heat the building more. That makes it drier, and more so on the second floor. I had nose-bleeds last year, and they're happening again this year. Admittedly, I shouldn't have been picking at the scabs. I apologize if this created any undue confusion for you."

His face scrunched up and his cheeks turned red.

"I appreciate you checking up on me," I added. "But I'll survive, I promise," I said with a *pinch* of sass.

I don't know why, but I declined to break eye contact with him. I got the sense that he knew, and that he knew that I knew he knew. The two of us stared at one another until he tossed the cloth on the table. He stuck his face inches away from mine.

"You had a bruise on your face this morning. I saw it with my *own eyes*. I don't know how you managed to get rid of it, but I assure you, I *will* uncover the truth. And when I do, you'll face the harshest punishment I have the authority to bestow upon you."

He brushed past me, slamming the door behind him. The way Tovin had killed me was clean. No blood, no mess...no clues. The only thing Vega could find was a rag that I used to clean the blood off my face, and that was *my* fault.

Had Tovin really been thinking this far ahead? I couldn't be sure.

The question remained: Why did Vega have it in for me? I'd had hardly any meaningful interactions with him, if any.

The only thing I could think was that he somehow knew it was me out in the halls that night, and he wanted to get rid of me for whatever it was he thought I saw.

I glanced at the clock. The confrontation hadn't lasted very long. With any luck, Vega was on his way back to the conference room. Axle might be able to pry something out of his mind. Any information would do wonders when we put our heads together later.

I tried to go back to studying, but my mind was everywhere else.

Why does Tovin all of a sudden care whether I'm expelled?

What secrets will Axle return with? Was Vega threatening me with disciplinary action...or something worse?

But more than anything, my mind was racing about the many-eyed monster. Seeing it again had been an incredible experience. Dying to witness it once more was almost worthwhile.

And this time it *spoke* to me.

Be not afraid.

What an interesting thing to say. I was a little afraid of it the first time I saw it, but the feeling subsided. More than anything, I was curious. What was it? Why was it visiting me in my time of death? How had none of the other students seen it so far, and if they did, why wouldn't they talk about it?

I decided to pay the library a visit. I pulled on a sweater and grabbed a few things: a pencil, my notebook, and for good measure, my tome. It was a sad state of affairs that I felt the need to be armed as I walked the halls of my own school, but having been killed once today already had me on edge.

The library was situated between the north and east wings, with entrances on both sides. ENU had spared no expense when it had constructed its library. Gold trim sparkled around thick iron doors that opened into a well-lit, massive, two-story room.

I'd forgotten that today was Sunday, the library's busiest day. Students were sitting at most of the tables, including the ones around the balcony high overhead. By sheer luck, the line at the help desk was short, only a few people ahead of me. I waited patiently until I was called.

"Next."

I stepped up to the desk and waited for the librarian behind the counter to acknowledge me. He had chestnut brown hair, a bowl cut, round glasses, and a wiry frame. He pushed a small stamp into a box on his ledger, indicating a book had been requested before looking up at me.

He pushed his glasses up the bridge of his nose, "Yes, sir."

"Hey, I'd like to search a book by a quote."

"It's got to be a good quote," he said, taking his keys out of his pocket and locking something under his desk.

"Come on," he said, waving me around the counter.

We went a short way to a less-used part of the library behind the staircase that led to the upper floor. An entire wall of thick, seemingly unlabeled books were stacked from the floor to the ceiling underneath the balcony.

"The way this works is pretty simple," he said. "If I speak the right words and then say in the clearest possible voice a popular or well-known quote, the spine of one of these books will glow. Observe." He cleared his throat. "Elinea odrix hasan, take your time, for time will take *everything* from you."

"Edgar, the Ageless," I said with a smile.

"Anyone would know the book by that quote," he responded. "So it should work."

The book in front of us emitted light. Runes ran down its spine casting a blue glow onto our chests. He grabbed the book, which filled almost his entire grip, and pulled it from its place. He opened it to the front page, where over a thousand numbers were written in tiny text. The number 399 glowed a soft blue, the same as the book's spine.

"So, you open this directory to page three hundred and ninety-nine," he said, resting the spine in the crook of his elbow and flipping to the corresponding page. "Then you'll look for the glowing text on the page."

Sure enough, the quote was highlighted, along with other notable quotes from Edgar the Ageless. The book's title was above each quote in bold, and the page number of the quote was in parentheses at the end of it.

"So *that's* how that works," I said as he closed the book and pushed it back into place.

"Yes, sir," he said, turning to face me. "So, what's the quote you want to search for."

"Be not afraid," I responded.

"Hmm." He placed his hands on his hips. "I'm not a hundred percent sure that's going to be specific enough. Conversely, it may trigger a number of books in this section, as it doesn't sound like a super-unique phrase, notwithstanding the strange word order. I'll give it a shot, but don't get your hopes up," he said looking up at the stack.

"Elinea odrix hasan, be not afraid," he spoke the words, and then took a step back to see the shelves better.

A book on a high shelf glowed yellow-orange. I waited for the librarian to see it.

"Yeah, see," he said, turning to me. "It's just not specific enough, y'know? Is the quote longer than that, or are there any other quotes you can remember?"

"Wait, what?" I asked, pointing at the glowing book. "It's right there. Don't you see it?"

He stared up at the indicated spot but seemed baffled.

"Right there," I repeated. He placed his head near my shoulder to follow my finger, shook his head and frowned. "No, I don't see anything at all. Are you sure?"

"Yeah, I'm looking right at it," I responded. "It's glowing a yellow-orange right there."

"Yellow-orange?" he asked with a chuckle. "They only glow blue." He shrugged. "Are you messing with me?"

"Can I use the ladder myself?" I asked.

"Certainly, just mind your footing, and show me the book when you get back down."

The ladder was attached to the wall, and I wheeled it back until it was next to the glowing book. I ascended the ladder, leaned out, and took it from its resting place. It was heavier than I thought it would be. I tucked it under my arm and began my descent back down the ladder.

When my feet touched the floor, I turned the book over to show him the spine, which was emitting a soft, fire-like glow.

"Let me see that," he said, taking it from me.

"By the gods," he muttered. "It looks like...*paint.*"

"Someone painted over the spine?" I asked, invading his space to inspect it. Sure enough, strokes of paint covered it. They were hard to see in the soft light, but someone went to a lot of trouble to keep the book from glowing at that quote.

"Who would do this?" he asked, wide eyed. "I'm not sure I can get the paint off without ruining the book. But you *can* see a faint blue light if you hold your hand over it, like this." He shot me a look of disbelief. "You got good eyes, kid."

He flipped the book open and sure enough, a number was glowing on the first page.

932.

He flipped to the appropriate page toward the back of the book. The quote was highlighted under a book titled, *Galgian Prehistory II: The Founding of a Nation.*

"Right there," I pressed my finger on the page.

The full quote read, *"Be not afraid, for with thee I am."* *(Page 22)*

"Galgian Prehistory two?" he asked, just above a whisper. "There's a second one?"

"Do you have this book?" I asked.

"If we do," he said, clicking his tongue a few times, his eyes absent, as though deep in thought. "It'd be in the nonfiction section under history, subsection Galgia. Between *Galgian Prehistory One*, and, I imagine, *Galgia: A Modern History Part One.*"

He tucked the book under his arm. "Thanks for helping me find this. I'm going to see what we can do about the paint on the spine of this guy." He pointed across the library. "Non-fiction starts over there. See the sign?"

I nodded. "Got it. Thanks. What's your name, by the way?"

"I'm Corrin." He shook my hand with his free one. "If you need anything else, ask for me."

"Will do, Corrin, thanks." I started across the library. I didn't know if the book would be related in any way to the creature I'd been seeing, but this was the first actual clue I'd come across in a really long time. I entered the indicated section and began searching the shelves for history books. When I finally found them, I didn't have to look far to find Galgian history. I perused the books, sweeping my eyes along their dusty spines.

Nobody had disturbed these books in ages, it seemed. To be fair, Galgian history was a pretty dry subject. Finally, I found the book. I couldn't believe it.

Galgian Prehistory II: The Founding of a Nation.

I pulled it from the shelf, and without bothering to find a desk, flipped to page twenty-two.

It had been torn out.

My jaw dropped.

Pages twenty-three and twenty-four were gone too—neatly torn right along the spine.

Someone didn't want whatever was on these pages to be known. Whoever had torn them might have also been the person who painted the spine of the reference book. I wouldn't have even gotten *this* far had I lacked the ability to see the magic behind that paint.

I gritted my teeth as I realized that I might have stumbled across another conspiracy.

Why is information about our prehistory being censored? What the hell is going on?

I thumbed back to the front of the book to find the table of contents. If they'd forgotten to remove it, that could provide a clue about what they were trying to censor.

I kept going. It seemed like chapter three went on and on about gods and goddesses, some of whom I was familiar with, but others who were unknown to me. It seemed, however, that all the missing information concerned *Galgalim, The Source of All*.

I found the missing pages but a small obstacle. I now knew that someone wanted to keep Galgalim a secret, but I didn't know why. I had a lot of research to do. I was mentally salivating as I closed the book and went back to the front desk as fast as was socially acceptable.

"I'd like to check out this book, please," I said, putting the massive text on the counter.

"You found it?" Corrin asked excitedly.

"Sure did," I said, doing my best to conceal my heavy breathing. "But pages have been torn out of it. Is it possible to order a new copy?"

"The reason I'm so surprised," he said as he hefted a ledger onto the counter, "is because this book isn't recorded in our ledger. As far as our system is concerned, the book on this desk doesn't exist. I'm not sure how to even order a book that isn't recognized by our library. It'll have to be the department administrator's decision."

It makes all the sense in the world now. When I first met the monster in the black abyss, I put in an order for all the books about old deities. This text never found me because the librarians weren't even aware it existed! Who would have gone to so much trouble to hide a book, and yet still leave it on the library shelf like that?

"I don't really know how to check this one out," he said. "Here, I'm going to make my own note of this book in the margins for now. I'm sorry it's damaged. I'll speak to the department head about ordering that new copy for you. What's your name?"

"Sure, thanks," I said as my thoughts scattered this way and that. "Gill Dragstenn. Two N's at the end of Dragstenn."

"Gill," he sounded it out as he wrote. "Dragstenn...All right. It's all yours. Let me know if you find anything interesting," he said with a wink.

"Thanks," I said as I scooped the book off the counter and made for the exit.

Why not just destroy the book outright if you're going to erase it from the ledger? Why leave the book out there for anyone to grab? The missing pages make it seem intentional. Maybe whoever was trying to hide it didn't want the librarians to find a gap and go looking for it. They'd put in a new order when they found out it was missing.

My heart and my mind were working overtime as I hurried back to my room. I cracked the book open on my kitchen table and read through everything about the old gods. Galgalim was mentioned in the intro to the chapter on page twenty—it's believed Galgia itself was *named after him.*

How was it possible that our nation was named after a deity, and we knew next to nothing about them? By now, it was clear that the information was being suppressed. Someone didn't want people knowing, but to what end?

Six thirty came around before I knew it, and I snuck out to the bathhouse to meet the guys. Axle was a hundred percent right, hardly anybody was out past the courtyard. As I neared the bathhouse, I could hear the muffed voices from within.

I changed into my shorts and went through the sliding door to the hot springs. Both jumped as though they'd been busted, Atlas even letting slip a high pitched yelp. They chuckled with relief when they saw me and settled back into the steamy waters.

"Gill," Atlas said as he closed his eyes. "You scared me."

"Nobody has any reason to be out here," Axle reassured him. "I've spent a lot of Sunday evenings out here. Never seen another soul, I promise."

I stepped into the water, and although it felt too hot at first, I quickly acclimated. I never had a problem with public spaces, but I had to admit, I liked having the bath-house all to ourselves. I closed my eyes, breathing in as the hot water soaked into my bones and steam wafted into my nose.

"Speaking of which," Atlas asked, "does having us here make it noisy for you? You know, mentally?"

"Not at all," Axle answered. "I've been meaning to tell you guys. Since I've started hanging out with you all, your voices have become like white noise to me. They're easy to tune out. It's not stressful, not even a little bit. In fact, it's become a comfort."

"Well, if that's not the sweetest thing," Atlas remarked. "Gill, did you hear that?"

"Not to be cold or anything," I replied, "but isn't there something more pressing to talk about, Axle?"

"Not yet," he said with a sly smile.

"Why?" I asked.

"Why what?" He stared back.

"Why are we *waiting*, Axle?" I said, frustrated.

The door slid open behind me.

Fena. In. A. Bikini.

"Hey, guys!" she said with a friendly smile, taking a few steps and dipping her toe in the water.

"That's why," he smirked at me.

You know that feeling in your stomach when you slide down a steep slide, where you're excited but aware of the potential danger? I felt *that*, but in my shorts.

I swallowed and turned my eyes forward. I didn't want Atlas to know anything, but the way I snapped my head away like that would have been a dead giveaway to anyone who *wasn't* a powerful young mage with his pinky in his nose.

She slid into the hot spring and made a noise in her throat that made my loins do a flip.

Axle. You absolute bastard. You didn't say she was joining us.

"Thank you for joining us," Axle said to her, as though he were suppressing a laugh.

I'm going to get you back for this.

"Good to have you back for this," he said to her, his smile widening. "Wouldn't have wanted to repeat this story."

"Oh, for sure," she responded, sinking down to her chin. "Wouldn't have missed it."

"I thought you weren't interested in the investigation," Atlas said to Fena, his tone dripping with snark. He might have enjoyed hanging out with us without his sister.

"Never said I wasn't *interested*," she replied as she closed her eyes. "I don't think we should put ourselves in compromising situations to *further* the investigation."

"Well, we're all here," I said, turning to Axle. "Come on. Did you figure anything out?"

Everyone stared at him as he closed his eyes and rubbed his chin.

He opened them and smiled. "You might just say..."

He paused for dramatic effect.

"I did."

Twenty-Four

The tension was as thick as the steam that filled the bathhouse. The three of us waited in silence for Axle's report as he organized his thoughts—or relished our undivided attention.

"The first thing I want to say is that although I did hear some interesting information, I'm not sure how it fits together or whether it's even related to our investigation. I made sure to write it all down in case it was important."

"Did you hide it somewhere safe?" I asked.

He blinked at me few times, surprised, "Um. I'm the guy with a boarded-up window and wards on his walls," he shot back. "*No*, I left it out on my table, Gill." He gave me an exaggerated thumbs-up and a wink.

"Just making sure," I said. "I'll tell you more later, but Vega broke into my room today and searched my dorm."

"Uh, whoa, what?" Fena blurted out. "Can they even *do* that?"

"Apparently so," Atlas said. "They did that to you, Gill?"

"Yeah," I affirmed. "It's the second time my dorm has been searched, actually."

"My room was searched today, too," Axle spoke up. "They broke in during my meeting with the headmasters. When I got back, the staff questioned me about my locks and wardings."

"Do you think it made them suspicious?" asked Fena.

"At first," he said. "But they laughed in my face when I warned them about what's really out there watching us and listening."

"Creatures from another planet," Atlas nodded knowingly. "Don't worry. I believe you, Axle," he reassured him.

"Means you won't be surprised when they come for us," Axle replied, leaning his elbows on the wooden walkway behind him. "We're awake in a world that sleeps, my man."

"I'm pretty sure this violates the contract we signed when we agreed to dorm here," Fena said in what was a refreshing return to reality. "I kept my copy," she added. "I'll be going over it with a magnifying glass one of these nights."

"The point is," I interrupted, "we need to be careful about what we keep in our rooms."

"Don't even worry, my man," Axle said. "I wrote it down in a language I invented. I call it Axillian." He grinned.

I only just stopped myself rolling my eyes. Of course, he had his own language. I sometimes forgot that he was crazy. *Correct* from time to time, but still crazy.

"Good," I sighed with relief. "I'm sorry I interrupted you."

"Can you teach me Axillian?" asked Atlas.

"So, I guess, break down what you can for us, Axle," Fena jumped in, ignoring her little brother's request.

"Right, right," he answered, clearing his throat. "Vega stormed out of the room before the meeting. I could hear him clearly; he must have been riled. One way or another, he knows for a fact that you're lying to them, Gill. There were no maybe's or probably's about it. He's got it in for you, pal."

"How could he know?" asked Atlas. "*Tovin* started that fight. Gill wasn't lying when he said he was innocent."

"I don't think it has anything to do with the bistro battle," Axle said, lowering his gaze to the water.

"I wager you're right," Fena piped up. "Vega is still riled up about finding out who was in the hallways the night Gill went looking for his lost money clip. That was never resolved, remember?"

"Yeah," I nodded. "I think pinning the fight on me was a means to an end."

"But if there was any provable way Gill could be tied to the Hall Monitor situation," Atlas contended, "he would be standing in front of the headmasters explaining himself, right?"

"Any *provable* way," Fena repeated, deep in thought. "Maybe he *knows* Gill is his culprit in some way that he can't prove to the other headmasters."

"Or," Atlas said, with a nod to his sister, "in a way that wouldn't also implicate *him* in something. Don't forget, the folks who chased Gill that night were trying to silence him."

"That's possible, too," I pointed at him. "Because I've got a hunch that Vega is doing something behind the other head-masters' backs."

"About that," Axle spoke up. "I had never *heard* Vega speak until this morning. He's not part of anything that puts him in every student's way, like Headmaster Rowan or Headmaster Alrune are." He paused, then looked me in the eye, "Gill. The thoughts I heard that night; the thoughts we assumed were the inquisitor's. They were *Vega's*."

"W-what?" I stared at him. "I don't understand!"

"Wait, so it was Vega who was chasing him?" asked Fena, glancing between the two of us. "Doesn't he sleep? How is that possible?"

"It *isn't* possible," I stated as I searched my memories. "I *saw* Imandr that night. He had the same beard and clothing.

Vega doesn't have a beard like that. I don't think he ever *has*, either."

"There *is* appearance-altering magic out there," said Atlas. "You have to take that into consideration."

"But at the meeting—" I stopped short. I'd only just caught myself. I looked at Axle.

He sighed. "It's okay, Gill. You can think it to me, and I can say it."

"But," I hesitated, "didn't they…"

"No," he said. "They didn't censor me. They said…I didn't have any friends," he looked away. "And that nobody on campus would believe a word out of my mouth anyway."

"Aww, Axle," Fena said as she shot me a hurt expression.

"It's all right," he said. "Means that they're not watching me. And that's a very good thing. What Gill was about to say is that during his meeting, they said the student in the hallway ran from Imandr. The headmasters appeared to agree on this fact, even in their heads. So, we can assume that it was Imandr, and not someone cloaked as him."

"But then how…" Fena asked.

"Maybe," I said, carefully considering my words. "Maybe he's a *telepath*."

"A telepath?" Atlas asked. "Like someone who can project their thoughts?"

"They *have* existed," his sister confirmed.

"And it's a strong possibility," Axle said with renewed vigor. "If Vega was sending mental messages to Imandr, it's a hundred percent possible I was hearing *his* thoughts."

"And if there *were* a living telepath," I cut in, "they would be among the powerful in this country. But why would Vega be cursing at Imandr's partner that night?"

"The miserable miscreation line," Atlas said, rubbing his chin. "It's been bothering me, too."

A long silence settled over us.

"The mystery deepens, I guess." Axle spoke up first. "But I've got a few more noteworthy pieces of information."

"Maybe it'll help glue all of this together," Fena said, nodding at him. "Lay it on us."

"I can say with a degree of confidence that Vega, Rowan, and Huede are investigating for a different reason than the rest of them."

"A different reason?" I prodded. "What do you mean?"

"Well, it was like you thought," he responded. "Headmasters Alrune, Norah, Edwin, and Anther were relaxed. I found it difficult to catch a snippet of their inner dialogues. Vega, Rowan, and Huede *dominated* the mental conversation. They were *worried*. Worried that whoever was in the hallway that night saw something they called *the procession*."

"The procession?" asked Fena. "As in a funeral procession?"

"I didn't get enough context," Axle said, "but there are different kinds of processions."

"Like festival processions," I spoke up. "Or processions as part of old ceremonies. I was reading an interesting book this afternoon about the old gods of this planet. Each of them demanded of the people an annual procession of worship."

"Eh?" Atlas cocked his head. "*I've* never heard of that."

"Worship," Axle said, deep in thought. "I heard that word twice among the three of them, but it never added up. You think they were talking about the worship of an old god?"

"But," Fena broke in, "that would be *heresy*."

"Indeed," Atlas's eyes rose to meet mine. "That would give them a *motive*."

"A reason to *kill* whoever might have seen the procession," Fena said, as she and Axle looked at me.

All three watched me with worried expressions. "Maybe we're jumping to conclusions," Axle said.

"I don't think we are," I said, folding my arms. "In fact, I'd say we're on the right track."

"Gill?" asked Atlas. "What's going on? Did you find something out?"

"I think I did," I answered. "Do you all remember when we were all in my room for the first time—right after the night I was chased through the halls? I told you Tovin killed me, but it was a long story, and I would explain it to you later. Well, it's later. It's time to tell you guys about the creature."

"The creature?" Fena asked, her eyes full of wonder. "Story time. Now."

"Yeah," I said. "When Tovin killed me that first time, I was surrounded by an inky blackness that was both calming and terrifying. An eye opened and settled on me. I was so scared I couldn't speak, couldn't move. Then there were *many*. Eyes opened all around its body, not pairs of eyes. Just...eyes."

I took a deep breath and let my arms fall to my sides. "Some of them moved together—oscillating around the main eyeball. But all of them stayed trained on me as though they belonged to the same creature. It's so hard to describe. I've tried thinking of better ways to explain, but I can't."

"Gill," Atlas spoke up, moving through the water until he was by my side. "That time, outside of Headmaster Alrune's office. When you asked me if I saw anything unusual when I died...was this what you meant?"

I nodded.

"Gill, are you serious?" Fena asked, moving closer to me. "You poor thing," she said as she wrapped her fingers around my hand beneath the water.

I squeezed.

"He's serious," Axle assured them. "I've heard you before, Gill. Thinking about eyes. Darkness. A creature. I've wanted to ask, but it never seemed right. Why have you been hiding this?"

"I...I didn't hide it from you on purpose," I explained, trying to stay focused as Fena cradled my hand in hers. "It just never came up. But now..."

"Now what?" Atlas asked. "Do you think that creature pertains to the investigation somehow?"

"That's kind of a leap," said Fena.

"Maybe so," I looked at her, "but I think he's right."

"Gill, what's going on?" Axle asked.

I explained *everything*. How the headmasters tried to pin the situation at the bistro on me, how Tovin covered for me by killing me, and how I had my second run-in with the many-eyed monster.

"You're telling me all of that happened *today?*" Fena yelled, splashing water at me. "Gill!"

"I'm only now realizing that your bruise is gone," Axle said, inspecting my cheek. "How could you keep all of that to yourself until now? I guess that explains what you were doing in the conference room today."

"That's a lot to carry all on your own," Atlas chimed in. "You should have told us sooner."

"I figured I'd wait until we were together again," I said. "It's a long story, and it's not done."

"Be not afraid." Atlas repeated the phrase. "Can you be certain that's what it said to you?"

I explained my trip to the library. How Corrin and I searched for the quote and found that the information had been obfuscated in every way short of outright destroying the book.

"There's an old deity called Galgalim, the Source of All," I announced.

"Gal-guh-lim?" Axle sounded it out.

"That's right," I said. "And that's about *all* I know about it. That and..."

"What?" Atlas inquired.

"I think Galgalim is the deity I've been seeing in the afterlife."

"I'd be...*careful* about where you say that," Fena warned, letting go of my hand. "The old gods aren't worshiped anymore. Heresy is one of the few things punishable by immediate execution."

"I'm not technically worshiping an old god," I said, defending myself.

"Just *acknowledging* an old god's existence in any way that suggests it's not wholly mythological," Atlas cautioned, "is *absolutely* grounds for being declared a heretic."

"Hahnahkordia, Atebe, and Olwoh," Axle said, "are the *only* gods considered to be old gods that are still worshiped in Galgia. Listen to us, man. This is no joke. We could be killed along *with* you for having a conversation like this."

"There's nobody around," I said. "You said it yourself."

"We're just letting you know that this conversation never happened," Fena looked around at the three of us. "And it never will *again*. From this point forward. Promise me."

There was no way I was about to stop chasing this lead now, not after all the time I had spent searching for answers. "I promise...Never to speak the name Galgalim. I'll call it the monster. Can we still talk about it if I do that?"

A brief silence, and then Atlas nodded. "I think that's sufficient. If anyone asks, you could say you're writing a book."

"Sure," Axle smiled. "I'm on board with that."

"Okay," Fena surrendered. "I suppose there's no harm in that. I'm willing to be expelled for you, Gill, but I'm not willing to die for anyone but my brother."

"That's super fair," I conceded. "Thanks, you guys."

"So let me put this all together then," Axle said, lifting himself out of the water and sitting on the edge of the walkway. "The working theory is that Vega, Huede, and Rowan are all heretics worshiping a monster late at night on school grounds?"

"And Vega was telepathically speaking with the inquisitor that night?" Atlas asked, glancing around at us.

"That's why the inquisitor was here in the first place," Fena folded her arms. "To investigate heresy."

"Of which, had I witnessed any of it," I said, "could have implicated the participating headmasters in a crime punishable by death..."

After a long silence, all of us sighed.

"Nah," we all said at once.

Even Axle shook his head, and he believed in moon people. The pieces didn't fit tightly enough together. If the inquisitor was on official business looking into whispers of heresy, then he would be working *with* the heretics.

"Well..." Axle said, "I'll keep my mind open for fleeting thoughts from the headmasters."

"I'll keep turning this around in my head too," said Atlas.

"We've got a lot of information here for sure," Fena concurred. "Any random clue could bring it all together. Maybe more can be found at the library."

"I put in an order for a new copy of the book," I added. "I hope it'll come in without any torn-out pages."

Atlas looked at me, wide-eyed. "You...you did what?"

I stared back. "I...put in a request with Corrin for a new copy of *Galgian Prehistory II*."

"Gill, someone is trying to keep that information out of peoples' hands," Atlas pressed. "Don't you think that was a little risky?"

"Well, at the time I didn't consider these two things to be connected," I said, shrugging. "How could I have known?"

"They still might not be," Axle interjected. "We're making a lot of leaps in logic here."

"Also, I've met Corrin," Fena spoke up. "He seems like a nice guy. I don't think he's in on the coverup if there is one."

"Well, the book wasn't in their system," I said. "He said he'd have to go through the administrative head of the department to order a new copy, so—"

"What?" Axle screamed.

Atlas jumped.

Fena stood up, her top coming loose in the process.

Atlas yelled about his neck as Fena dove back into the water.

Absolute pandemonium.

I stood and balled my fists. "Wh-what's the big idea screaming like that?" I yelled.

"The big idea?" he yelled back incredulously.

"Lower your voice!" I shouted.

"I can't!"

"Why?" I hollered.

"Vega runs that department, Gill!"

"What?" I grabbed my head with both hands. "Since freaking when?"

"This year," he cried out, grabbing his face.

I screamed in panic.

He screamed in panic.

"I saw my sister's boobs," Atlas sobbed.

"Everyone shut up!" Fena screamed over us as she fidgeted beneath the water. Her face was deep red. She eyed the three of us, "It's not that late. The library should still be open. Let's just get over there and cancel the request."

The bathhouse was silent, save for the sounds of our breathing.

"If they *are* connected..." Axle broke the silence. "Then this couldn't get much worse."

"I agree," Fena said, climbing out of the water. "The odds

are low, but we can't take the risk," she called back to us as she rounded the corner to the women's changing area.

"All right, then," Axle said. "That's the plan. Let's hope Corrin didn't submit that request yet," he said as he reached down and helped Atlas out.

"Gill, let's go," Axle offered me his hand.

I glanced at him sideways, "Why don't you give me a second..."

"What?" His face assumed what I can only describe as the most disappointed one he could make at me. "Oh."

"Yeah."

"What's going on?" asked Atlas.

"Nothing, he'll catch up," Axle said, grabbing Atlas by the arm. "C'mon, let's get dressed."

"What? Hey, you're hurting my arm!"

———

The four of us made our way to the east wing's main walkway. The sun had begun to set, and it illuminated the walkway up to the library's large, ostentatious doors. It was far less crowded than it had been—desolate even.

The doors echoed as they closed behind us.

"I've never seen it this empty," whispered Axle.

"Me either," Atlas said. "Not that I've been on campus for very long."

I didn't see Corrin or *anyone* for that matter. We walked across the massive room and stopped at the help desk.

"Hello?" I called out.

Nobody answered.

"Did they close already?" Fena asked. "I've been in here later than this by an hour at least."

"On a Sunday?" Atlas asked as I walked around the desk. The drawer was locked, and the keys were missing. I didn't know what was going on, but I didn't like it. If it really was Vega trying to keep that book out of people's hands, then ordering a copy of it would prove he was right to be worried about me; that I was investigating.

"What are you doing?" Atlas hissed.

"I was looking for the ledger," I said, looking up at him. "The keys are gone so..."

A tall, cloaked figure stood just inside the shadow of the shelves on the upper balcony at the far end of the library.

I wouldn't have noticed, had it not had a magic signature that blazed like a star in the darkness. All I could do was open my mouth as I stared at the masked man—the same one who'd been waiting for me on the other side of the door to the east wing thoroughfare that night.

Human or not—

It was watching us.

Twenty-Five

"Gill?"

"Hey, you okay?"

"What's the matter with you?"

Their voices sounded as though far away in the distance; I couldn't turn away from the mass of magical energy on the balcony. I could just barely make out the contours of its mask against the darkness of the upper floor.

Before I could gather the words together in my throat, Atlas followed my gaze to the balcony. Then Fena, and finally Axle. The four of us stared at it, speechless.

Axle moved his arms in semicircles then clasped hands in the direction of the balcony.

"Gill..." Fena whispered. "Is that the guy who chased you? The one with the mask?"

"Yeah," I said as quietly as I was able with my nerves on fire. "That's the one."

"Axle?" asked Atlas. "Does it...sound familiar? In your head?"

He swallowed, "Y-yeah. It's the thing I heard that night. No doubt about it."

"What's it thinking?" I asked without moving my eyes.

"It's the same," he said. "Single sentences—commands it seems—in the same tone and inflection. Something like... Protect the algorithm. Break and retrieve. Protect the algorithm. And so on. Now that I'm hearing it again, I can say for certain..." His eyes were wide and glossy. "That thing is *not* human."

"Break...and retrieve?" murmured Atlas.

Its magic began to swell within its chest. "Hey," I warned. "Its magic is riling up. It's about to do something!"

"Parameters. Four," Axle spoke as it thought. "Consider retreat. Ejecting sleep agent. Assess results. Act accordingly." Axle frowned. "What the he—"

Before he could finish his sentence, it opened its cloak with a clank. Four projectiles shot from its chest, and, had it not been for the glint of a glass object headed my way, I wouldn't have dodged it in time. I broke left as it whizzed past my arm.

I fell to the floor, then scrambled to my knees.

"What was that?" I screamed

Fena and Axle slumped to the floor.

Atlas stared at the syringe sticking out of his midsection, his face twisted up in fear and disbelief. He lifted his shaking hand and pulled the syringe out. He then searched around under his jacket and removed a pocket watch. Its face was cracked, and it leaked blue liquid.

He looked down at Axle and Fena, and then up at the cloaked figure on the balcony.

"Gill..." he asked. "Are...Are they...?"

"N-no." I cut him off. "Axle said the words *sleep agent* before the attack. I think...I think that thing meant to put us all to sleep."

"To retrieve us," Atlas finished for me in a wavering voice. "Its odds weren't good against the four of us."

"But now..." I trailed off as it stepped out of the shadows and hopped over the balcony railing. It landed with a crash on the other side of the library, down the main walkway.

"Parameters acceptable," it said in a bone-chilling monotone voice just loud enough to be heard in the silence of the library.

Axle was right; that was no human being. It was cold; alien in a way I couldn't describe.

"At...las..." A voice so quiet that I almost didn't notice it came from behind me. Fena's eyes were slits and she was struggling to remain conscious. "Atlas...D-don't...lose...no matter..."

With that, her head fell to the side, and her consciousness slipped away from her.

"I promise," he whispered back, tossing his busted pocket watch to the ground.

Atlas looked different. Normally he was reserved, almost docile.

But now...

His intensity almost looked out of place. The scorn in his eyes sent a chill down my spine.

I turned and faced the enemy with renewed vigor. Everything was riding on the two of us here. There was no telling where we'd end up if we let that thing drag us away.

"Ha-*ten!*"

My sword fell into my hand.

"Atlas, get ready," I said as I widened my stance.

"Right," he responded, his magic glowing within him.

The cloaked figure started toward us across the long carpet, each footfall echoing around the room. Its arms surfaced, each a sharpened sickle, like a praying mantis. Some kind of energy hummed throughout its being as it broke into a sprint, and the humming grew louder as it drew nearer.

"It can't kill you on school grounds," Atlas called out. "It'll try to render us unconscious!"

"Hence the sleeping agent," I responded, connecting the dots as I moved in front of him. "I'll take point. You look for an opening and fire away when you do. Don't worry about catching me in the blast either."

"You expect me to just *hit* you?" he asked.

"If that's what it takes, then yes. The school will resurrect me when my heart stops, but I'd hazard a guess that whatever that thing is, it doesn't have a heart."

"...All right," he conceded.

"Don't miss, okay? I'm counting on you, Atlas."

The masked creature was upon us, and it shed its cloak, spreading its sickles wide. Its body was the same color as its mask, but unlike the mask, its body wasn't humanlike. Its two legs separated, giving it four legs total, enhancing its speed and range of movement.

Its torso separated, giving it a height advantage. On its chest were four empty depressions—likely where it fired the syringes from. Hoses and thin cables ran along its body, and what looked like spinning pinwheels were mounted behind gates on both its shoulders.

It was the most horrifying thing I'd seen in all my life.

What in the name of the gods am I looking at? Can I really fight this thing? No. I have *to. Everything is riding on this. There's no room for failure; no room for doubt.*

There was no more time to think before the fighting began. It lifted its sickle-like appendage and brought it down fast, aiming for my shoulder. I stepped out of range and swung my sword at the joint on its arm. My strike was true, but the blade just bounced off it.

I reflexively looked up into its dead-eyed mask, and it bashed me with the back of its arm, sending me to the ground with a buzz running through my body. I rolled a few times before colliding with a bookcase; hardcover novels rained down on me as I got to my feet.

I glanced at my arm—all of my hair was standing on end.

I looked up to see the creature racing toward me.

Its arms. They're buzzing with electricity. *But this isn't any kind of casting I know. What's going on?*

I rolled out of the way as it took another stab at me and tripped backwards over a pile of books narrowly avoiding a follow up attack. The carpet hummed beneath each strike as I managed to avoid it again and again.

It seemed to have difficulty tracking me the way a real person would, but it was still too close for comfort. I backpedaled into a narrow aisle, and it marched in after me.

I envisioned the symbol for Aero Slice and cast it as soon as I was ready. Though it was one of my cheaper spells, it would help me gauge the toughness of the creature's hide.

I swung my sword, firing a gale of razor wind down the aisle. It lifted its arms to defend itself, but it broke through the shimmering blade of wind, seemingly unscathed. If Aero Slice failed to even dent it, my sword wouldn't do a *damn* thing. My options began to wane as I considered my next move. I would have to throw everything I had in my tome at it if I wanted to live to see tomorrow. Then, suddenly, Atlas appeared on the other side of the aisle behind the monstrosity as it barreled toward me.

"Gill!" he called across the library. "Duck!"

All I could do was trust him. I dropped backward onto the floor and lifted my sword to defend myself as it brought its sickle down. It glanced off my sword and into my shoulder, pinning me to the floor. A shock ran through me, and I couldn't help but scream—it felt like my body was allergic to itself.

All in an instant, it was blown away in a blinding beam of magical energy that passed just inches from my face. It crashed into the wall, and I managed to turn over onto my elbows to get a better look.

It fell to the floor in a crumpled heap. It scrambled to lift itself, but one of its sickles was missing. Furthermore, one of its hoses appeared to be severed, some strange liquid pouring out of it onto the floor.

Atlas appeared at my side and helped me to my feet, "Gill! You're bleeding!"

"I'm fine," I said through my teeth as I gripped my shoulder. "Thanks for the warning. I know I told you to hit me, but..." I watched the creature struggle around on the floor. "That looked *painful*."

The masked monster twisted its segmented body around once and discarded what remained of its severed sickle and tattered hose. It spun its head around, the hole where its hose used to be closing like a window as it did.

It stared at us through its cracked mask as if reevaluating its odds. The latches on the sides of its chest plate flipped open, until the plate clattered to the floor. Three cables fell out of each side and dangled down past its midsection, buzzing with static electricity.

It lowered itself to the floor.

"It's not done!" I called out just as it launched. It was somehow faster than before, and it ran toward us in a serpentine pattern.

"Encai Orah Hext!" Atlas screamed, throwing his arms forward. A violent tide of shadow rolled through the aisle as though it had a mind of its own. The spell was so powerful I had to brace myself against its backdraft, holding my arms in front of my face.

The dark energy manifested as writhing black tentacles that wrapped around the creature before hoisting it up past the second floor of the library. The tentacles almost reached the ceiling before coming down and slamming into the ground with concussive force, the rest of the energy dogpiling on top of it. The impact was such that it shook the entire building and blew out the nearest windows

I glanced at Atlas with wonder, surprise, and a tinge of fear.

"Atlas..." I said, a smile forming on my lips. "You're *incredible!*"

No sooner had the words left my mouth than the dark energy split from the source and coiled around Atlas's ankles and then his legs, working its way up to his chest. He gritted his teeth and fell to one knee before dropping his arms and ending the spell.

His mana reserves had been drained, but even atrophied, they were at least quadruple my own.

"Are you okay, Atlas?" I asked as I knelt next to him, the shadows receding.

"Shadow magic," he wheezed. "Every time I use it, I swear it'll be the last time," he said with a soft chuckle.

I let myself laugh with him, worried though I was. I turned back toward the enemy and found it lying on the library floor among a pile of scattered books, pinned, in part by a toppled bookshelf.

"I think that did it," I said standing to examine it from a distance. "Stay here. I'll make sure."

"Be careful, Gill," Atlas managed before he fell back on his hands. "I need a sec. The shadows really took me for a ride."

I made my way across the library, stopping about seven feet away. To my eyes, at least, it appeared to have gone dark; no hum, no magical signature. I sighed with relief and leaned against a bookshelf.

A noise caught my attention. The creature lifted itself from the wreckage, books and debris sliding off it.

"Wh-what in..." I stammered as I took a step back.

It whirred as it turned over and crawled away, one inch at a time. "Retreat," it said in a broken voice. "Pro...tect...the Gal...galim..."

A pop, and its form went limp. I stared at it for several seconds, repeating what it said over and over again in my head.

Axle had misheard. It hadn't been thinking *protect the algorithm*. What it *had* been thinking was much worse.

Atlas appeared next to me, trying to manage his breathing. "Did...that thing just say...?"

"Yeah," I affirmed. "I'm glad you heard it, too."

"Gill...You know what this means now?"

I paused. "...We should go see if Axle and your sister are all right."

"Yeah."

The two of us hopped over the destroyed bookshelf and hurried back across the library toward the help desk. I knelt next to Axle and propped him up, my shoulder surging with pain as I did.

Atlas picked Fena up the same way and examined her. "She's bleeding from her head," he said in a shaky voice. "Gill!"

I gently set Axle down and rushed to her side.

It wasn't a worrying amount of blood, but it still presented the possibility that she was concussed. It was probable that the best action I could take would be to kill her right here and now.

"What is the *meaning* of this?" came a voice from the east wing entrance.

Vega was standing in the doorway of the library. His eyes bore into us.

"*You two!*" he screamed, starting toward us. His face was shriveled up with a fury so intense I could feel it from where I stood. "You stay *right* where you are!"

Twenty-Six

"My goodness!" Alrune came through the other entrance to the library and made his way down the main walkway as quickly as his old bones allowed. "What happened here?"

Vega cursed under his breath and gritted his teeth. His face reflected his every emotion, and it was clear that he'd hoped to clean this up before anyone else arrived.

Unfortunately for him, Alrune was a sensory type like myself. Atlas's casting would have felt like fireworks to him, no matter where he was on campus.

I locked eyes with Vega, and we had a silent conversation.

By this point, he wasn't trying to hide it. He was after me, and now my friends, too.

Alrune gasped at the wrecked shelves.

"By the *gods*."

He turned, spying Atlas and me, and then Fena's and Axle's unmoving bodies.

His face softened. "What happened to these students?" His voice cracked with worry, assuring me that Alrune didn't have anything to do with this—he could be trusted.

I sighed my heaviest sigh ever and dropped my shoulders. The relief was overwhelming. If someone hadn't stumbled upon us, I didn't want to think what might have happened.

Anther and Wuthrand hurried in from behind Alrune. Wuthrand jogged down the length of the carpet toward us, his face wracked with concern.

"They were *fighting*," Vega interjected in a venomous tone. "In the *library* of all places!"

"We were fighting for our *lives!*" I snapped. "Against that...that *thing* over there!"

"You're trying to distract us!" Vega screamed, creating a spectacle. "I've had *enough* of you defacing our prestigious institution!"

"Just see for yourself," Atlas said, ignoring his obvious attempt at a smokescreen. "It's still over there."

Wuthrand took a detour toward the destroyed shelves, and I watched as a bead of sweat raced down Vega's brow. This was suddenly out of his control. He had probably never been this close to the web he was weaving.

After a couple of seconds, Wuthrand shouted, "This...this is *Diesel machinery!*"

A part of me worried that the thing had escaped while we weren't looking. The fact that they had eyes on it meant that the four of us would stand a chance against Vega's accusations.

That was some luck I wasn't used to.

"What?" Vega shouted, hamming it up. "Impossible!"

He and the other headmasters joined Wuthrand by the wreckage. Those gathered shared worried glances. They didn't need words to know what the others were thinking. A Diesel machine in ENU's hall presented major implications.

"To think their technology has come this far," uttered Anther just loud enough for us to hear.

"It's hardly recognizable from what they deployed in the

war," Alrune added, sparking up his pipe. "This is a wakeup call, gentlemen."

"But how did it manage to infiltrate the school?" asked Vega, predictably feigning ignorance.

Within moments, the library was packed with inquisitors and other staff. Atlas and I were ushered away quickly while Fena and Axle were hurried off to the infirmary for a medical evaluation. It wasn't until I was sitting in a chair being grilled by inquisitors that one of them noticed I was bleeding through my clothes. They argued with each other as I was whisked away to the infirmary. My consciousness was fading in and out as I stumbled down the crowded halls.

One of the last things I remembered before passing out was lying down in an infirmary bed. I hadn't even had time to process that we had likely just defended ourselves against modern Diesel machinery— and in some capacity, Vega was involved. I remembered thinking that it wasn't safe to fall asleep, then reminding myself that the school was filled with inquisitors. I wondered if they were trustworthy as I fought a hopeless battle against the complete mental shutdown that eventually swallowed me whole.

———

"Get up."

My eyes shot open, and reality flooded back in. I lifted my head to see two men in inquisitors' robes standing at the end of my bed. I had been moved to my room at some point. Atlas, Fena, and Axle stood behind them, pale-faced and in full uniform. Atlas managed a small smile for me as he wrung his hands. I couldn't form the words in my mouth, but it was great to see them.

"Get dressed," ordered one of the inquisitors. "Your cooperation is mandatory for the official incident report."

I lifted myself onto my elbows and winced from the pain in my chest. The gurney parked next to my bed told a darker story, but it seemed the medics had deemed me fit to heal naturally. I was still dressed in a medical gown with my butt hanging out. Before I could ask, the inquisitors turned around and ushered the others out of my room.

After I was dressed to the letter, the four of us were marched quietly down the halls toward the north wing. Students, it seemed, had been confined to their dorms. All of their doors were open, and they were sitting in their doorways discussing what had happened with their neighbors across the hall. It wasn't light-hearted or fun either; they were discussing the possibility of imminent war and watching us as we passed them by.

When we entered the meeting room, we were met not by the headmasters we had come to know and expect, but rather by unfamiliar and serious faces. Headmaster Rowan was the only member of the school's staff in attendance. The rest were inquisitors, senators, and even a member of the high priests.

I had never seen one of their order in person before, but for the way he was dressed, it was unmistakable. He was wearing a brown leather cloak trimmed in gold over a deep crimson robe encrusted with blue gems, over a white tunic made from the finest fabrics. Against his left shoulder were tied three scrolls which carried their creed— not that they would ever forget a single word written therein, but as dictated by tradition dating back generations.

The entire ensemble, however, was modest compared to the solid gold mask that each of them donned during public appearances. It was expertly crafted to look like a human face with a stern expression, a blue jewel set in the forehead, and a neatly sculpted and tied up beard. I couldn't help but marvel at the craftsmanship as we were shown to our seats. The mask of the high priest following me across the room instilled within me a new understanding of what a big deal this was.

I was living through the history that would be printed in future textbooks. I recentered myself as we took our seats. I glanced at the others before it all began. Where I had hoped to see Fena's cool and relaxed demeanor, I found a furrowed brow and an anxious glance. Axle's confident smile was a ghost on his lips; his eyes darted left and right down the table as a bead a sweat raced down his neck. Atlas was literally chewing his fingernails as the high priest's attendant opened her book. She placed her pen against the paper and the meeting began.

They peppered us with questions for hours, sometimes under the effects of spells that weren't familiar or explained to us. Axle attempted to interject a couple of times but was immediately shut down by the inquisitor nearest to him. It was made clear to us we were only to answer, not to ask. They would sometimes have one or more of us leave the room, and their questions didn't always make sense. After they had collected what must have been a satisfactory amount of data, they left the meeting room only to be replaced by the school's headmasters for a second round of exhaustive questioning.

Only this time we were allowed to speak more freely— and we did. While we didn't have the evidence to accuse a certain headmaster of a multitude of crimes, the facts were on our side when it came to the subject of immediate expulsion; a subject favored by the headmaster in question. Vega tried every avenue he could think of to cast blame on the four of us, but the other headmasters were having none of it. We were victims here and despite his efforts, Vega was unable to spin the events convincingly.

He stormed out, as I had become accustomed to watching him do when he didn't get his way. To my surprise however, we were separated and individually questioned about Vega specifically. They grilled us about Inquisitor Imandr too. Turned out he wasn't on the high priest's payroll at all. He was a rogue former member of inquisitors. How he had been cleared to be on campus was going to be an investigation all its own.

The Diesel machine had been recovered and disassembled. The higher ups had taken to calling it a *Stalker*, and I was questioned relentlessly about it. Atlas and I were the only ones who could speak to how it moved and operated, what kind of weapons it deployed, and how intelligently it adapted to combat situations. They were unable to verify my claims that it was filled with magic.

It seemed Atlas's final gambit to destroy the stalker with a tide of shadow devoured any traces of magic that existed inside of it, and as an unintended consequence, it scrubbed Vega's hands of the whole thing. Without being able to prove there was a magical element to the stalker's design, there was no avenue to suggest that someone at the college was involved.

We were held until sundown Monday night, all of us sent back to our rooms under strict supervision. The following morning the investigation continued with more high priests visiting the school. All four of us missed our classes to be interrogated further by the high priests and their inquisitors. Diesel hysteria swept through the college as students and faculty began reporting anything and everything as suspicious.

Vega's newest gambit was to scream about how the Diesel Empire had sent a machine kitted for retrieval of Atlas Grimbrooke, the new boy-prodigy. If it was meant to deflect suspicion from himself and turn peoples' attention somewhere else, it worked. It seemed the senators and high priests were willing to buy that explanation as Atlas became a main subject of the meetings that followed.

The syringe meant for Atlas had struck his pocket watch, sparing him the dose of serum administered by the stalker—

however the tip of the projectile had fully pierced the cover of the watch, injecting the liquid into the device itself. The inquisitors were able to retrieve a sizable enough portion to confirm that it was a sleep agent meant to immediately render the target unconscious.

After they were good and sure that I didn't know anything else, they finally released me back to my room around 4 o' clock. I was escorted back and informed that I hadn't missed my classes; they had all been cancelled for Tuesday, probably to ensure a speedy and unhindered investigation of the college. The inquisitors were *everywhere,* and I was grateful for it. I didn't feel safe at the school anymore.

By that night, we were given the okay to move around the east wing. Classes would resume in the morning, and one of the headmasters would talk about the situation in our first-period classes. Not long after we were given the okay to leave our dorms, I got a knock at my door.

I opened it a crack and peeked out to see Axle standing in the hallway, an inquisitor on patrol passing behind him. "Hey," he smiled. "Can I come in?"

I opened the door and before I knew it, he had me wrapped up in a bear hug.

"So glad you're okay, my man," he said, squeezing tighter before letting me go. He patted me on the shoulder twice. I winced in pain, and he retracted his hand as though I were on fire.

"Wait, *are* you okay?" he asked, looking me over.

"I'm fine," I said through clenched teeth as I closed and locked the door.

"Well, all right then. Don't know if you need to lock that, by the way," he said, falling into my mattress. "Inquisitors are *everywhere,* and I'm sure Atlas and Fena are on their way right now."

"Are you wearing your shoes on my bed?" I asked.

"Trust me," he said with a smirk. "You don't want me to take these off."

I grimaced.

Another knock came at my door.

"Two points for Axle," he said, mimicking a crowd cheering.

I rolled my eyes as I unlocked my door to let Atlas and Fena in. I pulled the door open to find the two of them in the hallway.

Fena had her hands held to her chest, looking down the hallway. A bandage was tied around her head, pressing what looked like a cloth to her wound.

She turned and made eye contact with me, gracing me with a small smile.

My spirits soared, and I stepped aside to let them in.

"Hey Gill," Atlas greeted me as he came in, followed by his sister. I closed the door and locked it as Axle got up and hugged Atlas, swinging him around in the air as he did.

"Whoa! Gla-ad to see-ee you too," Atlas said through the spinning.

"I'm so glad we're all okay," said Axle, setting Atlas down and wrapping himself around Fena.

She chuckled and hugged him back. "Yeah, by the gods' graces."

She then pulled me in for a hug. I didn't tell her she was pressing on my wounded shoulder. The pleasure outweighed the pain.

"Well, I'd say our friend Vega officially went too far this time," Axle began with a grin. "I didn't have to read anyone's mind either. I overhead a couple of the headmasters talking. Norah and either Huede or Alrune; it's hard to tell the difference between their voices through a wall."

"What did they say?" Fena asked as she pulled my kitchen chair out and sat in it.

"They're at odds with Vega right now," Atlas interjected, sitting down cross-legged next to my bed. "I overheard a little bit, too. I think our holding rooms might have been near one another, Axle."

"Turns out," Axle continued. "Vega was the one to check Imandr's credentials. He was solely responsible for allowing that fake inquisitor on campus."

"Wow, who'd have guessed," Fena said, her voice thick with sarcasm as she folded her arms and crossed one thigh over the other.

"I already got the sense that the other headmasters didn't care much for Vega," I said as I sat against my door. "Doesn't surprise me they're suspecting him now."

"Unfortunately," Atlas piped up, "I destroyed the Stalker with shadow magic. I thought that if I drained it of magic, it wouldn't work anymore. I wasn't thinking about preserving the evidence. It was short sighted of me." He looked down at his legs. "I apologize."

"It's not your fault," Fena assured him. "Nobody would have guessed that it was Diesel tech. I thought it was magically animated, same as you."

"My eyes were fooled also," I admitted. "That thing was *burning* with magic. I discounted the Diesel right away. And to be fair, it didn't last long after you smashed it to pieces. It's possible that devouring the magic inside of it *is* what stopped it."

"I guess that's true," Atlas said, his spirits lifting. "And hearing you scream like that," he looked up at me with a pained expression. "I just needed to destroy it as quickly as I could."

"I'd have done the same," his sister assured him. "We're all still here to discuss it. I could hardly ask for a better outcome."

They shared a smile.

"So, the working theory is," Axle said as he placed his arms behind his head and fell backward onto the mattress again, "that Vega, Imandr, and the stalker, were working together. If we could prove that Vega was using Diesel machinery to hunt us, then he would go on trial for treason against Galgia. Problem is that our tangible evidence is weak—*real* weak."

I chewed on my knuckles, as my thoughts consumed me.

Axle's right. The only way we're connecting Vega to all this is through his thoughts. From that, we got that Vega, Imandr, and the stalker are working together. Though the stalker mentioned Galgalim, that isn't tangible evidence, and we can't recreate it.

The idea that Vega is part of some cabal loyal to an old god doesn't seem as wild when all these pieces come together...but take away what Axle heard, and it's like taking the bottom out from a house of cards. Then there's also the fact that Axle doesn't always hear things correctly when reading someone. As far as the facts are concerned, we don't have a leg to stand on.

"Did you tell Axle?" Atlas asked me, as if on cue.

"No," I responded.

"Tell me what?" He sat up.

"Gill and Atlas heard the stalker speaking," Fena said, glancing at the two of us. "It wasn't saying 'protect the algorithm,' it was saying... 'protect the *Galgalim.*'" She mouthed the name.

Axle's eyes darted this way and that as he put the puzzle together and caught up to our current thought. "So then...It's true." He looked at me, eyes wide. "Vega's out to get Gill."

I rested my head against the door and stared at the ceiling. "From his perspective, I was walking around at night and saw a blasphemous act being committed by him and whomever else. Then I dug up knowledge about Galga...err, the *monster,*" I corrected myself. "It was knowledge someone worked hard to keep out of my hands."

"Ordering the new copy of that book," Atlas speculated, "was the final straw, wasn't it?"

"He panicked and closed the library," Fena said. "The stalker was probably watching to see if you'd come back to the building. It wasn't expecting all four of us."

"When it managed to catch us off guard and put two of us under," Axle said, picking up the conversational baton. "It figured those were good enough odds." He laughed to himself. "But it didn't know about my man Atlas, here." He ruffled the young mage's hair.

"Stop it," Atlas said suppressing a smile.

"What do you think would've happened," I asked, "if it got all four of us? Vega couldn't just *kill* us, could he?"

"That would explain the rumors about the missing students," Axle said, his tone serious.

"Atlas has made too many waves here," I said. "*Him* going missing would be national news."

"Expelled, is how the school probably would've put it," Fena grumbled.

"Suddenly expelled for no reason," Axle added. "I bet you that's what happened to those students."

"Nah," I shook my head. "Of all the rumors I hear at this school, that's the one I can't get behind. I'm sure the expulsions are quick and quiet. They're probably escorted off of school property and not allowed to talk with their friends. From an outside perspective, it probably just *seems* like they disappeared."

"Spot on," Atlas chimed in. "If students were really vanishing, wouldn't there be more outrage from the parents? I know *my* mom wouldn't keep quiet."

"They'd need a bigger gate," muttered Fena.

"And besides that," Atlas added, "doesn't expulsion require a majority vote? All the headmasters would have to be in on it for us to be suddenly expelled."

"It *does* require a majority," I clarified. "I was a part of one. I'm only here because Norah, Anther, Alrune, and

Edwin protested. Vega was the only vocal headmaster vying for my expulsion, but I got the sense that Huede and Rowan would have voted with him, if the others hadn't come to my defense."

I went back to gnawing on my knuckles. The student disappearances likely *were* just expulsions. But if sudden expulsion was Vega's way of dealing with his problems, and he was routinely failing to expel us... then we were in danger. I couldn't shake the feeling of underlying dread.

"So that's it then." Atlas spoke first. "Vega is out to get rid of us, and there's not a damn thing we can do about it."

"We can stick together," I asserted. "Atlas and Fena can sleep in one another's dorm rooms."

"And I can sleep in here," Axle volunteered.

"No," I lifted my hand. "No. But if I hear anything, I'm right next door to you."

"Sure." He nodded. "I'm a light sleeper. If someone has a distressed enough *thought*, I wake up. Like having a nightmare vicariously through someone else."

"I guess I don't mind sharing a room with my brother," Fena sighed. "Been there done that."

"Easy for you to say," he grumbled. "You snore like an animal."

"You want to run that by me again?" she snarled, standing up.

"I think what he said was," Axle interjected, standing and yawning, "is that it's late, we're all tired and stressed, and we need a good night's sleep."

"Fair," I said as I got to my feet. "We'll see what the headmasters have to say to us in the morning."

After hugging each of us, Axle went to his room.

"Why's he so huggy?" Atlas asked as the two of them left.

"I'll tell you later tonight," Fena said, waving at me and smiling.

I waved back and said goodnight before closing and locking the door behind them.

I went over everything we'd been through while I cleaned up and put my books in my bag; aside from that quick hangout, all I'd done today was study. It was still early, but I was ready to call it a night. I put on my pajamas, dimmed the fire, and laid down.

The stalker referred to Galgalim as "the" Galgalim. Is Galgalim its name, a title, or is that the name of its species? Could there be many of them? Does it really exist somewhere on campus? Where could they hide something so big?

A knock.

I sat up, unsure if that was *my* door or the door across the hall. I waited in silence. The knock came again, quicker this time. I swallowed and slid out of bed. I wouldn't be answering my door at all, but if it was Axle, I owed it to him to answer his call.

Besides, the campus was crawling with inquisitors. I should be safe, for the moment anyway. I unlocked the door and pulled it open to find Fena standing in front of me.

"F-Fena!" I stammered.

"Hey. Brought you some pain ointment for that wound."

A flat circular container with a screw-on lid rested in the palm of her hand.

"My mother sent me here with it. It's done wonders for my head. I don't think I'd have been able to sleep last night without it. Honestly thought about just killing myself." She chuckled.

"Wow," I said just above a whisper. "Thank you. I'm grateful. This thing really hurts."

"I can tell it does," she said, gently pushing past me. I hesitated a second before closing the door, following her with my eyes. She unscrewed the top and set it down on my nightstand.

"C'mere," she said. "I'll show you how to apply it."

I made my way over to her as though I'd forgotten how to walk and sat on the bed, arms at my side like a robot. My mind was doing gymnastics, but my body was rigid.

"Off with the shirt," she commanded.

"Um. What?"

"C'mon, shirt off," she commanded. "It's gotta go on the *wound*, dummy."

"Oh," I said, my face burning up. "Right."

I lifted my shirt off. It hurt to lift my left arm. I cringed in pain as she folded the shirt like an expert and set it down next to me.

The initial wound was about three-and-a-half inches across, stitched up, pink, and tender. Around the wound was a pattern like lightning captured in time reaching away from the wound in all directions.

She dragged my kitchen chair across the room to my bedside. She sat on it and dipped her fingers in the creamy substance in the container.

"This is gonna feel real good," she said, reaching toward the wound. "It soothes on contact."

My body blazed like fireworks as she massaged the cream into the wound, being careful not to touch the stitches. The cream felt like cold water on a nasty sunburn.

I closed my eyes as a sense of euphoria washed over me.

"I haven't said thank you yet," she said as she worked. "Y'know, for that business in the library."

"You've got it all wrong," I said. "Atlas was the one who saved our hides. I uh...bonked it with my sword, which did nothing, and then threw a wind spell at it, which...*also* did nothing. In fact, I'd say the most useful thing I did was get stabbed, so Atlas had a clear shot," I laughed softly.

"Atlas told me a different story," she said, dipping her fingers into the container again.

"Oh yeah?" I smiled at her.

"Mhmm. He told me the story..." she said as she worked around the stitches, "of a very brave mage who put himself on the front line. Of a man who took charge of the situation without regard for his own safety."

I couldn't deny that her words gave me the feels. My chest swelled. For Atlas to say such a thing...I had to stop myself from tearing up a little bit.

Brave? Fearless? I'd thought that those qualities were behind me, in a bygone age before Tovin drowned them out of my heart.

To hear it meant more than Atlas or Fena could ever know.

"You put yourself between that monster and my brother," she said, leaning back in the chair and screwing the lid back onto the container. "And for that, I've yet to thank you. So, thank you, Gill Dragstenn. You might not have dealt the finishing blow, but you're a hero to me all the same."

I smiled. Smiled in that way that you can't really hide or stifle.

I lowered my eyes and when I looked back up at her, she leaned in...

And kissed me.

TWENTY-SEVEN

Something I'd learned in the short time I'd lived was that life was filled with peaks and valleys: times when you're high, and times when you're low. Every now and again, you find that the gods have hewn you a deeper valley than ever before. Conversely, you delight in times when the mountains sing, when you're lifted upon a cloud to new heights, and you're dancing among the stars as your cup runneth over.

Never before had I been launched from such a deep pit onto the shoulders of the gods themselves.

Her lips were soft and warm. Her eyes were closed, and I was glad because mine were wide open.

I hadn't seen it coming at all. She had given no signs that she'd been at *all* interested in me, and I wasn't an oblivious person, either. Just like that, the kiss was over. Too soon.

She pulled away from me with a light caress along my jawline, sat back in her chair, and stared at me through eyes that shimmered in the firelight, silent save for my pounding heart.

"G'night hero," she said with a smile, making for the door.

My words caught in my throat. I wanted to ask her to stay up with me into the wee hours of the morning talking, to let me learn about her the way I'd wanted to from the beginning. We had a curfew though, and she needed to beat the clock back to her brother.

I understood that, but when I tried to convey it, what came out was, "You, but, hang on, you can, but curfew, I get it, sucks."

She giggled as she opened my door. "I don't mind applying that ointment for you on a nightly basis, if you like."

"S-sure, good, yeah," I said, recovering from the word salad I'd vomited at her seconds ago.

"Okay," she said, her dimples manifesting as she closed the door behind her.

I sat on my bed, immobile, staring at the door as my mind went everywhere all at once. I couldn't believe what happened. My heart was doing flips and my body was sweating for some reason.

Then I heard Axle through the wall. "Yeeeaaahhh!"

I was too over the moon to be upset with him for eaves-dropping. I laughed to myself for a moment before pushing my chair back into the kitchen. I walked to the wall that sepa-rated the two of us and leaned against it.

"Did you know, Axle?"

"Like the whole time, my man," his muffled response came through the wall.

"How?"

"We talk. Y'know, when you're not around."

I chuckled to myself, "Why didn't you say anything to me?"

"She'd have beat my face in with a brick."

"Fair." I nodded. "She *does* strike me as the type who can be scary when she wants to be."

"You have no idea. You're in it *now*, bucko."

"It almost scares me when you put it that way."

"No way, Gillbo, I'm super happy for you guys. Y'know what, Im'ma come over there and give you a hug right now."

"No, that's all right." I laughed. "I'll take an IOU for tomorrow morning."

"Yeah, all right."

"G'night."

"Sleep tight."

I locked my door and got back into bed. No chance I'd be falling asleep anytime soon.

In an instant, I saw our whole future together. Babies, a homestead, growing old—I would die first. I turned over, thanking the moons that she couldn't read minds, like Axle.

That's the kind of stuff that scares girls off, but I couldn't control my thoughts. Maybe it was because my body was trying to heal, but I drifted away far faster than I expected.

I fell asleep to thoughts of seeing her tomorrow. Would she try to play it as a spur-of-the-moment *I wasn't thinking* kinda thing? Or maybe she'd pretend it didn't happen.

I wouldn't know until after first period.

———

"Good morning, everyone," said Wuthrand as he walked into class, closing the door behind him.

The murmur of voices died down as he set his stack of folders on his desk and leaned forward on it. "All right. You're probably all wondering if we're gonna talk about it. We're *going* to talk about it; we're gonna have Headmaster Alrune in here in a moment. I want absolute silence while he's talking, or I'm going to double your homework."

He was talking to us like we were an elementary class.

As he walked across the room to his filing cabinet, the girl next to me turned to face me.

"Hey. Aren't you the one who fought that thing in the library?"

"I heard it was you, too," came a male's voice behind me.

"What was it like?" asked another from my right.

"Did it give you a scar?"

"What did it sound like?"

"Did it talk?"

As the questions rained down on me, the door to the classroom opened. By the slow movement, I could tell it was Alrune, though he paused, hanging onto the doorknob as he exchanged parting words with someone in the hallway.

Finally, he moved the rest of the way in, not bothering to close the door behind him. The room quieted as he made his way to the front of the desk and nodded at Wuthrand.

"Good morning, students," he said, looking around at all of us. "I trust you all took advantage of your extra study time yesterday?"

If it was meant to be a joke, it bombed. All of us waited in anxious silence for the update on just what the heck was going on around here.

"Hrhrmm," he cleared his throat. "Laugh or you're all expelled," he said.

That got soft, genuine laughter from the students, and he smiled at everyone. He leaned against the desk, half-sitting as he removed his pipe from a hidden breast pocket.

"First, I want to thank you all for your continued cooperation and patience," he said as he packed his pipe. "I want to assure you that the Inquisitors did a full sweep of the school. Not only that, but a select group of them will be remaining at the university with us until the Cape Exams have concluded. And yes, to answer the question you've all been asking," he took a puff from his pipe and looked up at us. "The Cape Exams *will* continue as scheduled."

The students murmured at the news. I had been wondering what to expect. I'd figured they'd be canceled, but in all likelihood, ticket sales complicated things.

"Rumors abound that certain colleges chose to pull their students from the exams; these rumors have merit. We're in talks with Conflux and Attainment. We think combat experience is more vital now than ever, and we're determined to make sure every college participates. But should they disagree, the pairings will be redone, and the exam schedule will change as needed."

It made sense to me that the colleges would withdraw from the exams. I was actually surprised only one college was getting cold feet about it. An attack from the Diesel against a college was unprecedented. It seemed, to me at least, that we didn't even have protocols in place.

It didn't matter to me whether we held the exams sooner or later, but I'd feel a lot better if Fena wasn't fighting Tovin. I was feeling better about Atlas's odds, having fought alongside him. Sure, he could only attack in an overkill sort of way, but who on Aurii could withstand that kind of onslaught?

"That being said," Alrune pierced my thoughts. "I'd like to talk to you all about what the investigation turned up. I'd like to remove all doubt here and now. The Diesel attacked ENU."

The class became noisier than they ever had before.

"I knew it. Gods be damned, I knew it."

"How could this have happened?"

"So, it's war, then after all..."

"By the gods. I can't believe this is happening."

"Everyone quiet down!" Wuthrand commanded in a more powerful voice than Alrune could manage. The class quieted and the headmaster took a couple of steps forward.

"Everyone, please," Alrune lifted his hands. "Make no mistake. This *was* an act of war. However, Galgia has its diplomatic strategies. The high priests will attempt to deescalate the situation before sending any of you to a battlefield. To this, we solemnly swear."

He puffed on his pipe as he chose his next words.

"It is also true, as I'm sure you've heard, that the machine was more sophisticated than we believed possible. Why, when I fought against the Diesel in the War of Red Rust, their machines were large and bulky, though formidable.

"This newer model is smaller, sleeker, nimble, and intelligent. Our enemy has made greater technological strides than we could have ever imagined. But as Mr. Grimbrooke and Mr. Dragstenn here, have proven," he gestured toward me with his pipe, "our students are more than a match for their advancements."

"Damn straight!"

"Way to give 'em hell, Gill."

"They *did* beat the damn thing after all."

"Bring 'em on!"

The students around me slapped my back, jostled me, and patted me on the biceps. I ignored the pain in my shoulder and stifled a smile. Alrune was making me out to be some kind of hot shot, but the truth was, Atlas could have handled that thing by himself.

Wuthrand marched to the front of the class. His eyes said that he'd had enough of asking us to remain quiet. Alrune touched his shoulder, stopping his impending wrath.

"It's quite all right, Professor. This is good," he said as the class buzzed. If I hadn't been sitting in the front row, I wouldn't have been able to hear him. Wuthrand lowered his shoulders and nodded, relaxing against the desk next to Alrune. He looked around, and he took on a faint, but proud smile. He wanted to be respectful of the headmaster, but he was gratified that his students were eager to take down the Diesel.

"The next thing you should know," Alrune continued, lifting his smoldering pipe and waving it around. The classroom quieted. "The next thing you should know is that for the next week, curfew will be an hour sooner. I know, I know," he said as the students heaved a collective sigh.

"But your safety is our number one concern, and I promise you we will do all that is within our power to make sure you feel secure here. Thank you for having me in your classroom, and take heed—the first round of battles will begin this weekend, barring any further disasters. Mind your studies, be in your dorms by no later than eight o'clock, and rest assured the Diesel threat is being handled by our nation's top talent. Thank you again, and have a wonderful week."

He stood up, saying something to the professor as the students' conversation picked up again. He shuffled out the door, waving to us one last time and closing the door behind him.

My mind drifted back to everything that had happened the night prior, and class zipped by. I'd be seeing her after this. I didn't know why, but I felt nervous about it. I knew I shouldn't; *she* kissed *me*.

When the professor dismissed us, I made my way to the hallway. My stomach was turning over as I looked around.

I waited and waited. We usually walked down the hallway together. I chewed on my bottom lip as I fidgeted with the edges of my textbook.

"Yo!"

"Ah!" I jumped.

Axle snickered. "Expecting someone else?"

"Shut up, man," I said, holding my chest. "She should be here by now, right?"

"Yeah, you're both usually standing here by the time I show up. Wonder what's holding her up."

"I don't know, but I can't stand here forever. Thatchett locks his door and shames anyone who's even a minute late."

"Ugh, I know," he groaned. "I have his class for my final period; he does the same thing to us. If you want to head to class, I'll let her know you waited. My class is right there," he gestured to a nearby door.

"Your class is right there?" I asked.

"Yep."

"You walk all the way down toward the restrooms with us, and your class is all the way back here?"

"I like hanging out with you guys," he defended himself.

I laughed to myself, wiping my hand over my face. "All right," I said, turning. "I'm gonna hit my locker, switch out my books, and if she's not here by then, say hi to her for me."

"Sure thing, Giller Killer."

I rolled my eyes; he was always calling me something ridiculous like that, and I was losing my will to fight it. I changed out my textbook and waited a little longer than I should have; no sign of her. I waved to Axle, and he waved back as I hurried to class.

I couldn't focus on my test. My mind was going nuts.

Why didn't she come see me? Did I say something wrong? Should I have asked her to stay? Have I hurt her feelings some-how? Am I bad kisser?

I sat up.

Do my lips taste bad?

I closed my eyes and shook my head. Need to focus.

7.) Which of the following nations was the second to fall in the War of Red Rust and served as the tipping point for Galgia's race to militarization?

a.) Lang

b.) Tauri
c.) Raeche
d.) Hanouru

What if she really does feel like the whole thing was a big mistake and she's trying to figure out how to break it to me? What if Atlas knows, and he's pissed at me? What if this breaks the group in half?

I set my pencil down and pushed on my temples with my palms. I had eighteen more questions to go, and the last one was an essay. I glanced at the clock. I had twenty minutes left. I needed to move. I circled my best guesses and moved on.

8.) Which spell type is best for piercing the Diesel's thickest machines?
a.) Shadow
b.) Light
c.) Force
d.) Beam

I knew that one. I circled "beam" and continued.

9.) Reasons she's not into you.
a.) Your breath is bad.
b.) You didn't kiss her back.
c.) You stared at her like she had a void slug on her face.
d.) She realized right just then that you're ugly.

I blinked hard, opening my eyes to find a question about known Diesel battle tactics.

I'm losing my mind. Why am I like this? Why do I always overthink everything? It's probably nothing. It's possible the kiss meant nothing to her! I'd like that better than her being angry with me. How can such an amazing thing turn bad this quickly?

I failed my test and made my way out into the hall. I wanted to wait for her, but my anxiety had given me diarrhea and I needed to make an emergency stop at the restroom. My body always rebelled when things were terrible.

I left the restroom and looked up and down the halls. No sign of her at all.

I hated this.

I wished she'd never kissed me.

I wanted things to go back to the way they were—back when I looked forward to seeing her every time. Back when—

"H-hey." Her voice came from behind me.

I turned around. Her eyes were trained on the tile beneath my feet.

"Fena!" I exclaimed. "Where um...where have you been?"

"I uhh..." she stammered, looking at everything but me.

It was weird seeing her like this. She was always so confident and in control. It was awful seeing her struggle for words. It felt really out of character for her. Like seeing Tovin laugh or something.

"It's all right," I assured her. "We don't have to make it a big thing or whatever."

She locked eyes with me and smiled, "Gill...It's...Look, I'm just not sure...I mean..."

"Just walk with me to class," I said in the chillest voice I could fake, moving toward the gym. She caught up with me and matched my stride.

"Wild announcement, right?" I asked, trying to change the subject and break the tension.

"Oh, yeah!" she perked up. "I'm surprised they're going ahead with the exams. We had Norah in our class; how 'bout you? Been wondering how different Vega's presentation was."

"Alrune," I responded as we turned a corner. "He singled me out in front of everyone. Made me feel like a real star, but I gotta say...I'm feeling major imposter syndrome."

She laughed. "Gill, ya big dummy. I told you that you need to think more highly of yourself. You're a lot more impressive than you know!"

"Keep telling me that and I'll start to believe it," I joked.

"I'll remind you as often as it takes," she said with the confidence that I'd come to expect.

"Gill," she said. "Thank you."

I couldn't help but smile at her; she seemed back to her old self. I realized right then and there that her being *her* was enough. Seeing what she was reduced to when she was trying to explain herself to me was painful. I didn't want to see her like that again.

She was dealing with an internal struggle about the entire thing. As much as I'd have loved to relive it over and over, we were better like this.

It was clear to me now. I loved her.

Her caring heart, her sense of humor, her competitive cockiness, and even the fact that she seemed way smarter than me. I prioritized her happiness over my own, and if she never wanted to talk about it, I'd never ask her to.

———

The week went by as usual, and neither of us mentioned it. But our eye contact was a little more prolonged, and our hugs dug a little deeper. She made good on her promise to come by every night to help me with the pain ointment, but we found ourselves talking about anything and everything, sometimes laughing so hard that it hurt.

Axle was kind enough to let us "honeymoon," as he put it, and he gave us our space, even though I invited him over. I was surprised to find that Fena and I had way more chemistry than I'd imagined.

Our relationship was simple when everything else was so complex, and it was exactly what I needed.

But when we got the news that Conflux & Attainment had chosen to remain enrolled in the Cape Exams, it made that much more difficult.

Without new pairings, Fena would still fight Tovin.

I'd have to watch one of them die tomorrow afternoon.

Twenty-Eight

I managed to sleep, but I was plagued by nightmares all night long. Visions of Fena being slaughtered like an animal as a crowd cheered around me.

A spectacle.

That's all it was to them. These living, breathing, thinking human beings with beating hearts would suffer, and the crowd would cheer for it. It wasn't that I didn't understand; to them, death was trivial as long as we died within the stasis field.

What they didn't know was how much dying changes a person, or how much one carries it with them after the fact... how much it hurts.

And it hurts *a lot.*

I didn't want that kind of pain for Fena, for *anyone.* But she especially didn't deserve it—having to fight that monster head-to-head. I'd have preferred to fight her or Tovin *myself.* I couldn't keep the worry out of my heart, and I wasn't alone in my sentiments either. The students existed beneath a thick blanket of anxiety, anticipation, and jitters. You could literally feel it in the hallways of the university.

When I saw Axle in the cafeteria that morning, I knew

that something was off. He had bags under his eyes and his face was pale.

"Axle," I said as I saw him. "You look...terrible."

"Couldn't sleep," he mumbled as he sat down with two mugs of coffee and a croissant. "Everyone was having night-mares all night long. Kept waking me up."

"I...may have contributed to that," I admitted.

"Can't wait for this weekend to be over," he grumbled. "I think I'm gonna have to sleep in the gods-be-damned hymna-sium tonight."

"Axle," I said. "Do I have to remind you how dangerous—"

"I know, I know," he interrupted, waving his hand around in an exhausted stupor. "Only kidding."

I sighed and scanned the cafeteria. It was quieter than normal. Everyone seemed to be in their own heads as they ate. Some merely stared at their plates. The overwhelming majority of them had never died before. They had never even put their lives on the line.

Maybe the headmasters were right. They weren't ready for war.

"How are things with Fena?" Axle asked, drawing my attention back to him. "You guys dating or what? You spend enough time together."

"Oh, well." I scratched the side of my head. "I don't really know *what* we are. I don't think she does either, and that's all right with me."

He made a 'not bad' face at me as he picked up his second mug of coffee and took a drink. He set it down and nodded. "I think that's a really mature way to think about it, my man."

"Other than that, we're right as rain," I added. "Have you seen her today?"

"No, but I ran into Atlas on the way here. He was headed back to his room with a coffee to go. He said she needs some time alone before her fight. She's one of the main events, y'know. Probably trying to psych herself up for it."

I hadn't thought about that. I'd been so worried about watching her die that I hadn't considered it would probably be the most-watched battle in the whole event. That had to be a lot of pressure.

"When is her fight, do you know?" asked Axle. "I only looked at my own schedule."

"She's fighting Tovin at three," I answered. "I think it's the final fight of the day, too. Their fight is one of the few scheduled for a specific time."

"Mine too," he thumbed at himself. "I'm scheduled for one thirty against Miss Meridia."

"Atlas is fighting Leo at noon," I said, resting my head in one hand. "My fight is the only one out of the four of us that isn't scheduled."

"I don't understand." He shook his head. "How are they handling this?"

"Well," I said, "anyone ranked under like twenty is considered unimportant. They broke the tickets up by major bouts. Depending on which ticket bracket you buy, you get six fights: five among lower-ranked students, and one big one. My fight is one of the earlier ones. I'm headlining for Atlas and Leo."

"Oh, no way, you're fighting first?" he asked, with as much interest as his pre-caffeinated state allowed.

"Yeah. Some guy named Tanz Hauley. Could be a girl for all I know; I've never heard a name like that before. Whoever they are, they're ranked nearly four hundred tiers higher than me."

"That's a drastic difference," he responded with concern. "How do you feel about that?"

"Well, they're from BEA. They don't have as many students as we do, like mid-five-hundreds. So the difference isn't as great as it sounds. But if I win, I'll jump in the rankings."

"Still a big difference, Gill," he said, gesturing toward me with his mug. "Someone's got a lot of faith in you."

"Or they put me up against big odds hoping I'd lose in front of everyone. Y'know, someone who might get a kick out of watching me get destroyed. Someone who's overseeing the Cape Exam matchmaking this year." I held eye contact until it clicked in his eyes.

"I forgot that was Vega," he said in a frustrated tone, dropping his head. "You think?"

"I can't say I'd be surprised, but he's not the only headmaster working the exams this year." I folded my arms. "Makes me want to win all the more, though."

"That's the spirit," he smiled with a long, tired blink. "Let it drive you. Spit right in his face."

"Yeah," I said trying to smile. "I'm gonna win today, Axle. I can feel it."

"I like what I'm *hearing!*" he said in a loud voice as he stood, the caffeine hitting him in real time. "We're *all* going to win today!"

I couldn't lie; his enthusiasm helped. For so much confidence as I was showing on the outside, I had my doubts. I'd be fighting head-to-head against a real mage. What made a mage dangerous was that you'd never fight the same one twice.

All of us had a bag of chosen tricks. Too bad for me, but my set of skills was small and straightforward. I had only so many combinations I could throw before my foes figured out how to counter them.

"I'm just glad all of our fights are scheduled for today," I said, glancing out the window. "We can just take it easy tomorrow and hang out."

"You don't want to watch?" he asked.

"Nah, I don't care about anyone else's fights. I want to relax tomorrow. Maybe make it a bathhouse day?"

"It *is* gonna be chilly," he said, nodding at the clouds through the big cafeteria window. "They're headed this way."

"Sounds good to me." I picked up my trash. "I'm gonna go get ready. I don't think any of these fights are going to take the full ten minutes, and I'm expected to be on deck."

"We'll all be rooting for you, Gilla-Gorilla. Let him have it."

"Okay, that one *especially*."

He lifted his mug and grinned. "Never again."

———

I didn't see Atlas or Fena before I entered the stadium and went down the corridor to the competitors' cages. We weren't literally caged, but we sat behind thick warded glass on the ground floor and watched the matches while we waited for our turns. After mine was over, I'd be able to join the others high up in the stands.

I turned down a long hallway off the main tunnel, went all the way to the end, turned left and pushed through a set of double doors. I stepped into the cage and eyed the other three competitors. There were supposed to be *four* others.

"Gill Dragstenn?" came a voice from behind me. One of the proctors was sitting on a bench looking over the clipboard as he chewed on something.

"That's me," I responded as I turned to face him.

He sighed and shook his head. "If our friend Mr. Colloway isn't here in five minutes, your match is getting pushed up to first."

"F-first?" My extremities went numb.

"Mr. Colloway was supposed to fight Miss Regoul in round one, but he's nowhere to be found. Miss Erigun here," he motioned to one of the women, "was scheduled to fight second, but her opponent is late, too. You're third, so you're next in line if neither of them shows."

"How could they be late for their *Cape Exam?*"

"First-years," muttered Miss Erigun. "I *knew* it was a bad idea."

Headmaster Edwin made his way to the center of the stadium. My heart sank. I knew all along I would be fighting early, but I didn't want to be *first*.

"Good morning Galgia!" he said, his voice amplified by magic. The crowd was still gathering in the stands, some of them only now getting seated. It was a poor turnout for us pissant competitors.

"In just a few short minutes, you'll be treated to one-on-one combat between our nation's finest mages! Let's hear it for them!"

The small crowd gave a half-hearted cheer. I knew it was half-hearted because of what came only a few seconds later.

Edwin moved his arms in wide arcs and then slammed his fists into the ground. The green grass of the stadium inverted in a wave that traveled along the surface to the outer edges of the arena. The grassy floor of the stadium had been transformed into earthy soil.

The crowd roared as he slammed his fist into the ground a second time, flattening it all into a stable dirt floor. The onlookers screamed as he looked up at the stands and smiled.

"You ready for some *magic?*"

I didn't know such a small crowd could make so much noise. I also didn't know Edwin was so capable with the earth element. I'd never *seen* an earth-element spell taken to such heights. For the life of me, I couldn't stop underestimating the headmasters.

"One minute till showtime," called the proctor from behind me.

My stomach was doing summersaults. I wished I had used the bathroom first. I scanned the student section of the seats—far more of *them* out there than civilian spectators. I couldn't spot the others in the stands. You'd think Fena would be easy to spot with her blazing mane.

I turned around and took a deep breath as I attempted to steady my nerves.

"All right, Mr. Dragstenn," called the proctor. "Both of your weapons were approved. You'll find them in that box by the door. Sorry for the surprise, but you're going to have to get out there right now. Good luck to you, sir."

I doom-marched over to the box and found both my weapons. I picked up my tome and fastened it to my belt before gripping my sword and making for the door. I walked down the long hallway to the tunnel that led to the arena.

My heart was pounding, and my thoughts were scattered as I placed one foot in front of the other. When I exited the hallway and turned to move into the arena, I found myself face to face with the last person I wanted to see, pretty much ever.

Tovin stood in my path; his arms folded. My already scattered thoughts were dashed against the rocks. His eyes bore into mine as the two of us shared a moment of silence.

"Gill," he said firmly. "You're not allowed to lose to this clown. Do you *understand* me?"

I swallowed and found myself lost for words, as I often did when confronted with imminent death.

"Prove it," he said as he started toward me. I stiffened, and he stopped beside me, facing the opposite direction. "I *know* you're better than him. So, prove it. Prove it to them all."

He started toward the back of the stadium, and I turned around.

"Tovin," I called after him.

He stopped and looked over his shoulder.

"You're fighting Fena today," I said, turning around to face him fully. "Please don't do anything...unnecessary. I'm not asking you to take it easy on her, but, if you have to kill her...*please* make it quick. Clean." I folded my hands. "Can you do that? Please?"

He scoffed, "Some faith you have in your girlfriend. Just for that," he said, "I'm going to *crush* her in front of everyone, and I'll let her in on a little secret: that you *begged* me not to kill her."

My mouth opened but no noise came out. All the air had been sucked out of my lungs, and he hadn't even used a spell.

I didn't know what else to say; what else to do. I closed my eyes tightly before turning and making my way toward the stadium. I had inadvertently made things terribly, terribly worse.

If she found out about it, she would be pissed to no end, competitive as she was. But what was I supposed to do? I didn't want to see her in pain. I knew what Tovin was capable of as well as what he *wasn't*: mercy, restraint, and empathy.

I stepped out of the shadows and into the morning light. The Cape Exams had seemed so far away. Some far-off date that I didn't have to worry about. The idea of standing at the edge of the arena might as well have been imaginary, until now. But the date had found me, and fate was calling my name.

"Entering now is Eye of Newt University's lowest-ranked student! The underdog who has chosen to specialize in tome-casting and wields a sword in his offhand. Everyone let it out for Gill Dragstenn!"

The crowd mustered a small cheer for me as I made my way toward the center of the stadium. Did he really have to tell them I was the worst student at ENU? Like I was some kind of appetizer for better fights to come?

Over the small collective sigh from the spectators, one small group of students made a racket. Fena and Axle were screaming their heads off. I also heard my mother's trademark bird-squawk-cheer from somewhere else in the stands.

My face was burning as I managed a smile and a half-hearted wave. Atlas must have been in the cage preparing for his battle, and I needed to be prepared for mine. I didn't want my parents to have to watch their son die horribly.

I faced my opponent as he strode out of the other side of the stadium.

"And his opponent, hailing from the Brightroot Elemental Academy! With his unusual blazing fist style, he has chosen to specialize in close quarters mage combat. Everyone welcome Tanz Hauley!"

He drew nearer. I couldn't believe what I was seeing.

"Ha!" he guffawed, stopping about ten feet from me. "Would you look at this? The gods smile on me, this day!"

I gritted my teeth and tightened my grip on my sword.

Short brown hair. Pierced left ear. Bushy beard, and a scar over his right eye.

The very one who had hit on Fena right in front of me a week ago. The same coward I'd tackled to the ground to stop him from carrying out a sneak attack. Tovin's words made more sense now.

Tanz stood across from me, smiling from ear to ear.

"Fate has a funny way of working out doesn't it, little man?" he asked as his magic rose from his midsection to his arms. He made the motions, the same he'd been trying against Tovin that day.

His fists all the way up to his forearms ignited brightly, exciting the onlookers.

"I wasn't done beating the life out of you when your friend intervened," he said with a smirk. "Nobody can save you this time. I'm gonna pop your head like a zit in front of *everyone.*"

I lifted my sword and Fortified myself as I widened my

stance and prepared Jetstream on the soles of my feet. I took an extra preventative measure and activated Heatshield. Aside from my summoning spells, it was my cheapest one, and I used it to keep cool on Galgia's hottest days.

I didn't know how effective it would be against literal fire, but I was not about to lose for *any* reason that I could have better prepared for. Not while Fena was watching, not while my mom cheered from the stands.

And Tovin...

"Competitors!" Edwin's voice rang throughout the stadium. "Begin!"

Twenty-Nine

agic swelled in his feet. I recognized it; it wasn't very different from my own battle preparations.

Without a second thought, I strafed left, avoiding his fiery fist as it passed by my face. I never would have imagined he was that fast. Had I not had the ability to see his magic, had I not had that brief window of warning, I *never* would have dodged that punch. I maneuvered around and gleaned everything I could from the first attack.

He had covered the fifteen feet between us in nearly the blink of an eye, but he seemed to be having trouble stopping. The spot where he'd been standing had a small but noticeable crater in it.

I see. It's not speed so much as a magically enhanced lunge with the potential to end a fight before it begins. He'll never catch me off guard as long as I can see him building magic.

Considering that he's only now managing to turn around, it's safe to assume he can only attack like that in a balls-out linear swipe. Not only can I dodge it, but I might be able to take advantage of it if he tries it again.

He whirled around and glowered at me, lowering his stance. "How did you do that?" he growled.

I held my sword out in front of me, choosing silence as I anticipated his next attack. He sent more magic to his feet, but far less than before.

No doubt this next attack would be quick, but he seemed to be opting toward more control after his opening gambit failed. I needed to be ready for whatever was about to come next.

"Let's see you get away from *this!*" he called out before launching forward, his arms outstretched, the flames trailing behind him like a speeding comet.

It's exactly as I suspected. He's running at double his normal sprint speed. Two or three seconds to impact. Let's see if this slows him down.

I charged my blade with an Aeroslice and swung my sword in a horizontal arc. The sword hummed with energy as it released a slicing gale of wind directly in his path.

He slid beneath it, hardly losing any momentum as his arms blazed with energy. He tucked them behind him, propelling himself on explosions from the base of his palms.

I wasn't ready for that at all.

He wound up and threw a haymaker, connecting with my chest. I was bathed in torrid flames and flung backward several feet. It hurt, but not as badly as it would have without Fortify. The flames were mitigated by my Heatshield as well, staving off the secondary damage of his attack.

Both of those defensive spells working together had likely saved my life.

I skidded to a stop, still on my feet.

He was glaring at me again, frustrated and confused.

"How...are you *alive?*" he seethed. "You should have damn near exploded!"

"Guess I'm made of tougher stuff," I responded, buying time to strategize.

I took a powerful attack head-on. Fortify held up well. He'll never catch me by surprise with his lunge, and he'll never damage me if that's all he's got. Between Fortify, Heatshield, and my eyes, he'll never be able to take me out.

I think it's safe to say I've got the upper hand now.

I focused my magic in my feet. It was time to go on the offensive.

I tore forward, aloft on pressurized water streams beneath my heels, closing the distance between the two of us. He gritted his teeth and dropped into a battle stance. I eased up on Jetstream on one foot and added pressure on the opposite foot, putting myself into a spin.

Within seconds I was a spinning buzzsaw with a blade in my hand. With my eyes, I tracked him by the magic burning in his arms. I increased my speed at the last second, throwing off his timing as I ripped through him.

My blade passed through flesh, and I came to a stop when I was a decent distance away.

I fell back on my right foot as I shrugged off the dizziness, and his multiple images converged into one. He was holding his left arm and watching me as he backpedaled.

The crowd was on their feet.

I'd *hit* him.

There was wet blood on the edge of my sword. I had cut him pretty deep. Now was no time to let up. With his left arm wounded, I only had to worry about attacks from the right.

I launched myself, weapon in hand as I watched his magic for sudden changes. His right arm blazed as he prepared a right hook.

When I was about six feet away from him, I turned and closed in on his damaged side. The blazing inferno on his right arm switched sides as he cocked his left arm back and focused his magic in his right foot.

I saw the change, but I was too close and going too fast to react in time.

He leaned forward and caught me in the jaw with what was *supposed* to be a damaged arm. I caught only a glimpse of it before I reeled backward.

He hadn't been holding his arm because it was painful; he'd been cauterizing the gash, feigning weakness in the process.

It was a trap, and I had fallen right into it.

My fortification spell faltered; my armor was cracking.

Not content with a single good connection, he exploded into a follow-up attack.

He struck me from behind before appearing in front of me, catching me under the chin with an uppercut that lifted me off my feet.

Each strike was stripping me of my fortifications; he seemed to be everywhere at once.

I couldn't react.

He drew his arm all the way back and kicked off, punching me so hard in the stomach that the world turned over as I was blasted across the arena. I touched the ground once, twice, three times before slamming into the wall.

Somewhere along the way, I'd lost my sword. Fortify had ended. Heatshield had taken all it could take and had also expired.

I lifted my head. Tanz was rushing toward me at breakneck speed.

I have to do something. I can't let it end like this. I have to reapply Fortify. If I put Heatshield back up, that's one less Aeroslice. That could also bar me from using Starspear depending on what I have to cast in the meantime. It's my most expensive spell, but if it connects...

I made up my mind as I lifted myself from the ground.

I watched his magic course through his body; it was dimmer than before. One of the spells he was using was *taxing*. He was probably sitting at half of his original reserves.

By my count, we had only been at it a few minutes. If I could wear him out, he'd have to give up on at least one of his problematic spells.

Like me, his entire kit had a lot of synergies. If one of his spells were to end, it'd be like watching a chariot break a wheel.

I didn't have any more time to think. He was on me.

I refortified myself, using Jetstream to avoid his next strike. His fist passed my head by mere inches and collided with the wall, sending reverberations through the entire stadium. The wall exploded into a maelstrom of dust and debris at the impact site, and his magic reserves dimmed in real time.

I get it now. It's not the flames on his arms or his speed—he's using some kind of spell or combination of spells to enhance his strength. Any strength-enhancing spell is going to be expensive to maintain.

Is he only activating it at the points of impact? It makes sense now, why I was paired against him of all people. We have fine magic control and close-combat styles. We're natural enemies.

I put a little distance between the two of us and strategized as he yanked his arm out of the crater in the wall. I was thinking about every possible combination in my spellbook that I could cast in the next several minutes.

A higher number of smaller spells or a smaller number of more potent spells? Which spell to save for last? Which to lead with?

My mind raced as he found me. He was breathing hard; desperation would set in soon, more so if I goaded him. If I could get him to wear himself out chasing me around, I could find an opportunity to tip the scales.

As things were right now, I was losing this fight.

"I get it," he called out to me. "You're applying some kind of armor to yourself," he said, starting toward me, working his shoulder out. "I felt a difference last time I hit you. I forced you to reapply your defenses, didn't I?" He grinned.

"I forced you to whiff on one of your more expensive spells, didn't I?" I shot back. "Thought you were going to finish me off that easy?" I smiled. "You've got a long way to go."

His eyes narrowed and his arms flamed to new heights, "Tch. Look at you, talking tough. All you can do is run from me now!" he shouted in a blind fury.

He blasted toward me again. I took a deep breath and watched the magic coursing around in his body as he moved. He was focusing his power in his arms; he was trying to end it with a strike.

As soon as he was close enough, he threw a right hook that I ducked, then a cross from which I was just out of range. The heat coming off him stung my face as each strike passed by.

I watched his magic surge into his leg and lifted my arm to block as he localized an explosion on the back of his heel into a powerful roundhouse kick. I blocked the blow, and my body surged with pain. If I hadn't been fortified, a strike like that would have broken my arm.

I managed to stay out of range of his strikes as he attacked again and again, though I had to admit that without Heatshield, the molten temperatures were getting to me. It was a price worth paying; his magic was dimming with each swing.

It was as I'd predicted; desperation was setting in.

"Stop running!" he screamed, whipping his arm out to the side. Flames leaped from it and fanned outward into an almost tangible whiplike state.

I stepped back in surprise, but I couldn't have predicted what would happen next. He swung the entire arm of flames around in a way that I couldn't block or escape.

I did the only thing I could; I renewed my Heatshield as he picked me up off the ground with his flames. They reconfigured into a fist around me. Even with the Heatshield active, the temperatures were almost too much to bear. I gritted my teeth as sweat rolled off my forehead.

He laughed maniacally as he held me in place. "Where are you going *now*, little man?" The flames squeezed me and greedily devoured all the oxygen around me; I couldn't breathe.

The crowd was roaring, probably in his favor. I looked down at him. My Heatshield was at its limits.

"You can't talk! You can't move! You can't sing!" he cried out, laughing like a madman. "All you can do now is *burn!*"

This is it.

He was grinning like the devil as he watched my defenses peel away.

All my other spells be damned. It's going to cost everything.

He grabbed his right arm with his left, and he winced in pain.

He's about at his limit. My defenses are about to break. Now's the time if ever there was one.

Through the pain, through the crushing flames, and for the first time in actual combat, I envisioned the symbol for my most powerful and expensive spell: Starspear.

I extended the index and middle fingers on my right hand and pointed them at him as I poured almost all that remained of my magic into the attack. At my command, a radiant spear of bright energy leapt from my fingers and pierced Tanz straight through the chest.

The crowd quieted.

His eyes widened.

The flames that choked me dissipated.

I fell to the ground, landing hard. Fortify had ended again, and Heatshield was down. I inhaled like I'd never taken a breath before and turned over on my side as Tanz looked down at the glimmering spear of light sticking out of his chest.

I had missed his heart by only inches; I might have punctured a lung. I got to a kneeling position as the magical spear of energy faded away, leaving a hole in his chest. He dropped to a knee and coughed a pool of blood onto the dirt.

"I couldn't talk," I said as I stood up. "Or move." I steadied myself as he looked up at me in surprise. "But I don't cast like the rest of you. I don't need words. I don't need broad movements. And you're *lucky* I don't sing." A pained laugh escaped me.

"Do you..." he growled as he stood, "think this is some kind of *joke?* That it's over and you've won?" he asked through labored breaths as he gripped his chest.

"You've got next to no magic left," I countered. "And that was a light elemental spell I put through your chest. Your casting is gonna be messed up for at least the remainder of the round."

"Who says..." He looked at me with wild eyes. "That I need *magic* to end you?"

I was taken aback. I had to stop myself from taking a step backward as I stared at the hole in his chest. I couldn't fathom where his energy was coming from.

I had almost no magic left, either, but he couldn't know that. I decided to bluff like I still had energy to spare. I figured maybe he would just give up; it would be the sensible thing to do when one had a gaping hole in their chest.

"You're in no condition to continue," I advised him. "You're going to die in *minutes*—if even that."

"Heh..." he scoffed. "As if I need more time that!" he shouted, kicking off into a sprint straight toward me.

I couldn't hide my surprise. I probably couldn't win a fist-fight against him. But pride stopped me from running away. He tackled me to the ground with more force than I expected him to generate in his condition.

I lifted my arms to defend myself as his fists rained down on me.

Each blow was *heavy*.

His arms were thick, his veins bulging as he swung again and again and again, the blood from his wound spraying all over me as he did.

Then he broke through my guard.

The first punch that connected with my face struck me with so much force that my head bounced off the ground.

Gods...He might actually *pop my head with another one of those. I only need to hang on long enough for him to keel over. If I can only maintain consciousness...*

Another fist blasted me in the jaw, and I could swear I saw one of my teeth bounce away to safety. I struggled to guard myself, but the blows kept coming. There was a moment during the pummeling when everything seemed to slow down.

In the stands, Fena was screaming. I don't know how my eyes landed on her, but they did.

Axle was holding her with all his might as she reached for me. The panic in her eyes...I couldn't stand it.

I didn't want her to look; I didn't want her to see.

Then the fists stopped. I looked up to see if he'd finally died, but instead, he was standing over me. His shoulders rose and fell with his ragged breathing as red energy glowed in the center of his palm. First a flicker, then a flame.

I had underestimated his magical control. Even with his mana dwindling and his control scrambled, he was pulling together one final spell.

"I'm...gonna...end you first..." he wheezed. "I...won't die while you're still...alive."

But I had one spell left too. It wasn't a combat spell. In fact, it was the cheapest spell I knew how to cast, and I had just enough magic in the reserves to pull it together.

"Ha-*ten*!"

My sword fell into my hand, and I flung the wet blood still resting on its edge into his eyes. He shut them tightly and lost control of his spell, a gout of flame rushing past me as I rose toward him and rammed the entire length of my blade through his stomach.

He spewed blood all over my shoulder and lifted his hands against me in vain; he was weak. His vitals were leaving him as he clawed at my chest. His final struggle felt awful. Each little movement he made ran down my sword and into my hands. I had never taken a life like this before.

He gurgled something into my ear as his eyes fluttered, his consciousness hanging on by a thread.

"It was a good fight," I said, loud enough that he might have heard it.

He'd busted my face up. I found it painful to talk. I pulled my sword out of his stomach, and he fell backward onto the ground. "You've got heart," I added as my breathing steadied. "I'm glad you're on *our* side and not the Diesel's." I laughed weakly.

I was interrupted by raucous applause from the stands. The stadium had become packed. I looked around as they cheered for me.

"Yeah, he's done," came a voice from behind me.

I turned to see one of the proctors kneeling over his body. He had his finger under Tanz's jawline, feeling for a pulse. He gestured to Edwin that the fight had concluded. The headmaster nodded in affirmation before moving up next to me.

"And the winner of our first Cape Exam exhibition is Gill Dragstenn!"

I gasped in surprise as he grabbed me by the wrist and

lifted my arm. My right eye had swollen shut, but through my left eye, I took in a sight that I would never forget.

Thousands of people were on their feet cheering for me, validating all the hard work I'd been doing and filling me with hope that I hadn't reached my full potential yet. On top of that, the fight itself was exhilarating in a way I hadn't expected it to be.

I heard a noise behind me. Tanz was sitting up and holding his head. He was coming to grips with what had happened. He'd just died for the first time; it was all in his expression.

Seeing him awake and in good condition did wonders for my mood, though. I didn't like killing him, but I did somehow enjoy the fight. As long as we were on school grounds, I could enjoy one without the other.

"Up you go," one of the proctors said as he helped him to his feet. He smacked the proctor's hand away and glared at me. "This isn't over."

"I hope not," I called to him with a bloody smile. "That was fun! I hope we can do it again sometime."

He eyed me, folding his arms defiantly. He smiled, despite his loss and shook his head. "Heh...It *was* kinda fun, wasn't it?"

After the fight, I was to report back to the cage and receive my new projected ranking from the proctor stationed there. I was light-headed, my face hurt, and my body felt like it was going to fall to pieces, but I was so excited that I'd won that I couldn't help but be in high spirits as I exited the stadium.

I turned down the long hallway and pushed through the double doors. The gathered students had all manner of kind words for me, but I was so shell-shocked that I didn't manage to hang onto anything they said.

"Mr. Dragstenn," the proctor said with a smile as he handed me a large wooden cup filled with cold water. I hadn't realized how much I wanted water until the cup was in my hands. I downed the entire cup and then half of another before rinsing the blood out of my mouth and spitting it into the dirt.

"Congratulations," he said, placing his hand on my shoulder. "Headmaster Vega should be sending me your results any moment," he said, looking up at the judge's booth.

Huh. So, it is *telepathy. I just learned something.*

"In the meantime, feel free to wash up in the sink over there."

I decided it might be best to get all Tanz's blood off my face, and I put my whole head in the sink. The cold water felt like heaven as I ran it through my hair and over my face. I hoped it would do something for the swelling, too, before I saw my mom.

I pulled my head out of the sink and let out a sigh of relief.

The proctor's eyes lifted as though someone had called his name. His gaze moved this way and that as he jotted down numbers on his clipboard. After a few moments, he stopped writing and sent a thumbs up to the judge's booth.

"All right, Mr. Dragstenn, here's a copy of your scores," he said, ripping out a page and handing it to me. I took it and looked it over.

"The judges this year are headmasters from all four schools. One from each of the other three schools, and our very own Alrune and Vega. They'll be anonymous on your sheet, but this is how all five judges viewed your performance."

Judge	Power	Intelligence	Adaptability	Stamina	Resilience
Judge #1	4/10	7/10	9/10	3/10	8/10
Judge #2	4/10	7/10	8/10	4/10	9/10
Judge #3	2/10	3/10	4/10	3/10	5/10
Judge #4	5/10	9/10	10/10	4/10	10/10
Judge #5	4/10	8/10	9/10	3/10	8/10

"These scores aren't bad," I said to the proctor.

"Certainly not," he responded. "You were phenomenal out there, kid. I can't say I've ever seen someone put up such a fight with a tome and sword before. You've got an unusual fighting style, Mr. Dragstenn. I'm surprised you're not at BEA with Tanz over there. That school is full of students with creative styles."

"Thanks," I said bashfully. "But I wanted to attend ENU. Always have."

"I'm receiving your new projected ranking right now, hang on." His eyes moved skyward and darted around before he smiled and nodded.

He placed a hand on my shoulder. "Guess where you're projected ranking is."

"Aw don't do this to me," I said with a grin. "Just tell me."

"No, guess!" he insisted.

"Six hundred," Miss Erigun guessed for me.

"Higher," he said.

"Five hundred," guessed another one of the students.

"Keep going," the proctor pressed, not bothering to hide his enthusiasm.

"Wow," I exclaimed. "Two-fifty?" I guessed. "It couldn't be higher than that, could it?"

"Keep going," the proctor responded, glancing around at all of us.

"No way," Miss Erigun spoke up. "That would be the biggest leap in the rankings for like...all of this school's history, wouldn't it?"

"That's what I was told," the proctor said, matter of factly.

"N-no way," I muttered. "Did I break the top one hundred?"

"Mr. Dragstenn, you're ranked ninety-ninth in the school now," he said with a big pat on my shoulder.

Like that night when Fena kissed me, I had a smile I couldn't fight to save my own dignity.

"How is that even possible?" one of the students asked.

"Well, if you're asking me," the proctor answered, "I would say Mr. Dragstenn was ranked lower than he ever should have been to begin with, probably because of the tome and limited mana reserves. All they needed, I imagine, was to see him in action against a real-life opponent. Now that they have, they probably think that they were right to take a chance on him."

"Un...Unreal," I said, a feeling of faintness overcoming me.

"I would imagine the same of his opponent as well," the proctor continued. "Both proved that their unusual styles are applicable in real-life combat situations. Even though he lost, I'd wager he jumped a couple hundred ranks himself. And also," he turned to me, "that's an *estimated* ranking. It could rise or fall tens of ranks depending on how the other students score, so it's not a surefire number."

"Wow," one of the students behind me remarked. "You can go up in rank even if you lose?"

"I didn't know either," replied Erigun. "I bet Gill falls though. He's good, just not top 100 material."

"You should be proud, nonetheless, Mr. Dragstenn," interjected the proctor. "The difference between ranks one hundred and seven hundred isn't *nothing*, but the real climb starts here. The difference between rank one hundred and rank one is *immense*. You've been recognized as one of the greats today, kid. Be worthy of it."

I didn't know the rankings worked like that, but the more I thought about it, the more it made sense. How much stronger could rank 450 be than rank 451? I looked at the page with my scores on it and smiled again.

I couldn't believe this was happening. I'd had dreams of this kind of thing for over a year, but it was *happening*. A drop of blood fell from my mouth onto the page, and I looked up at the proctor as I remembered a question I'd been meaning to ask.

"Hey, can you tell me if I still have all my teeth?" I opened my mouth.

This got a big laugh out of the other four students, but I was serious. The proctor snickered as he did a cursory sweep of my mouth. His eyes widened as he focused on my left side.

"Gods, you *did* lose a tooth out there!"

The others gasped and gathered around me as he pointed it out for them. I couldn't believe the bastard had knocked one of my gods be damned teeth out.

"You're missing one from the top row on your left side. It's not a bad spot to lose a tooth, for what it's worth. It's not one of your molars, and it shouldn't show unless you smile. You might be better off dying and fixing all of that damage up."

I closed my mouth and thought about it a moment. I shook my head, "No. I think I'll just heal up."

"Are you sure?" asked the proctor with concern in his tone. "If you wait too long, the stasis field may not fix *everything*."

"Yeah," I nodded. "I think it's a battle scar I can be proud of."

"Scars are hot," Miss Erigun chimed in.

I smiled. "Y-yeah?"

"And it looks pretty good on you," she added, for good measure.

A missing tooth looked good on me? I was starting to think she had a weird kink.

The proctor turned and looked up at the judge's booth and nodded. "All right, Mr. Colloway, please make your way out to the arena."

"Oh, you made it," I chastised him as he passed me.

"Bite me, ninety-nine," he said with a small smile as left the room.

"You're welcome to remain down here and watch the battles if you like," the proctor offered.

"You're welcome to sit next to *me*," Miss Erigun added, without looking away from the arena.

"Nah, I've got my mom waiting up in the stands to talk to me," I said as I started toward the doors.

"Congratulations again, Mr. Dragstenn. You're gonna be a tough act to follow!"

I waved a thank you as I made my way toward the exit to the stands. A lone figure waited for me at the end, but it was tough to make them out against the sunlight. As I drew closer, I wondered if Tovin was waiting to tell me how terrible I looked.

The figure started toward me, and I recognized the fiery red locks as she stepped beneath the stadium walkway. She walked with determination in her gait and worry all over her face.

"Hey," I said when I was within speaking distance.

She responded by throwing her arms around me and squeezing me tight, both the best and worst feeling in the world.

"Gill," she whimpered.

"What's the matter?" I asked. "I won."

She sobbed on my shoulder. I didn't know what to do. Comfort her? Ask her what was wrong? Because, really, I couldn't think of a single reason she would be crying.

"Fena..." I said, attempting to get a word in through her tears. I lifted my eyes. Axle was leaning against the entrance of the tunnel with his arms folded.

I rested my chin on her shoulder, "C'mon...We should be celebrating."

She held me at arm's length, nodding with a forced smile,

"Gods! You're right! I'm sorry. I just..." She pulled me back in and cradled the back of my head.

"I didn't like watching you get beat on like that. My heart...it ripped right in half," she said in a wavering tone.

She leaned out of the hug and stared into my eyes. Two vibrant green irises that shined like sparkling ocean waves washed my weariness away. Her lips were pressed together as though the words behind them were fighting to be spoken. Her dimples manifested on her cheeks as her lips pulled back into a tight smile.

I felt like my heart was about to burst out of my chest. I'd been holding something back too; something I couldn't contain any longer.

"I know what you mean—how you're feeling, that is. I don't think I could bear the sight of you in pain either. My stomach twists up in knots thinking about it," I chuckled. "You've become one of my best friends; someone I would do anything for. You've become...irreplaceable to me."

I stared at her at her a little longer than I meant to, but, to me, she was art. Every curve, every freckle, every stray strand of her sunset locks.

I decided now was the time if ever there was one.

The words tumbled out of my mouth almost without my permission.

"Fena...I love you."

Acknowledgments

I want to start by thanking my best friend, my rock, and my wife, Crystal. From reassuring me when doubt crept in, to designing artwork for my stories, to providing helpful edits and insights. You're my everything, love. I couldn't have done it without you.

Thanks to everyone on my publishing team. Danica, this couldn't have been done without you. I believe God set up our chance arrangement that fateful day. I remember I just wanted to ask some questions about meta data. You pretty much had to beg me to tell you about my book. I had no idea who you were; the greatest mentor a fledgling author could ask for. Thank you for your kindness, your patience, your encouragement, and your hard work. I hope we can work together for many years. Clare, your edits were top-notch. You caught so many things that I didn't— things that would have totally embarrassed me if they made it to the final copy. Melanie, I read the book probably 20 times and *still* missed some of the stuff you caught. Your suggestion completely transformed one of the later chapters and made it so much better. The three of you are a dream team, and I enjoyed working with you immensely.

Thanks to my original readers who waited patiently for chapters to drop week by week. You were my entire motivation. It wouldn't have ended up being a novel without you all commenting and pushing me forward. You're a community that I consider family. I love you all so much. This is a big day for us. Let's hope the rest of the world loves *Of Oil & Sorcery* as much as all of you do. I especially want to thank my Sojourners, who helped finance this book by supporting me on Patreon. Garrett Mitchell, Jason Hirsch, Lucas Whitelaw, Matthew Brown, Eathan Corona, Linus Jathe, Sam Tobias, Jeremy Arena, Chris Anderson, Rebecca Rowe, Ellen Yu, Gandalf171, LarryZilla, Haggisllama, Pythagon, Shoop83. Ben, Half_a_Shadow, Rayn_7, TonySkar, Christoper N, UmJustDino, Kamilla and Reading Owl.

I'd like to thank my mother for being my biggest fan since day one (literally), and always pushing me to follow my dreams. She always told me that if God puts a desire in your heart, he'll give you a pathway to success. If I thanked you for everything you deserve thanks for, this would need to be a second novel at the end here. I love you mom.

Glory to God. I'm blessed to be able to share the worlds in my head with all of you.

And lastly, thanks to everyone I didn't thank personally here. You're all a part of my story, and I love you.